Logan

The Craigdon Family Dynasty

Book Eight

CHRIS TAYLOR

LCT Productions Pty Ltd
18364 Kamilaroi Highway, Narrabri NSW 2390

ISBN. 978-1-925119-88-6 (Paperback)

Logan is a work of fiction. Names, characters, places, brands, media and incidents either are the product of the author's imagination or are used fictitiously. Any resemblance to actual persons, living or dead, events, or locales, is entirely coincidental.

Published in the United States of America.

Books by Chris Taylor

THE MUNRO FAMILY SERIES
The Profiler
The Investigator
The Predator
The Betrayal
The Deception
The Negotiator
The Christmas Vigil
The Ransom
The Defendant
The Shooting
The Maker
(Available in Audio)

THE SYDNEY HARBOUR HOSPITAL SERIES
The Perfect Husband
The Body Thief
The Baby Snatchers
The Final Bullet
The Debt Collector
The Lab Test
The Stolen Identity
The Cliff-top Killer
The Likeable Fraudster

THE SYDNEY LEGAL SERIES
An Accidental Murderer
At the Hand of Her Father
A Woman Scorned
Lies and Deception
Ordinary Evil
The Ties That Bind
The Perfect Crime
A Toxic Inheritance
Malicious Love

THE CRAIGDON FAMILY SERIES
Callum
Joel
Isabella
Nicholas
Sophia
Flynn
Noah
Logan
Elizabeth

THE BARRINGTON FAMILY SERIES
Broken Lives
Broken Promises
Broken Bonds
Broken Spirits
Broken Vows
Broken Minds
Broken Dreams
Broken Hearts
Broken Homes

THE FAIRFAX FAMILY SERIES
A Cattleman in Disguise
A Cattleman's Quest
A Cattleman's Daughter
A Cattleman's Secret Baby
To Catch a Cattleman
The Doctor and the Cattleman
To Rescue a Cattleman
A Cattleman's Heart
For the Love of a Cattleman

BACHELORS AND BRIDES SERIES
Matilda

Austin
Farrah
Benjamin
Verity
Denver
Ebony
Tyrone
Willow

Chris Taylor writing as
BELLA CHRISTIAN

THIS IS WHERE IT ENDS SERIES
(in order)
Jessie's Story
Ryan's Story
Holly's Story
Sarah's Story
Veronica's Story

Get a FREE book when you sign up for Chris Taylor's
newsletter at: www.christaylorauthor.com.au

Love Audiobooks? Check out Chris Taylor Books on audio
on Audible.com, Amazon.com and Apple Books.

Join Chris Taylor's Facebook reader group/fan page and be
among the first to receive news of book releases, read and
review books prior to release and other amazing offers. Join
Now at: www.facebook.com/groups/1758023621144744/

Find out more about all of Chris Taylor's books, by visiting her
website at: www.christaylorauthor.com.au

Dedication

This book is dedicated to Detective Superintendent Michael "Mick" Kilfoyle (ret). Thank you for being my "go to" person for all things policing. You lend my stories credibility and for that I am deeply grateful. Any mistakes are all my own. Thank you.

And as always, to my husband, Linden. My best friend, my soul mate. I love you to the moon and back.

Acknowledgments

As usual, no book comes into being without a lot of help and support by my friends and family. A world of thanks must go to my wonderful editor, Pat Thomas. Thank you for everything that you do to make my stories even more amazing than I could ever dare to dream. To former Detective Superintendent Michael Kilfoyle, thank you for lending my story credibility. Any mistakes are wholly my own.

To Mary and all of the team at Miblart, thank you for the fantastic book cover. To my sister, Nicole Guihot and to my friends, Ally Thomson and Sue Ricardo, thank you for your excellent editorial comments, proof reading skills and suggestions. I hope you like the final result.

To Amy Atwell, Kirby and the dedicated team at Author EMS who are so much more than book formatters. Amy, once again, thank you for your magic.

To the fantastic writer organizations such as Romance Writers of Australia, Romance Writers of America and Romance Writers of New Zealand for all the help, support and encouragement they offer new and aspiring writers, including me.

To my readers, thank you for your support and love for my stories. Your encouragement and enjoyment make this journey all worthwhile.

And lastly, to my friends and family, especially my husband and children. Thank you for putting up with late dinners and even later conversations as I've emerged day after day from the sometimes scary but always enthralling world I've created on my computer.

Chapter One

For the past three years, the third week of January had been painful for Logan Craigdon. This year was no different. Mainly because it brought back memories of the accident that had changed his life forever. He'd been competing in a sailing regatta. They were more than halfway through the day's races and were well ahead on the leaderboard when it all went to hell.

The wind had risen and the water had become choppy. The change in conditions shouldn't have posed a challenge for an experienced sailor like him, but then an unexpected squall took the whole crew by surprise. Logan was hit hard by the boom and knocked off his feet. He'd fallen awkwardly. Even now, three years later, he could still hear the snap of breaking bone and feel the immediate rush of excruciating pain and nausea that filled his gut.

He'd paid a heavy price for any over-confidence that day. He'd fractured both shin bones in his right leg in several places. They hadn't mended well. He'd spent miserable weeks lying flat on his back in a hospital bed and then even more weeks doing rehab—and still he'd been left with a permanent limp. But the worst of it was he knew he'd never sail competitively again. All his hopes and dreams and aspirations of being world number one in sailing disintegrated before his eyes, destroyed by the power of the very thing he loved the most—the ocean.

In retrospect he realized there had been nothing he could have done to prevent it, but that didn't mean he didn't replay the accident over and over until it nearly drove him mad. It was hard not to feel resentful. Even in the rehab ward, where there were patients far worse off than he, the resentment festered. He'd been all of twenty-two years old and his hoped-for life was over. He'd never sailed again. Well, that is, not until now.

Logan frowned darkly at the ten sailing dinghies lined up side by side on Balmoral Beach. This was the last place he wanted to be. He was only there because his cousin, Callum, had badgered him into it. Callum, the guy who'd been on his way to becoming a priest and was now happily married to the love of his life. He might have given up on ministering the Good News, but he sure as hell hadn't given up on being a do-gooder.

He'd approached Logan a couple of months earlier with the idea of running a sailing school for needy kids. Apparently there were plenty of them in Sydney. Kids who had no hope of ever knowing what it was like to sail. Or do anything exciting, so far as Callum had led him to believe.

While the major hurdle was their limited finances, more important was the lack of people willing to offer them opportunities to experience things most people took for granted. Though offering sailing classes for anyone was the last thing Logan wanted to do, Callum had been persistent. In the end, Logan had agreed, simply to get his cousin off his back.

And so here he was. Day one of a five-day course. Ten kids filled with excitement, looking to him to make the experience something they'd never forget.

Logan's lip curled up in disgust. *Great. Just great.*

Unfortunately, he'd left it too late to make his escape.

Some of the kids had already arrived. They wore wide grins and were chattering among themselves with nervous excitement. Logan closed his eyes and prayed for the strength and patience to get through the next five days. As if sensing his discomfort, Callum jogged over to where Logan stood with his arms crossed over his chest.

"You want to make sure the wind doesn't change," Callum teased. "I'd hate for you to have to go through life glaring like that."

"Fuck off, Callum." Logan took the sting out of his words by offering his cousin a half-smile. It felt more like a grimace.

Callum touched him on the arm. "Hey, I just want to say thank you again for doing this. I can tell it's not easy for you to be here. I'm guessing it brings back a lot of bad memories. That's what makes me even more grateful. And for you to be volunteering too… I just want you to know your sacrifice will make a huge difference to these kids."

Logan's frown deepened. "I should be in my office, finishing the design on my latest super yacht, not wasting my time out here."

Callum's expression remained calm and filled with understanding. "It's not a waste of time. Once you meet these kids… You'll see what I mean."

Logan grimaced. "Right. I'm doing it for the kids."

Callum nodded. "Right. And they're going to love you."

Damn Callum for guilting me into being part of this! There's a reason I've stayed away from the water for so long. It hurts too much to remember all I could have been and all I've lost.

"Hey! Logan! You ready to get started?"

Logan was pulled from his black thoughts by his brother, Noah, who stood beside their oldest brother, Flynn. They were surrounded by a bunch of noisy kids. Though Logan had reluctantly agreed to be part of the Tackers program, he'd done it on the condition his brothers also came along and helped out. He was glad to see they'd kept their word.

With a heavy sigh, he muttered a disgruntled farewell to Callum and walked toward the shed where everyone had gathered.

Ten pairs of eyes filled with a combination of excitement and apprehension watched his approach. Logan came to a halt a few yards from the group and clapped his hands to get their attention. Within seconds, silence descended. Logan nervously cleared his throat and forced a smile.

"Hi. I'm Logan Craigdon. Welcome to the Tackers program. Thanks for showing up. I know from your applications that all of you can swim, but I'm betting most of you have never sailed before. Am I right?"

His question was met with nervous laughter and a few nods and uncertain grins. Behind the children stood a handful of adults. Mostly women. Moms of the kids, no doubt. They looked almost as nervous as the participants. Logan felt an instinctive need to reassure them. He might have given up sailing three years ago, but he was still more than competent to teach. No one was going to drown on his watch.

He offered a few words of reassurance to the parents. He even managed to throw in a joke and saw them visibly relax.

"For those of you who don't know anything about the Tackers program, let me explain," he continued. "In a few words, it's a sailing school for beginners. We utilize a poly-plastic sailing dinghy. It's a simplified version of the international Optimist sailing dinghy."

"Never heard of that," a chubby kid in the front row muttered.

"That's cool," Logan responded with a grin. "I don't expect any of you to have heard of that. The main thing to know is that the type of dinghy we use is a small, single-handed dinghy that is very kid friendly. It's one of the most popular sailing dinghies in the world."

He looked around the crowd. Some of their nervousness

seemed to have dissipated. They stood in silence. Their wariness had been replaced by a mixture of curiosity and impatience.

"Right. A few things to remember before we start. You're going to be split into three groups." He pointed toward Noah. "This here is my brother, Noah. He's in charge of the first group." Logan then directed his attention toward Flynn. "And this is my other brother, Flynn. He's in charge of Group Two. I'm going to take the last group."

Logan scanned the crowd. The kids were still paying attention.

Good.

"Now, it's really important that you listen to your instructor. If everyone does as they're told, we can hopefully avoid accidents, including anyone getting hurt. No one wants that, right?"

There was a murmur of agreement, mostly from the adults at the back.

Logan nodded. "Good. Now, the most important thing to remember is to have fun. Are you ready?"

His question was met with cheers of excitement. Logan smiled and then addressed the parents.

"We'll take good care of them, I promise. You're welcome to stay and watch. Otherwise, we'll see you back here in an hour."

As the adults dispersed, Callum moved up beside him. "Thanks again, Logan. You're doing great."

Logan shot him a level look. "It's fine, Callum. You don't have to look so worried. I agreed to do this and I'll see it through. I understand a lot of these kids belong to people who frequent your soup kitchen and that's why you're so concerned, but I promise to show them a good time." He shot his cousin a disparaging smile. "Who knows? They might even learn to sail."

Callum merely smiled in that calm way of his and slapped him on the arm in a friendly show of support before moving away. For a moment, Logan watched as his cousin approached some of the women. He greeted each of them by name. Their faces lit up as he spoke to them. Callum was one of those guys who was good and kind and compassionate all the way through. For a second, Logan wished he was more like that.

Who am I kidding? I don't have a hope of being the kind of man Callum is. I've followed a different path and made choices that have led me in a different direction… Besides, I'm way too damaged for that…

With a sigh of irritation, Logan turned away and joined his brothers who were surrounded by excited children, all keen to start. Logan had gone through their applications a week earlier. Of course, he'd received ten times as many as he could handle. That had surprised him a bit and for a moment he'd thought about the disappointment many of them would feel. Then he'd put the matter out of his mind. He'd agreed to one class. That was it.

He'd culled the applications ruthlessly. First to go were those kids who couldn't swim. Though everyone wore a lifejacket at all times, there was no way he was going to complicate things by taking on non-swimmers. Next were the kids who were on medication. It was tough, but he wasn't a doctor and he didn't want to have to deal with some kind of medical emergency in the middle of the ocean. He was doing this as a favor to Callum. A quick, five-day sailing school. In and out, get it over with. And then he'd return to his cave to dwell on the unfair hand life had dealt him and to lick his wounds in private.

After hours of culling, he'd gotten down to the chosen ten. Then he sorted the kids into groups. As the more experienced sailor, Logan would take four kids under his wing. Flynn and Noah each had three. Unfortunately, they were also limited by the number of dinghies they had. It had been mighty decent of the Balmoral Sailing Club to loan them the ten. That was all the club had.

It was Callum who'd approached the club president and explained the situation. It didn't surprise Logan that the president had immediately come on board. Callum had a way about him that drew people. They wanted to help him out, do his bidding. Not many people could say no to him, Logan included.

Swallowing a sigh, he clapped his hands together to get everyone's attention. The kids fell silent. Logan forced a grin. "Right. Who's ready to learn how to sail?"

Amelia Ivanov—Mia to her friends—kept an anxious eye on her brother. So far, Mikhail seemed to be having a good time. She'd seen the notice about sailing lessons in her local church bulletin and, after considering it for a day or two, she'd signed Mikhail up. Though Mia had never sailed and didn't particularly care for the ocean, her younger brother was an entirely different matter.

He loved the water and was an excellent swimmer. She was sure he'd also enjoy the challenge of learning something new. Things didn't come easily for him, but he always gave it his best. Learning a new skill would be good for his self-esteem.

She eyed the three male instructors. Even if the one who'd introduced himself as Logan hadn't mentioned they were brothers, she would have guessed. They looked a lot alike. Flynn was taller and Logan had lighter hair, but their resemblance to each other was clear to see. All three were strong and muscular, with broad shoulders and slim hips. Noah wore glasses and looked friendly and cute. Flynn was casual and relaxed. But it was Logan who kept drawing her gaze.

While most of the other moms and caregivers had left, Mia

had elected to stay. She was nervous for Mikhail. Though she was certain this would be good for him, she wanted to make sure he'd be okay. After all, he was among strangers, learning to sail for the first time. And though he'd turned fourteen last birthday, he also tended to be a bit rambunctious, like an overeager puppy, and she wanted to be close by in case she needed to intervene.

She often felt this way about her little brother. He'd had a rough start in life. Through no fault of his own, he struggled with many things most people took for granted. He was born with fetal alcohol syndrome, which had caused him to be developmentally delayed. Even thinking about it made her feel equal parts anger and sadness. One thing was certain. She was determined he'd always know what it was like to be loved.

Protectiveness surged through her. She was ten years older than he was and the only family he had left. She took her responsibilities toward him seriously. He was her little brother, her responsibility, now and for always.

Glancing toward him, she was relieved to hear his excited chatter and see the animation on his face. The other kids in his group also appeared to have accepted him without comment. She detected no snide remarks, sideways glances, snickers… All the things she looked out for and was super-sensitive about.

She eased out her breath in relief. The mid-morning sun was warm on her skin. It sparkled off the blue waves like diamonds. She found a spot on the grassy bank above the beach and sat down, filled with a mixture of excitement and apprehension.

She watched the class from a distance. Mikhail was in Logan's group. The sun-bleached, surfer dude who looked right at home on the sand. No doubt he spent hours right there, on the beach, catching waves. She wondered what he did for a living.

As he moved from one child to the next, answering questions, showing them how to tie knots, instructing them in the ways of sailing, she noticed he limped. She wondered if it were a recent injury or something more permanent. And then she shook her head and smiled inwardly.

What do I care if the hot instructor has a limp? It's obviously not interfering with his ability to teach.

Her brother was watching the instructor's every move. Even from a distance, she could tell he was enthralled. His eyes were bright with curiosity. He was taking everything in, seeming to hang on every word. Mia held her breath as he tried one of the knots. He laughed uproariously when he got it all tangled. Logan chuckled and knelt down beside Mikhail and patiently showed him again.

Mia's heart turned over. She was a sucker for anyone who showed her brother kindness. Because of his age, a lot of people expected him to behave with more maturity, more self-control. They didn't know about his condition; that he couldn't process information the same way as most other teens. But Logan didn't seem to have a problem with him at all and that knowledge helped Mia to relax.

All too soon, the first class was over. Mikhail bounded up the hill toward Mia. She got to her feet just in time before he threw himself against her, laughing.

"That was so much fun!" His eyes lit up with laughter.

She ruffled his hair. "You did so well out there, Misha. I'm proud of you."

"Logan's the best!" Mikhail smiled widely and turned back to face the beach, searching for his new hero. "There he is! Come on, Mia! Come and say hello!"

Before she could murmur a protest, Mikhail had taken her hand and began to drag her down the hill.

"Misha! Stop! Let me go!"

Her demands were met with laughter. Her brother

continued to tug her along until she was face to face with the man Mia had struggled to keep her eyes off for the past hour. He was half-turned away from her, speaking to another parent, but the pull of attraction was strong and swift. Her heart leaped in her throat.

"Logan!" Mikhail shouted.

The man swung around in surprise. He was even more good looking up close. A rush of nervousness flooded through her. His eyes were an intriguing gray-green color that seemed to change, depending on the light. His bleached blond hair was wet and messy and hung over his face. An attractive three-day growth shadowed his chin.

"Logan! Logan! This is Mia! My sister!"

Logan smiled at Mikhail and then his gaze moved to her. Mia froze. For a moment she was too mesmerized to utter a word. She felt like she was butter and melting… He was the sexiest man she'd ever set eyes on.

Mikhail beamed, looking from one to the other. Logan held out his hand toward her. With an effort, Mia gathered her wits and managed to greet him with a handshake.

"It-it's nice to meet you, Logan," she stammered. Heat crept over her cheeks. She wished the ground would open up and swallow her.

Ignoring her awkwardness, Logan gazed at her with frank interest. "Nice to meet you, too. Thanks for bringing your brother along. He's a natural."

Mikhail looked at Logan with adoration. Mia's heart skipped another beat.

Good looking and kind…and interested… A heady combination.

And straight on the heels of that thought was another.

He's Misha's sailing instructor. What am I thinking!

Chapter Two

The moment Logan's gaze fell on the woman who stood beside Mikhail, it was all he could do not to do a double take. With her flawless olive skin, rich chestnut-colored hair and huge blue eyes that looked right into his soul, he was immediately interested. Her hair was swept off her face with some sort of wooden clip. The style emphasized her high cheekbones, her pert nose, her luscious mouth. All he could think about was what she would taste like…

Belatedly he remembered his manners. He held out his hand toward her. After a slight hesitation, she took it. Her handshake was warm and firm and…oh too brief.

What the hell's gotten into me? Working with the kids has obviously sent my brain to mush…

He shot her another quick look. Yep. Just as desirable, just as attractive as he'd thought the first time. Out of nowhere came the awareness he really wanted to sleep with her. Every curvy, delectable inch of her. Would it be too forward if he asked her out? She was the sister of one of his pupils. Did that matter? Did that mean she was off limits? Surely not.

Logan wasn't blind to his own attractiveness to women. Despite being jilted at the altar by his fiancée, he'd never had any trouble pulling a date. So, he'd lost count of the number of one-night stands. *What does that matter?*

He'd been recovering, having fun along the way, and he sure as hell had made certain his heart wasn't involved. After what had happened with Virginia, it was the only way he knew to protect himself. There was no way he'd ever leave himself vulnerable to such hurt and pain again. That didn't mean he couldn't enjoy women and the one standing right in front of him seemed more than a tasty treat.

But something about her made him hesitate. She wasn't like the usual girl he picked up for the night. There was something about her fresh innocence that told him she wasn't a girl who did one-night stands.

No. Women like her were looking for a life partner. They were in it for the long haul. He sure as hell didn't fit that bill and he didn't want to be the one to disillusion her or dash her dreams—or, quite frankly, waste her time.

Still, as she politely thanked him for the lesson and the time he'd spent with Mikhail, he couldn't deny the exceptional pull of attraction. Mesmerized by her beauty, he mumbled an appropriate response and then watched with reluctance as she and her brother slowly turned and left.

Mia brought the last of the groceries inside and then set about with Mikhail to unpack them. He was good at stacking things such as tinned tomatoes and boxes of cereal on the shelf. He inevitably ate more of the green grapes out of the bag than what he put in the fruit bowl, but that didn't matter. She'd bought the makings of beef tacos—her brother's favorite meal.

All afternoon he'd talked non-stop about the sailing class. She was thrilled he was so engaged with it, but every word drew her thoughts back to the hot instructor. *Logan Craigdon.* He was the sexiest surfer dude she'd ever seen. Even hotter than the men on the TV show, *Bondi Rescue.*

When she'd signed Mikhail up for the course, she'd been

worried about how he might cope. Good-looking instructors had been the last thing on her mind. With that added element, she anticipated this was going to be even more fun than she'd imagined. She couldn't wait for the lesson tomorrow.

Fortunately she'd already negotiated with her assistant, Katerina, to cover for her while she took Mikhail to his lesson. When she'd set that up she'd done it on the off chance Mikhail might need her close by. Now there was an extra motivation to hang around for the hour. The thought made her smile.

She also felt good about being able to spend more time with her little brother. Between her hours at the shop and the time he spent at school, their time together was often reduced to a few hours in the evening before Misha drifted toward the television and she spent the time tallying the day's takings, balancing the books and responding to an ever-growing number of emails.

She ought to be thankful she received so many inquiries for the dresses that graced her shop. Selling the gowns and accessories gave her the financial freedom to take time off when it suited her. Like now.

Spending time with her brother was even more important now that it was school holidays. They still had ten more days of summer break. Then it would be shopping for school things: shoes, uniform, backpack, lunchbox. Misha loved to start off a new school year with new things. It was fortunate—thanks to their father—she was able to indulge him.

Still, there was nothing more precious than creating memories together and providing him with interesting and challenging activities. His regular pediatrician continued to emphasize how important it was for Misha to gain new skills. That was one thing she hoped to achieve with the sailing classes. If she got to ogle a sexy sailing instructor along the way, all the better.

Logan busied himself dragging dinghies out of the shed and pretended he wasn't waiting for a glimpse of Mia. Every time a car pulled up on the promontory above them, he glanced up and felt his gut drop with disappointment when it wasn't her. It was Day Two of their five-day course. Most of the other kids had arrived. Surely Mikhail hadn't thrown it in already? He'd appeared to have a good time the day before. Still, there was no telling with kids. Some of them surprised him with their lack of resilience. He couldn't remember being like that when he was a kid.

"Logan! Logan! Logan! I'm here!"

At the excited sounds of Mikhail, Logan looked up and smiled. Mikhail was bolting down the incline at full speed, his focus only on arriving at his destination. He threw himself at Logan and hugged him around the waist. With any other kid, Logan might have felt embarrassed, but with Mikhail, it felt just fine.

Logan looked over Mikhail's head and spotted Mia walking toward them. She looked just as stunning as she had the day before. This time she wore a white tank top and navy-blue cotton pants. Her lips were covered in some kind of pink, shiny gloss.

She smiled at him as she drew closer. Though her eyes were concealed behind huge sunglasses, his heart still skipped a beat. He was sure he could feel the warmth and appreciation in her gaze. He immediately scowled with annoyance at himself.

What the hell? We've only just met… Why's my heart beating like I've just gained the lead in an offshore sailing event? Who cares if she's gorgeous? She's just another woman…

He didn't even know her. Knew nothing about her, save her name and the fact she had a brother. Mikhail was dressed in black and green Billabong boardshorts and a long-sleeved rash shirt. He offered Logan a toothy grin.

"Can we go sailing now, Logan? Can we go sailing now?"

Mia ducked her head and gently touched her brother on the arm. "Misha," she said quietly. "Slow down, mate. We've only just arrived. Logan has to work with all the other kids. You're not the only one in the class."

Logan's heart thumped at her nearness. A waft of her exotic perfume reached his nostrils, sending his pulse into overdrive. He forced his gaze away and then chuckled at the look of disappointment on Mikhail's face.

"Hey, buddy. It's all right. We're just waiting for Jackson and then we'll be able to hit the water. Do you remember Jackson?"

"Of course I do! Jackson's my friend!"

"He sure is. In fact, we all had a lot of fun yesterday, didn't we?"

"Yes! Fun! Come on, Jackson! Hurry up! It's time to go sailing!" Mikhail cried.

Logan laughed. "I love your eagerness, Mikhail. It's great. So, what can you tell me from yesterday? Do you remember what we learned?"

"Of course I do! I'm not stupid."

"No, you're not stupid. In fact, I think you're one of my best students. You caught on so quickly yesterday. I don't think I've seen someone tie knots as good as you. Are you sure you haven't been sailing before?"

"No." The boy's brow furrowed in thought. "At least, I don't think so." He turned to his sister who stood a short distance away. "Have I, Mia? Have I been sailing before?"

She gently shook her head. "No, Misha. This is your first time. Well, second counting yesterday."

Logan ruffled the boy's blond hair. "Then that means you're a natural, Mikhail. The very best kind to teach. It makes my job kind of easy and so much fun."

Mikhail's wide smile reflected the pride he felt. Mia shot Logan a soft smile of gratitude. His heart lurched.

Thank you, she mouthed.

He gave her a wink and when her face became suffused with a delightful pink his body hardened instinctively.

God, she's so beautiful.

And so not for him. She was fresh and sweet and innocent. Way too good for the likes of him. He'd be wise to keep his distance. It would be best for both of them.

The classes began to fill as the rest of the students, including Jackson, arrived. Flynn and Noah led their groups away. Logan did the same. Callum wasn't there yet, but no doubt he'd show at some point. He wanted to do his bit to help out and reassure the parents all was well.

Throughout the lesson, Logan did his best to ignore Mia. Today he'd taken the class out into deeper water, but from her position perched up on the grassy knoll, she commanded a good view of the beach and the activity below. Though her gaze was still concealed behind sunglasses, he had the feeling her attention stayed on him and her brother.

More likely her brother. That's who she was there for, after all. Logan was an idiot to think his interest might be reciprocated. Then again, she appeared to be as aware of him as he was of her. She'd blushed when he'd teased her, hadn't she? That had to be a good sign…

Logan made a sound of impatience in the back of the throat. Since when did he waste time wondering whether a woman was into him? It was ludicrous. If he wanted a willing woman for the night, all he had to do was walk into a bar and find one. There were usually plenty to choose from. He didn't even have to try.

And that was the problem. It was all so easy. A smile, a wink, an offer to buy a drink. A few anecdotes, a joke or two. A couple of well-placed questions. It was all so predictable and boring. He wondered when he'd become so jaded.

He looked across to where Noah and Flynn were teaching

their groups. A few of the kids, like Mikhail, had already started to get the hang of it. That didn't surprise him. Logan and his brothers had learned to sail from the time they started school. It had been something their father enjoyed. A fun way to spend a Saturday afternoon. For Logan, it had become much more than that and at the age of eighteen, he'd turned professional. At nineteen, he was selected for the Australian Olympic team. They hadn't won gold, but they'd come close.

Logan assumed he'd spend the rest of his days sailing competitively around the world. But that wasn't meant to be. Life and a nasty accident had had other plans. Everything he'd taken for granted was tossed up in the air. He'd been forced to reevaluate his future. To say he'd struggled to readjust was an understatement.

"Logan! Logan! Look at me!"

Mikhail's excited cries broke into Logan's depressing thoughts. He looked across at his young student and grinned. Mikhail was in his dinghy hanging on to the line for dear life. Logan grinned. The Tackers program usually catered to beginners who ranged in age from eight to twelve. At fourteen, Mikhail was the oldest of the group, but he didn't seem to notice or mind. Instead, he happily listened to everything Logan said and obediently followed all instructions.

The wind caught Mikhail's sail. It snapped taut. His yelp of joy could be heard clear across the harbor.

"Way to go, Mikhail! Hold her steady now. You're doing great!"

Logan threw a quick glance over his shoulder in Mia's direction and was disappointed to see she appeared engrossed in her iPad.

What did I expect? That she'd be glued to my every move? She's here for her brother. No one else. And a good thing, too. She's so not for me.

He had a momentary frisson of alarm when Mikhail was becalmed on his tack. The sail was luffing but then a gust of wind caught it and the sail shifted, swung out over the water, taking Mikhail with it—plunging him into the water… Logan was soon put at ease when the boy surfaced with a grin from ear to ear.

"Logan! It's freezing!" he chimed, pulling a face.

Logan laughed and made his way over to where Mikhail clung to the side of his sailboat. Logan helped the boy back into the dinghy and settled him on the seat.

"There you go. The wind took you by surprise, that's all. That will happen many more times before everything starts to fall into place, I promise you. But you're only on your second lesson. You can't expect to know everything just yet."

"But I want to be the best, Logan!"

The earnest look on Mikhail's face tugged at Logan's heartstrings. His chest tightened on a sudden rush of emotion. He could still remember feeling exactly like this when his father first taught him to sail. He'd been a few days past his fifth birthday.

A rush of warmth and sentimentality flooded through him, catching him off guard. It had been so long since he'd associated sailing with anything other than negativity. Three years, in fact. Three long years when he'd hated the thought of anything to do with the sport because every time his mind drifted in that direction, he was cruelly reminded of how much he'd suffered and what he'd lost.

As if on cue, a familiar shaft of pain arced down his leg and momentarily stole his breath. He winced and closed his eyes until the feeling eased. It wasn't always like this, but the pain made itself known often enough for him to be tired of it. He yearned for the time when he'd be free of this pain. If that day ever came.

"Logan! Logan! Look at me!"

Once again, Mikhail's cries of excitement dragged Logan from his sad reverie. He looked up in time to see Mia's brother sail his little boat expertly across the water, his sail full of wind. A moment later, the wind turned and the sail collapsed, along with Mikhail who toppled into the water once again. He came up laughing like he'd done the last time and Logan chuckled with him. Wading over to where the boy was, Logan helped him up again.

"Good job, Mikhail. You're really getting the hang of it."

Mikhail beamed up at him. Logan high-fived him and then turned back to the rest of the group. "Okay, guys, let's head back to shore. Class is over for today."

They all slowly made their way back, accompanied by Noah and Flynn. Most of the kids had pulled up the centerboards, climbed out of their dinghies and were pushing them back to shore. Once all of the students were safely out of the water and the boats, lifejackets and other equipment stowed away, Logan gave them all a few words of encouragement before dismissing them.

From the corner of his eye, he saw Mia stand and dust off her pants before heading down the hill. Turning away, he busied himself with the equipment.

"Mia! Mia! Mia! Did you see me? I was sailing!"

"You certainly were, buddy. Good job!"

Logan continued to pack away the last few lines and life jackets that had been left on the shore. As hard as he tried to ignore Mia's presence, it proved impossible when she stopped a few feet away from him.

The first thing he noticed were her shoes. She wore hot-pink converse. An unusual choice this close to the beach, but whatever. The color was sexy. His gaze drifted slowly up her crisp navy-blue cotton pants, across the white tank top and finally came to rest on her face. Her eyes were still hidden behind her oversized sunglasses, but a friendly smile turned up her lips. Despite his best efforts, his heart rate kicked up a notch.

"Thank you for another great day Logan," she said.

"All good," he muttered, staring at the ground.

"It was all Mikhail could talk about last night. He couldn't wait to get here today."

Logan smiled involuntarily. "He's doing so well. He's a great kid."

"Yes, he is."

Suddenly, Logan was filled with curiosity about Mia and her brother.

Does she still live at home with him? Where are their parents? Why is she the one bringing him to a sailing lesson? Doesn't she work? Is she his primary caregiver?

He opened his mouth to ask one of the many questions circling in his head, but then closed it again. It was none of his business. *They* were none of his business. He'd agreed to teach the class of keen young sailors only because Callum had hounded him to do it.

The class was set to run each week-day morning. Five lessons in total. And then he'd be done. Once he'd completed his obligation to the kids who'd signed up for the course, he had no intention of returning to the water again and he was even more determined to steer clear of the likes of the woman who stood before him.

"Um… I was wondering…um… Would you like to grab a coffee?"

From the expression on Mia's face, he could only guess the invitation that came out of her mouth had surprised her as much as him. All the reasons why he should decline crowded his mind, but he found himself nodding.

"Yeah, why not? Sounds great."

"Yay! Can I get a milkshake?" Mikhail asked her.

She laughed and ruffled his hair affectionately. "Of course. Chocolate, right?"

"Right! Chocolate's the best!"

Mikhail turned and started running up the grassy bank that led to the car park. Logan had a quick word with his brothers and updated them on his plans. They agreed to pack away the last of the gear. He caught up with Mia and together they followed Mikhail at a more leisurely pace.

"So, do you live nearby?" he asked, filling the silence.

"Not too far away. We live in Mosman."

She mentioned an affluent, lower north shore suburb about five minutes' drive away. "Nice," he responded. "I live just down the hill, right here in Balmoral."

"Balmoral's a lovely spot."

"Not too shabby," he agreed.

"Mikhail loves to come down here to swim."

"Yes, I can tell he's a water baby. Have you been in Mosman long?"

"Long enough. I've lived there most of my life. My father was in…the construction industry. He built our house. When he died, he left the house to me."

"Oh, I'm sorry."

She compressed her lips. "That's okay. He passed away a bit over a year ago."

"You must miss him."

She shrugged. "Living in my family home reminds me of him every day. He was also responsible for a lot of the apartment blocks you see on the lower north shore. You could say he left a substantial legacy."

"Nice," Logan responded. "My uncle was also in property development. It's been nearly twelve months since he died. He left his company to me."

She smiled. "So you're a property developer. I can imagine that keeps you busy. Especially around these parts. How are you able to volunteer your time to a project such as this?"

They'd reached the car park, saving him from having to respond. He didn't feel like explaining he was there under sufferance and would never have agreed to be part of it if it hadn't been for his cousin's constant badgering.

"This is me," he said, indicating the steel gray CLA 250 coupé Mercedes.

"Nice," she repeated, a cheeky expression lighting up her face.

His heart somersaulted. "You know cars?" he teased.

She indicated a shiny black Tesla. "This is me."

"I'm impressed," he said.

"Good." She winked at him.

Mikhail bounced up and down on the balls of his feet, waiting impatiently to climb in. Mia pressed the button on her remote and the doors came open, lifting out and upwards like the car out *Back to the Future* movie, a movie Logan had seen many years earlier and still loved. With a brief wave, she turned and walked around to the driver's side and slid behind the wheel. "I'll meet you at Café 2088," she said, mentioning a popular coffee shop in the heart of Mosman's shopping precinct.

"See you there," he murmured and did his best to ignore the acceleration of his heartbeat. He reminded himself, they were just two new acquaintances sharing casual conversation over coffee. Nothing more.

Yeah, right.

Chapter Three

Mia wiped her sweaty palms down the sides of her pants and tried to quell the nervous excitement coursing through her veins. She found a parking spot within walking distance of the café and, together with Mikhail, made her way down the street. Café 2088 was one of her favorite places to hang out. It was only a few doors down from her shop. This time of day the breakfast crowd had dissipated and the lunch goers had not yet materialized. It was the perfect time to be there. The owner, Joanna Penberthy, greeted them with a smile.

"Hi, guys! It's good to see you. What are you up to?"

"We just thought we'd pop in for a coffee," Mia replied.

"Let me guess: One skinny latté and a large chocolate milkshake." She winked at Mikhail. "Am I right?"

"Yay!" Mikhail cheered.

"And a short black, thank you," Logan added, stepping inside the shop and closing the door behind him.

"Oh, I'm sorry, I didn't see you there," Joanna said, blushing.

Logan waved away her embarrassment. "It's no problem."

Mia made the introductions. "Joanna, this is Logan Craigdon. He's been teaching Mikhail to sail."

"Oh, that's wonderful. I remember you telling me

something about that awhile ago." She smiled at Logan. "It's a great thing you're doing."

Logan shrugged and looked away, a flush of embarrassment staining his cheeks. "It's nothing," he mumbled.

Mia indicated a table by the large bay window that looked out onto the street. "Should we take a seat?"

Mikhail bounded over and sat down. Mia and Logan followed. The table was only big enough to seat four people. With Logan's shoulders broader than the average man's, all of a sudden the space seemed too small to seat them. When Logan sat opposite her he dominated the space, felt so close she suddenly found it hard to breathe.

He was really good looking. She'd barely even noticed his limp. It certainly hadn't appeared to hamper him in the water. During Misha's sailing lesson, she'd done her best to remain immersed in dealing with her email, but the truth was, she'd been hard pressed to keep her attention on anything but the Adonis in the harbor.

Logan shifted his weight on the chair and then winced.

"What did you do to your leg?" she asked.

His expression went blank and his eyes shuttered. "I broke it."

"How long ago?"

"Three years."

She raised her eyebrows in surprise. "It must have been a bad break."

"Yep. And it's breaks. Plural. One healed well; the other…not so much…"

"How did it happen?"

His eyes flashed with annoyance and his lips compressed. *So, he finds my questions irritating…*

"It doesn't matter." His tone was brusque, closing down any further discussion.

She bit her lip and nodded. It was none of her business.

She hardly knew the guy. She had no right poking into his life. A new tension reverberated off him in waves. His expression was taut. Gone was the easy-going sailing instructor of a few minutes earlier.

Okay, so even after three years, he's still sensitive about his accident. She burned with curiosity to know what had happened but was wise enough not to push it for now.

For now? What am I thinking? Am I hoping this is only the first of many personal conversations we might share?

Of course she was. The man who sat before her was tall, broad-shouldered, sexy. He was also kind and thoughtful and funny and treated her brother like he was just another teenager. The latter was more important to her than any of the other qualities, but there was no denying he ticked a lot of boxes. The romantic in her couldn't help but dream of possibilities.

Good God! I'm being ridiculous! I've only just met the guy! Give it a break!

To her relief, Joanna arrived with their order and Mia was forced to put her wayward thoughts on hold. All three of them murmured their thanks and then started in on their drinks. Mikhail slurped noisily through his straw and both she and Logan laughed.

"Good?" he asked Mikhail with a smile.

"Good. I love chocolate—and milkshakes are the best!"

Logan laughed. "You won't get an argument from me, buddy. Although I usually go for caramel."

"I like caramel, too," Mikhail replied. "But chocolate is the best!" He laughed boisterously and Logan joined in.

She took another sip from her coffee. Logan continued to regard Mikhail with curiosity. Mia could see the questions in his eyes, but he either wasn't as curious about Mikhail as she was about him, or he had more self-control. Either way, he remained silent.

"So, what made you think about starting the sailing class?" she asked, unable to help herself. She had an innate curiosity about people and in the moment she wanted to know everything about the man who sat across from her. It was almost a physical yearning.

Logan set his coffee cup down and shook his head, a rueful expression flooding his face. "You have my cousin to thank for that. Callum Craigdon. He was headed for the priesthood until he met the love of his life. Now he runs a soup kitchen in the city and is in the middle of constructing affordable housing. He's always had an active social conscience. He thought a class like this one would be a good idea."

"Well, I'm certainly grateful to him. This has been a nice opportunity for Mikhail and it's only the second day. I understand he's not disadvantaged in the way we usually mean, but he's disadvantaged in other ways. I thought this might be good for him. When I saw the notice about it, I just had to check it out."

"I'm glad you did."

"So am I."

Their gazes caught and held. Mia's heart skipped a beat and then galloped away so fast she felt breathless. With an effort, she looked away and did her best to regain control of her run-away pulse.

"You mentioned your shop," Logan continued in such a smooth voice she could only assume he hadn't been as affected as she had by their prolonged exchange.

She blinked to clear her thoughts. "Yes. I-I own a bridal wear shop in Mosman. It's only a few doors down. Wishes and Dreams. Do you know it?"

Logan stared at her in horror. *Did she just say she owns a bridal shop? Oh, God. This is worse than I thought! I should have followed my*

instincts and stayed the hell away from her. She was as fresh and innocent as he'd imagined. She owned a bridal shop, for God's sake! She believed in love, in happy-ever-afters… Oh, God. This couldn't get any worse.

Despite everything, he'd managed to ignore the warnings in his head and accept her invitation for coffee. The truth was, he liked her and his cock had been hard from the very first moment he'd spied her approaching from the car park near the Balmoral Beach wharf. She was an incredibly attractive woman and he was only a flesh-and-blood man.

But then he'd talked to her and had realized she was the exact opposite of the women he usually flirted with and who he eventually took home to bed. And yet, here he was. Sitting across from her, sharing conversation, getting to know her and wanting to know her a hell of a lot more.

I need to get out of here…

Almost clumsily, he pushed back his chair and stood. He glanced at his watch and then at Mia. "I'm really sorry. I just remembered a meeting I have scheduled. A…staff meeting…at Craigdon Enterprises. I…usually leave them to my cousin, Nicholas, but I promised to be there today. I'm sorry. I'm really sorry."

She blinked away her surprise and merely offered him a genuine smile of disappointment. "Don't be silly. Go. There's no need to apologize. It's been fun, hasn't it, Mikhail?"

Her brother turned to look at Logan and gave him a wide grin. "Yes! Fun, Logan. See you tomorrow, Logan!" Mikhail waved enthusiastically and Logan half-heartedly waved back.

"See you tomorrow," he mumbled and feeling like the coward he was, he threw down enough money to cover their drinks, then spun on his heel and left.

"Turn off the TV, Mikhail. It's time for bed." Mia braced herself for the familiar argument.

"But, Mia! It's only nine o'clock! Just another hour!"

She remained firm. "No, Misha. It's bedtime."

"But it's holidays!"

"Exactly! You're normally in bed by eight."

When her brother looked like he was about to argue further, Mia took his hand and pulled him off the couch.

"You have to go sailing again tomorrow. You don't want to be all worn out before you get there."

His expression brightened. "Sailing! Yay! I love sailing!"

His wide grin lit up his face, making him look even younger. Tenderness surged through her. She drew him close and hugged him. A few seconds later, he wriggled out of her embrace.

"Will Logan be there again tomorrow?"

She nodded. "Yes. He's your instructor. You'll have him all week."

"Yay! Can we invite him for a milkshake again?"

Mia laughed at the eagerness on Mikhail's face. "Maybe."

Her brother punched the air. "Yes!"

She patted his cheek and chuckled. "I don't know which one you're more excited about—spending time with Logan or having another milkshake."

Mikhail grinned. "Both!"

She laughed and walked down the hallway toward his bedroom, relieved when he followed without further protest. She turned down his bed and fluffed his pillows. He walked in behind her.

"Don't forget to brush your teeth," she reminded him.

With a sigh, he went into the adjoining bathroom. She heard the water running and the sound of him brushing his teeth. A few moments later, he walked back into the bedroom and climbed into bed. She perched on the edge beside him.

"Did you have a good day today?"

He smiled happily. "Yes. A good day. Tomorrow will be even better!"

She leaned over and brushed a lock of hair out of his eyes and winked. "I'm sure it will."

He let out a huge yawn. She smiled. "Goodnight, Misha. Have a good sleep. I'll see you in the morning." She stood and kissed him on the forehead and then leaned over and switched off the bedside light.

"Goodnight, Mia. I love you."

Her heart clenched at the sweetness of his words. "I love you too, Misha." With that, she turned and left the room, leaving the door to his bedroom open.

Making her way back to the living room, she poured herself a glass of soda water and added a fresh piece of lime before she settled on the couch. It had been a tiring day. Even though Mikhail was fourteen, his mental age was closer to ten. She wasn't game to leave him at home alone all day so during school holidays, when she was working he came to the shop with her. She was fortunate she owned the business and this option was available to her.

Mikhail spent hours in her office at the back of the shop, mostly playing games on his iPad or watching Netflix. He rarely complained, accepting without protest that he had to stay there. Occasionally she let him walk to Café 2088 and do a coffee run. Then he also got to buy himself a milkshake.

She took a sip from her glass and sighed quietly. It was these moments after Mikhail had gone to bed that she treasured. Though she loved him unconditionally and never got tired from the responsibility of raising him, it was always nice to have some quiet time to herself.

There were only ten years separating them, but more often than not she felt more like his mother than his sister. She supposed that was only natural. She'd been taking care of him all his life. Their mother had died when he was seven, but even before then Mia had been his primary caregiver.

Their mother's parenting skills had been non-existent and with their father absent more times than he was present, the responsibility of seeing to her brother's daily needs had inevitably fallen to Mia. Not that she resented the intrusion.

Mikhail was her brother and she loved him. It wasn't his fault their mother had been an alcoholic and drug addict long before he was born. It wasn't his fault his physical and mental development had been impaired as a result. It made Mia all the more determined to give him the life he deserved. She refused to allow anything to hold him back. Signing him up for sailing lessons was a perfect example of that.

With that reminder, her thoughts returned to Logan Craigdon. She groaned aloud in renewed embarrassment. She still wasn't sure what she'd said to frighten him off, but she guessed it had something to do with the mention of her bridal wear shop. She'd barely finished speaking and he'd torn out of there like his pants were on fire.

Did he think I was angling for a husband? Is that why he'd left so quickly?

She'd done a bit of research on social media the night before. She'd discovered Logan was well known on the social scene. According to the Internet, he partied long and hard and was currently single. No doubt a man with good looks, charm and money was a much-sought-after prize for the women of Sydney.

Perhaps he assumed I was of the same vein?

In that case, she couldn't blame him for his hasty departure. It was a shame he hadn't hung around long enough for her to assure him that owning a bridal shop didn't mean she was looking for a husband. She might be an incurable romantic who believed in love and happy-ever-afters, but she was also a pragmatist. After all, nearly half of all marriages ended in divorce. That was a sobering statistic.

Of course, no doubt someone like Logan was propositioned more times than he could count. After all, he was a good catch. Most everyone in Sydney had heard of the Craigdon family. They were one of the richest families in the state, with much influence and standing in both business and political circles.

And before his death, Henry Craigdon had headed a multimillion dollar property development enterprise. Apparently the same business Logan had inherited. No wonder he was antsy when he came into contact with females of marriageable age, and even more so when said female owned a bridal wear shop.

She sighed and took another sip of her drink. It was getting late. She ought to go to bed, read for a bit and then call it a night. Mikhail had always been an early riser, which meant she was an early riser, too. It was hectic in the mornings, getting breakfast for the two of them, packing his school bag, including his lunch and making sure he could find his shoes.

Normally she'd then drop him off at his very expensive, very prestigious school and head off to work. At least during the school holidays she was spared that part of the routine. Doing the school run during peak hour traffic was never fun.

Signing her brother up for sailing lessons had been a stroke of genius. Not only did it get Mikhail outside and learning a new skill, it was just down the road from where they lived. A five-minute drive. How good was that? And Mikhail was having fun. Watching him laugh and learn and splash in the water was a nice distraction from her usual work day. And then there was Logan.

An even nicer distraction…

With an impatient sigh, she forced her mind away from the too-handsome-for-his-own-good Logan Craigdon. She'd spent way too much time thinking about him already. It was time to give it a break.

Yet to be sure, there was always tomorrow…and another sailing lesson. With that thought in mind, she finished her drink and, with a smile tugging at her lips, she switched off the lights and headed for bed.

Chapter Four

Logan slept fitfully and arrived at Balmoral Beach tired and out of sorts. His brothers were already there, pulling dinghies, life jackets and other equipment out of the boat shed. So was his cousin, Callum.

"Glad to see you managed to drag yourself out of bed, lover boy," Noah teased.

"Looks like you had a rough night. Not enough sleep?" Flynn joked.

Logan merely grunted.

"What's her name?" Noah asked.

"I don't know who you're talking about."

"Of course you do," Flynn said. "We saw you leave with her yesterday."

Logan held up his hand in a sign of surrender. "Okay, okay. It's Mia," he mumbled.

"Mia," Noah replied, savoring the name. "You two looked kind of cozy for two people who'd only just met. Still, you've never been backward about coming forward where women are concerned. Especially ones as cute as her."

"She has a nice butt," Flynn commented in a casual tone.

"I didn't notice," Logan muttered.

"Liar." Noah chuckled.

"Hey, you two are spoken for," Logan protested. "You shouldn't be noticing anything."

"He's right," Callum said, joining the conversation. "I couldn't even tell you whether she had blond hair or black."

"Yeah, right," Flynn replied with an exaggerated eye roll. "As if we believe that! You got married, Callum. You didn't go blind."

They all laughed and then Logan spied Mia and her brother walking down the hill toward them. His belly clenched with nerves.

This is ridiculous! She's just a woman!

And he'd already decided she was off limits. There were millions of available women in Sydney. He'd go out and find one that very night. One that didn't have a wide, sweet smile. One who didn't listen to him like she was really interested in what he had to say. One who wasn't intelligent, intriguing and who didn't own a god damned bridal wear business.

Mikhail bounded toward him, waving enthusiastically. "Hi, Logan!"

Logan smiled. "Hi, Mikhail. Good to see you, buddy. How're you doing?"

"Good."

"You ready for some more sailing?"

Mikhail grinned. "Yes! Let's do it!"

"Well, just take a seat. We need to wait for the rest of the class to arrive."

The boy nodded obediently and moved over to where Logan's brothers and cousin waited. They all greeted him with friendly words. Mia moved close enough to Logan that he caught a whiff of her perfume. His gut clenched again.

"How are you, Logan?" she asked in a casual tone.

He was determined to match her attitude. "Fine."

"Good."

An awkward silence fell between them. He was suddenly filled with guilt. He owed her an explanation.

"Listen, about yesterday. I'm sorry. I left rather abruptly."

She waved his apology away. "It's fine. Don't sweat it."

"No, I mean, I want to explain."

"You had a meeting. I understand."

"Yes. No. I mean… I didn't have a meeting. That was just an excuse. The thing is… I… I got scared."

She frowned. "Why would you be scared? It's not like either of us were about to attack you."

He flushed and heat crept up his neck and spread across his cheeks. "Of course not. I didn't mean that. Scared is probably the wrong word. What I mean is…"

She stared at him expectantly. He cursed beneath his breath and then decided honesty was the only way to go.

"Look, Mia. I like you. You're a great girl. But I'm not marriage material. I get that a girl like you could have any man she wants and I sound like such an idiot even suggesting you might like me in that way. No doubt I've offended you, but—"

She laughed. "Oh, Logan! You haven't offended me in the slightest! I get it. You're one of Sydney's most eligible bachelors and I own a bridal shop. I totally understand your panic."

A surge of relief went through him. He stared at her, almost unable to believe how well she'd taken it.

"You do?"

"Of course I do. I'm not stupid. The kind of people who own bridal wear shops are dreamers, romantics of the highest order. You have to be, or you'd go crazy surrounded by all that love and happiness. And I freely admit I'm both of those things. But that doesn't mean I'm on the prowl for a husband."

Relief flooded through him. "Oh, wow! That's great! You can't imagine how relieved I am to hear that!"

Her smile faltered slightly and he suddenly realized what he'd said. Heat crept up his neck again. He hurried to explain.

"I don't mean you're not the kind of woman any man would be proud to call his wife. It's just that… I'm not the marrying kind, no matter who she is or how wonderful. And you are. At least, you seem…wonderful."

By the time he'd finished, his face burned with embarrassment. He'd made a complete hash of that. But to his relief, she merely laughed again.

"Hey, I get it. Don't beat yourself up. It's okay, Logan. We're cool."

Once again, he was filled with relief. He gave her a rueful grin. "We are?"

"Yes."

This time, he sighed aloud. "Great. Because I like you and I like Mikhail. I like hanging out with the two of you." He held out his hand toward her. "Friends?"

She nodded and reached out to seal the deal. Her grip was firm and sure. Heat tingled across his palm as he registered her soft, slim fingers.

"Friends," she repeated and once again gave him an open smile.

"Are you nearly done over there, lover boy?"

The question came from Flynn and sent a fresh wave of embarrassment washing through Logan. With a brief nod of farewell, he turned away from Mia and jogged over to where his brothers and the students stood waiting.

He couldn't stop grinning.

Later that same day, Logan was at the Craigdon Super Yachts production yard, working in his office. Though he loved to be on the floor building the luxury super yachts he and his father were renowned for, he was also very much involved in their design. Right now he was finishing a custom-made design for a new client.

Logan had been referred to Winston Simpson II by one of Logan's existing clients. Richard Harrington was a billionaire who put in an order for a new super yacht every few years. The budget was flexible and Logan was given free rein on the design. Each time, the luxury inclusions reached new heights. Richard was a client Logan loved to work with.

Winston Simpson II wasn't any different, although he was more inclined to question Logan's design decisions and seemed a little more concerned about the cost. It didn't bother Logan. He worked for all types. Some, like Richard, were over-the-top casual about the millions they were spending, others not so much. Either way, Logan worked hard to produce the best product possible to the client's specifications. There wasn't a Craigdon super yacht on the market he wasn't proud of.

A sharp knock on his door caught his attention. Logan looked up and frowned. His father filled the open doorway.

"Hi, Dad. Is there a problem?" Logan asked, deliberately keeping his voice neutral.

It was no surprise his father was unhappy. Logan chose to spend his time at CSY getting his hands dirty, rather than dealing with the everyday minutiae of running a business. The truth was, despite his father's insistence Logan step up and take on more responsibility, the business side of things bored him to tears.

"No, there's no problem," Archie said slowly, coming into the room. "I just wanted to see if you'd given any more thought to my proposal."

Logan scrubbed at his hair with impatience. "Dad, we've been over this before. I get that you want to take a step back and slow down and you want me to pick up my game so you can make that happen, but I don't want to run a business. How many times do I have to say it?"

"I'm sixty-three, Logan. I want to retire. Or at least cut back my hours. I can't do that if you keep refusing to take on the added responsibility."

"So employ a manager, Dad. That's what other people do."

Archie looked pained. "I don't want to hire a manager. I started this company from nothing. I poured my blood, sweat and tears into this business. I don't want to leave just anyone at the helm. I want you. My son."

Logan's jaw tightened in a familiar surge of stubbornness. "I'm sorry, Dad. I wish I could help you out. But I can't."

"Of course you can!" Archie cried on a sudden surge of anger. "What you meant to say is, you won't."

Logan shrugged. "Can't. Won't. What's the difference?"

"The difference is, you're my *son*! My flesh and blood! You should want to take over the reins of our family company. One day you might have a son of your own. Then you'll know how it feels."

Logan merely waved him away, infuriating him further. "Save your breath, Dad. That's never going to happen."

Archie turned red in the face. For a moment, Logan was concerned his father might be having a heart attack, but then Archie merely swore under his breath and spun on his heel and left, slamming the door behind him.

Logan drew in a deep breath and eased it out, trying to regain his equilibrium. He hated arguing with his father, but there was nothing he could do to appease the man. He wasn't going to take over responsibility of the company and that was that. Archie needed to accept that and move on.

After spending the morning with his brothers and cousin, teaching the kids to sail, he'd bought a coffee and a sandwich and then eaten them in his car on the way over to the factory. Though his time on the water wasn't proving to be as tiresome as he'd thought it would be, he was still glad he had another job to go to and a way to spend his time that didn't involve sailing.

He'd taken a job at Craigdon Super Yachts only at the insistence of his father after it was clear Logan would never sail competitively again. Though he never wanted to run the company, working on designs wasn't all bad. From the moment he'd stepped foot in the factory, he'd come alive. The scream of steel and aluminum as it was cut and folded and molded into place… The sound of hammers, planes, chisels as a sleek new yacht was outfitted… The energy of the place.

On a normal day he'd be completely immersed in his work and loving every minute of it. The design process of a super yacht could be incredibly demanding, not to mention tedious, as well as exciting. Using his skills and his imagination to come up with something not only unique and beautiful, but practical and on budget was a bundle of challenges he enjoyed.

But now his thoughts kept straying to a certain bridal shop owner and her little brother. The truth was, despite the argument with his father still fresh in his mind, he couldn't stop thinking about Mia. She was unlike any other woman he'd met. She seemed genuine. Refreshing. Honest. Beautiful—inside and out.

He wondered, not for the first time, about her family. He wanted to know more about her. Was desperately curious. Surely that was okay? They were starting a friendship, weren't they? Friends got to know each other. Learned more about each other's lives. There was nothing wrong with that.

Before he could clearly think things through, he tapped on his keyboard and opened the spreadsheet he'd created with the list of enrolment details for the sailing course. Moving his mouse down the entries, he clicked on Mikhail's name. The boy's full name, address and other contact details, including the contact details of his parent/guardian filled Logan's screen.

There it was. Mia's name and phone number. Did he dare call her? Picking up his phone before he lost his nerve, he dialed her number. She answered on the third ring.

"Hello? Wishes and Dreams bridal wear. This is Mia."

Nerves rushed through him. He almost ended the call.

"Hello?" she asked again.

"M-Mia," he stammered. "It's Logan." Heat suffused his face. He felt awkward, embarrassed, tongue-tied. The insecure feelings were so foreign, especially when it came to dealing with women, he was taken aback.

What the hell's this woman doing to me? She has me tied up in knots!

"Oh, Logan. How are you? Is everything all right?"

"Yes, of course."

"Is it about the class tomorrow? You need to re-schedule, right?"

"N-no. I should be fine for the class tomorrow." He paused. The silence dragged on.

What the hell am I thinking? This is a stupid idea.

"Logan? Are you still there?"

He cleared his throat. "Yes. I'm still here. The thing is, I was wondering if you'd like to go somewhere for a drink? Not right now, but maybe later. Tonight."

"A drink?"

He could hear the surprise in her voice and didn't blame her. He was acting totally weird. Still, he'd come this far. Might as well finish it.

"Yes. A drink. We could meet at that new bar down at Balmoral Wharf. The one that opened last month. Do you know it?"

"Um, no. Look, I appreciate the invitation, but the thing is, I don't drink."

Now it was Logan's turn to feel surprised. "Okay, well how about dinner?"

"I'm sorry. I don't like leaving Mikhail alone."

"He's fourteen…"

"And?" she replied.

"And… What about your mother?"

"She's dead."

"Oh. I'm sorry."

"It's fine. It happened a long time ago."

So she'd lost both parents. No wonder she was such a central part of Mikhail's life. She was his primary caregiver. She rose even higher in his esteem. It made him want to get to know her even more.

"Okay, so how about I bring dinner to you? Would that work?"

She paused and he could tell she was fishing around for an excuse to say no.

"Please?" he added.

She cleared her throat. "It's just that, we agreed only to be friends, remember?"

"Yes, and friends spend time together, don't they?"

Finally, she laughed a little uncertainly. "I… I guess so."

"Good. I'll see you at seven."

He ended the call before she could argue. Her address details had also been provided on the enrolment form. He had everything he needed. Now all he had to do was decide on the menu. He didn't have a clue what they liked to eat or if either of them had allergies. What if Mikhail had a special diet? It was possible. Hell, this could end in disaster if he made the wrong choices. He could call her back and ask her, but he didn't want to give her another opportunity to turn him down. Suddenly he was beset by nerves.

What the hell's wrong with me? It's not like I'm trying to impress her.

They'd already agreed they were only going to be friends.

It felt like he was preparing for a date. A real one… One like those that usually ended with him in his date's bed.

But not this time. And not this woman. Mia deserved better than that. Especially since he had no intention of taking things any further. No. There was no way he was going to find himself waiting at the altar again. Being jilted once was enough for anyone. And that meant he and Mia would never be anything more than friends.

The trouble was, he couldn't stay away from her. The more he got to know her, the more he wanted to know. There were so many questions he wanted to ask. She intrigued him, tied him up in knots, threw him off balance. It had been a long time since he'd been so interested in a woman.

When he was in her company, he forgot about his leg, his lost career and every other piece of bad luck that had come his way. He enjoyed being in her company. She made him laugh. The knowledge that in such a short period of time she had so much power over him was scary, but he seemed helpless to resist her. He had to see her again.

Chapter Five

Mia checked her appearance in the bathroom mirror for what seemed like the tenth time and patted a stray lock of hair back into place. Ever since she'd agreed to Logan's suggestion, nerves had filled her stomach. Her concentration had been shot. She'd messed up two orders at work and snapped at Katerina. In the end, Mia had collected Mikhail and left the shop early.

Swallowing a nervous sigh, Mia touched up her lipstick and added a bit more rouge. With a final glance in the mirror, she left the bathroom and returned to the kitchen. Mikhail was bouncing around like an excited puppy. Mia couldn't help but grin.

"Is Logan really coming here for dinner?"

"Yes, Misha."

"Cool! What are you cooking?"

"He's bringing dinner with him."

"I hope he brings Chinese food. I love fried rice."

Mia smiled indulgently. "Yes, you do. But I'm afraid I'm not sure what kind of food he's bringing. We didn't talk about it."

Just then her phone rang. She walked over to the kitchen counter and checked the screen. Her heart sank.

"Who is it? Is it Logan? Don't tell me he's not coming!" Mikhail looked about ready to cry.

She waved his questions away and turning her back on him, answered the call. "Dimitri. I thought I told you last time you called that I never wanted to speak with you again," she said in a no-nonsense tone.

"Amelia, just listen to me. You were overwrought, shocked about the death of your father. We all were. But that was more than a year ago. It's time we talked."

"No, Dimitri. I don't want to talk and I don't care how long it's been. I have no interest in being involved in my father's business."

"But you're perfectly situated to help us, Amelia! Your shop—"

"Don't you dare bring my shop into this! I built that business all on my own. I didn't take a cent from anyone. I'm not having it tainted by you or the ghost of my father. Do you understand?"

Behind her, the doorbell rang. Mikhail leaped up from his chair to answer it. Mia heard him greet Logan enthusiastically before the two of them reappeared in the living room. She quickly ended her call and turned to face them.

Logan looked breathtakingly handsome in a pair of Levis and an emerald green polo shirt that darkened the color of his eyes. Mia had spent an inordinate time on her wardrobe. She'd finally decided upon a pair of loose, colorful, Balinese-style cotton pants and a long-sleeved, white linen shirt. She'd rolled the sleeves up to her elbows and had tied the bottom of the shirt into a knot around her waist. She'd surveyed the results in the mirror in her bedroom and had been pleased with the overall effect. It was stylish, yet casual. She'd left the top two buttons undone, which allowed for a glimpse of cleavage. Sexy, but not over the top. After all, he'd made it clear they were only friends.

That didn't mean she couldn't try and change his mind. She'd told him the truth when she'd said she wasn't on the hunt for a husband, but that didn't mean she wasn't a hopeless romantic who dreamed of one day finding someone to love and adore and build a family with.

Of course, it wasn't as easy as that. Her Mr Perfect would also have to be willing to take on the responsibility of Mikhail. It would be a long time before her brother was able to stand on his own two feet, if ever. She'd accepted years ago that she'd probably share her house with him for the rest of her life. And she was perfectly fine with that, but it would take a special man to accept that. Something told her Logan Craigdon could be that man. She wondered what had happened in his life to turn him so against marriage and was determined to find out. With that thought in mind, she offered him a wide smile.

"It's great to see you again. Thank you for coming."

He smiled back. "Thanks for inviting me. I hope you like Chinese food. And if you don't, there's Thai, Indian, Mexican and oh, some Italian. Just pasta and a pizza." With a rueful grin, he held up his hands which were laden with plastic bags filled with takeaway containers.

She laughed and shook her head. "You bought all of that? I hope you're hungry."

He looked abashed. "I forgot to ask what you and Mikhail liked to eat, so I got a bit of everything. You can always pack away the leftovers for later."

"Or you can take them home. There's enough food here to feed a stadium full of people."

"Like I said, I wanted to cover all bases."

"Do you have any spring rolls, Logan? Or fried rice?" asked Mikhail with a hopeful look on his face.

"You bet," Logan replied with a grin. "Spring rolls, prawn toast, fried rice, honey chicken, garlic prawns and so much more."

Mikhail chuckled in delight. He looked at Mia. "It's just

like when we go to the Chinese restaurant on banquet night, right Mia?"

She shot him a tender look. "Right, Misha. It looks like Logan's thought of everything."

While Mia fetched the plates, Logan set about lifting lids off takeaway containers and setting the food out along the counter, like a smorgasbord. Mia looked again at the amount of food and shook her head.

"You really shouldn't have. Chinese food alone would have been fine."

Logan shot her a quick grin. "I'll know better next time."

Mia's heart turned over, both from his casually sexy smile and to the reference of a next time. Though she cautioned herself not to read anything into his comment, it was hard not to while he looked at her with a gaze so filled with appreciation that it looked like he wanted to eat her up.

Dinner passed uneventfully among platefuls of good food and pleasant conversation. After he'd declared himself full to bursting, Mikhail took his plate over to the sink and asked to be excused. He drifted off to the living room to watch TV.

Logan pushed away from the table and took Mia's empty plate. She joined him in the kitchen and together they stacked the dishwasher. She insisted Logan take the leftovers with him.

He laughed. "I live on my own. What am I going to do with it all?"

She shrugged. "I don't know. I guess you could always donate it to the soup kitchen. I'm sure your cousin won't say no."

"Great idea. See, I knew it wouldn't go to waste."

"Thank you once again for your generosity. You shouldn't have."

He shrugged. "Like I said, I wasn't sure what kind of food the two of you ate. Then I wondered if Mikhail had food allergies or a special diet or whether he just didn't like certain foods and I kind of went overboard trying to cover every possibility."

"It was very sweet of you," she replied softly. Their gazes caught and held. Her heart thumped. Without conscious thought, she drifted closer toward him until there was barely a whisper of space between them. Her eyes fluttered closed.

"So, tell me about Mikhail."

Just like that, the moment was broken. She flushed hotly with embarrassment and awkwardly turned away, busying herself at the sink even though the dishwasher had already been stacked and there was nothing left to clean. She forced herself to face him.

"Sure," she said in an overly bright manner. "What do you want to know?"

"Well, I already know he's fourteen, but he seems a little small for his age and…"

She nodded briskly, now all business. She was used to people asking questions about Mikhail.

"You're right. He's both physically and mentally delayed. Our mother was an alcoholic and a drug addict. She drank heavily and used drugs the whole time she was pregnant. Mikhail was born with Fetal Alcohol Syndrome. Have you heard of it?"

"Yes. I'm sorry. Shit. Poor kid."

She compressed her lips against a familiar surge of anger. "Yep. It's something he'll deal with his entire life and none of it was his fault."

"It makes you angry."

"Of course it makes me angry! What kind of mother does that?"

"What about your father? Didn't he have any say in it?"

Her shoulders slumped on a wave of defeat. "Dad wasn't around long enough to notice. He was busy with…other things."

Logan leaned against the kitchen counter, his arms folded casually across his chest. "Tell me about your parents."

A wave of familiar pain and sadness mixed with anger and frustration washed over her. She took a few moments to rinse her hands and dry them before turning to face him once again.

"Are you sure you want to hear this? It isn't pretty."

"I'm sure."

She sighed. "I was adopted by Marina and Alexander Ivanov when I was five. By that time, Marina had lost four babies to miscarriages. They'd opted to try another route. My father once told me they'd gone to the adoption center seeking a boy, but he heard me laughing with some of the other kids and decided he'd prefer me." She shrugged. "I got lucky."

"Were you orphaned at birth?" he asked gently.

"No." She sighed again. "My birth mother was killed in a car accident when I was five. She was a single mother. I never knew my biological father. After my mother's death, I was in and out of foster care. Then the Ivanovs came along."

Logan's face flooded with surprise and compassion. "Wow. You've had a rough time of it."

She compressed her lips. "I was one of the lucky ones. I was adopted. There are plenty of kids in foster homes who aren't as fortunate."

"You're right." He paused. "My mother was also killed in a car accident. It happened ten years ago. My uncle was behind the wheel. He lived with the guilt of it for the rest of his life, even though none of us blamed him. There was a kangaroo. He swerved to miss it. The police ruled it an accident." He paused and then added, "A few weeks ago we discovered Uncle Henry had every reason to feel guilty. He'd been drunk behind the wheel. It was just as shocking to discover my mom had cocaine in her system."

Mia's body flooded with shock. "Your mother took illegal drugs?"

Logan shrugged. His expression went blank. "That time, at least."

Mia frowned, her heart thumping. After the toll illegal drugs had taken on her family, she wanted to keep herself and Mikhail well away from them. She had to know how Logan felt about them.

She narrowed her gaze on him. "Do you use drugs?"

If her bald question surprised him, he didn't show it. His expression turned somber and his lips thinned. With his gaze steady on hers, he shook his head.

"No."

"Never?"

"Never."

He said it with such conviction, she was filled with relief. His mother might have used illegal drugs in the past, but it wasn't fair to blame Logan for that. He had no control over his mother's decisions. Mia knew firsthand from her father that family didn't always act the way you wanted.

"Good," she said. "Because it's a deal breaker for me, even for friendships. My adoptive mother—Mikhail's mother—died of a drug overdose. The very thought of illegal drugs and the damage they do makes me angry beyond belief." She looked him straight in the eye. "I could never be friends with someone who took them, even for fun."

"That's fine. I'm not into drugs. Never have been."

She nodded, satisfied with his answers.

He sighed quietly and ran a hand through his hair, setting it askew. "I take it your adoptive mother wasn't always an alcoholic drug addict?"

"No. At least, not like she was by the time Mikhail came along. They'd always thought they couldn't have children. Mikhail was their miracle baby. It was too bad Mom didn't see him that way. It might have given her the incentive she needed to rid herself of her addictions."

"And your father didn't try to intervene?"

"Not really. Neither of them knew she was pregnant until she was more than halfway through her pregnancy. Dad spent many hours working outside the home and when he was there, he didn't seem all that interested in what my mom was up to. I guess the love they'd felt for each other in the early days had dissipated by then."

"And yet you own a bridal wear shop," Logan mused with a tinge of disbelief.

She shrugged, a little embarrassed. "What can I say? In spite of my upbringing, or maybe because of it, I'm a hopeless romantic. I want to believe in everlasting love, in knights in shining armor, in happy-ever-afters. I refuse to let the sadness and tragedy that seemed to follow me all through my life define me."

She paused and then added, "I made a conscious decision to put that behind me and to focus only on the good in this world. I wanted to create happy moments to replace the sad. What better way to do that than with a bridal shop? How many unhappy brides do you know?"

She'd said it lightly, but noticed a darkness come over his face. His eyes shuttered. She could almost feel his withdrawal, but this time she wasn't going to let it go unchallenged.

"What is it, Logan? What did I say?"

He shook his head, his voice brusque. "Nothing."

"Please, tell me," she urged softly.

"It's just the whole thing about happy brides and weddings and everything. That's not the way I've experienced it."

She started in surprise. "You've been married?"

"No. Well, not quite. My fiancée jilted me at the altar. We'd been together since high school."

She gasped in shock. "Oh, Logan! I'm so sorry! That's awful!"

His expression remained grim. "Yeah."

"When did it happen?"

"Just over a year ago. Feels like yesterday."

Her heart clenched at the pain in his voice. "You still haven't gotten over her."

He shook his head, his eyes flashing. "No, that's not right. I've gotten over her all right. It's just the unanswered questions that I can't let go of. Mainly, *why*. She'd declared her eternal love. We'd been together forever. Marriage was the next logical step. I proposed and she accepted." He paused and then seemed to make up his mind about something. "It seemed she didn't even mind my leg," he added.

Mia remembered asking him about his leg back in the coffee shop. He'd closed down their conversation. She wondered what had happened to change his mind.

"You told me you'd broken it in several places. How did it happen?" she asked.

He grimaced. "A sailing accident. I was racing. We were flying along. Forty or fifty knots. We were out in front. Then a rogue wave came across the bow and caught me by surprise. I was knocked over. My leg got caught in a loose line. The next thing I knew I was hanging over the side of the boat. The only thing keeping me there was my leg."

He shook his head as if to clear the memories. "It all happened so quickly. One of my crewmen managed to reach me and haul me back into the boat, but by then the damage was done. The bone in one leg didn't mend well. I'm lucky I didn't lose it."

"There are worse things than losing a leg. You could have drowned," she said quietly.

"There was a time when I wished I had." His lips twisted in a humorless laugh. "Hell, what am I talking about? There are still times when I wish I had."

She stared at him in surprise and with a growing anger. "How could you say such a thing? You have your life. From what I can tell, it's a good life. Some people would do anything to have what you have, limp and all!"

Her breath came fast. Heat suffused her face. He frowned down at her, perplexed. "Whoa! Steady! It's easy for you to say. You're not the one with a useless leg that aches at night, and other times. That's the reason my career came to an end. My life is shit and that's the truth. Besides, what would you know about it? You might have suffered some knocks early on in life, but from what I can see, you've come through it all right."

He looked around at their comfortable surroundings, the designer furnishings, the waterfront views. She wasn't about to tell him most of those things had been purchased by her father from the proceeds of his illegal drug business, including the multimillion dollar house they stood in. She'd inherited everything on his death.

While she'd wanted to turn her back on everything his dirty money had bought, she wasn't stupid. She and Mikhail needed somewhere to live and as profitable as her little bridal wear shop was, she could never have afforded something like this. So she kept the house and its expensive furnishings and transferred the balance of her father's bank account into her name for Mikhail's benefit, and vowed never to take another dollar of her father's money.

Not that she'd ever been tested on that vow. The drug money had dried up on her father's death. Without him at the helm, there was no drug business. She'd found an address book crowded with names and phone numbers in a safety deposit box that she could only assume related to his business operatives, but she quickly returned the book to where she found it and tried to put its existence out of her mind. She'd donated the stash of cash she'd found to charity.

But Logan knew none of this. In fact, he knew very little about her and her life and yet he had the audacity to judge her. Her anger found its head.

"How dare you! You know nothing about me!"

His eyes narrowed. "I know enough."

"Yeah? You don't know about *this*." With that, she lifted the loose leg of her pants, pushing it up above her knee. "See?" she cried.

He stared down at her leg in confusion and then slowly comprehension flooded his face. "You… You have a prosthetic leg?"

Chapter Six

*L*ogan stared at her in shock. Never in his wildest dreams had he imagined Mia with an artificial leg. With a closed expression, she dropped her pant leg and it fell back into place. Spinning on her heel, she strode to the opposite side of the room, as if needing to put some space between them. Her breath came fast. She crossed her arms over her chest and drew in some deep breaths. It was obvious she was working hard to get her anger back under control. She looked at him.

"I'm sorry. I didn't mean to spring it on you like that. I was upset. I lost my temper." She drew in another deep breath and looked at him. "Yes. I have a prosthetic leg."

He continued to feel dazed. "H-how? What happened?"

She stared at the floor. "Remember the car accident I told you about that killed my mother?"

"Yeah."

"What I didn't tell you was that I was also in the car. A vehicle ran a red light. It collided with our car, on the driver's side. I was seated behind my mother. My leg was crushed. They couldn't save it. They amputated just below the knee."

Logan stared at her, still feeling shocked. "God, I'm so sorry."

She was calm now. It appeared she was almost relieved he knew. She looked at him, obviously expecting more.

Logan was flooded with guilt. "I feel like an ass."

"Good. You were an ass."

"Does it hurt?" Is it uncomfortable?" he asked tentatively.

"No, not anymore."

"I never guessed. You walk easily. There's no indication."

"I'm lucky. I had good doctors."

"I had good doctors, too. The best money could buy. It wasn't enough."

"At least they saved your leg."

"Yes. They did. And I'm…grateful," he said, realizing for the first time that was true.

"That's not what it sounded like to me." She wasn't going to let him get off that easily.

"You're right." He hung his head in shame. "There's always someone worse off. That's what my father always tried to tell me. I didn't want to listen." He looked at her.

Her eyes flashed with anger. She clenched her fists. "Don't go feeling sorry for me."

He threw up his arms in a sign of surrender. "I don't. I admire you. You have every reason to be bitter and resentful. You've suffered more than your share of hard knocks. Yet you haven't let it define you. Or defeat you."

His voice lowered a notch, got husky with emotion. "I don't know you very well, but you're probably the strongest woman I've ever met. A warrior. Taking all the blows life has thrown at you and still smiling." He paused and then added, "I've never met anyone like you."

He moved closer and reached out, unable to help himself. He cupped her cheek and stroked his thumb across the silkiness of her skin. "You're so beautiful."

Almost in a daze, he leaned forward and touched his lips to hers. They were as soft as they looked. Sweet, full, sensuous. He tasted her momentary surprise and then her lips opened beneath his, as if she was as powerless as he was to stand against the magnetic attraction that had been between them from the start. He pulled her hard against him and deepened the kiss.

Her tongue came out tentatively and touched his, igniting a flame inside him. With their lips fused together, he plundered her mouth, greedily taking all she was willing to give. When they finally broke apart, they were both breathing hard. She stared up at him, her face flushed with desire.

"Logan…"

He pressed a finger against her lips, silencing her. "*Shh. Don't speak.*"

"But… What about what you said? About just being friends?"

He shot her a rueful smile and then pulled her in for a hug. She felt so right in his arms. "Did I say that? I'm an idiot. You and I could never just be friends."

She pulled slightly away from him. "What are you saying?"

"There's something about you, Mia Ivanov. Something special. I've been fighting my attraction to you, but now I realize there's no point. It's obvious we both want this."

A tentative smile broke out across her face, stealing his breath. "Things are moving so fast."

"Does that scare you?"

She nodded. "Yes."

"Good, because it scares me, too. But something inside me keeps pushing me forward, wanting me to take the risk. I want to get to know you, Mia. I want to see you again. I want to be more than friends."

She looked up at him, her eyes wide. "Do you mean that?"

"I've never been more serious is my life."

"And my leg…doesn't bother you?"

"Does my leg bother you?" he asked instead.

She frowned. "No, of course not."

"You haven't even seen it. There are lots of scars from the surgery. Most of them permanent. It's not pretty." He wasn't smiling.

Impatience flooded her face. "I don't give a toss about what your leg looks like, or whether it works or not. I like you for who you are. I like you a lot. And that's the truth. Nothing else matters."

Relief poured through him. "You're right. That's the only thing that matters."

Their second kiss was slower, sweeter, less frantic. They took their time to get to know the curves and crevices, the light, the shade, the heat. He buried his fingers in her hair and slanted his mouth across hers. Their tongues met and danced, entwined, flooding him with need. His cock throbbed, pressed hard against her. He longed to lie down with her on a bed of softness and bury himself inside her, but there was Mikhail to think about. This wasn't the time or the place. Reluctantly, he set her away from him.

"Logan…?" She blinked up at him, confused.

"There's nothing I want more than to follow this through to its natural conclusion, but I don't think that's such a good idea right now. Mikhail…"

Sanity returned to her gaze. She nodded. "You're right. I don't know what I was thinking. I got carried away. I'm sorry."

He framed her face in his hands. "Don't be sorry. I want it as much as you. But I also want our first time to be special. I want to take my time. It could take…hours."

Her eyes widened. "Hours?"

He grinned. "At least three or four."

She laughed. "Oh, only three or four. I'm disappointed."

He swatted her playfully on her butt. "Brat."

She laughed again and then slowly turned more serious. "Thank you for tonight. I had a really nice time."

He moved close enough to press his forehead against hers. "So did I. Let's do it again sometime."

"It's a date," she murmured against his lips.

"You bet."

Mia felt like she was walking on air. She floated around the bridal shop, straightening dresses, checking sizes, cataloguing stock. She'd fallen asleep with the feel of Logan's lips on hers, the warm and shivery feeling she got whenever he was near, still swirling through her veins. She'd shared some of her deepest secrets with him. She'd told him about her childhood, her accident, about Mikhail, her hopes and dreams. She'd even told him how much she liked him and he hadn't run for the hills. She was the luckiest girl in the world.

The only black mark on the whole evening was the phone call from Dimitri. Fortunately he'd called before Logan had arrived. Though she'd shared so much of herself with him, she hadn't dared to tell him the truth about her father or the pressure Dimitri continued to exert from afar.

At the thought of her father's henchman, a wave of anger and some fear washed over her. She hadn't seen the man since her father's funeral, but he'd called her a couple of months afterwards and had put forward a business proposition. The members of her father's cartel had been talking. They'd all agreed she should be offered her father's position at the table. It was hers for the taking.

She'd been shocked and outraged that they'd thought she'd want to have anything to do with the illegal business that had killed both of her parents and left her and her brother orphans. She knew firsthand what that felt like. There was no way Mikhail would be sent to a foster home.

Fortunately, she was old enough to take care of him. Eventually she'd been appointed his legal guardian. Mikhail knew nothing of the life of crime their father had led and that's the way it would stay.

The bridal shop turned a decent profit. Enough to cover their needs. She hated that she'd had to use some of the money in her father's bank account to pay for Mikhail's expensive school and the upkeep on the house, but she was prepared to do whatever it took to give her brother a comfortable life. That didn't mean she was willing to become involved in the illegal drug trade. She could only hope she'd convinced Dimitri he was wasting his time.

"Hi, Mia. I just checked the appointments. You're booked solid today."

Mia looked up in time to see her assistant, Katerina Popov, walk in from the back where Mia kept her office.

"Oh. Do I have time to take Misha to his sailing lesson?"

Katerina shook her head. "I don't think so. Your first appointment's due any minute."

Mia felt a surge of disappointment at the thought of not seeing Logan again. "Oh, too bad. I've been enjoying… getting outside to catch some sea air."

Just then, Mikhail came bounding out of her office. "Mia! Come on! It's time to go sailing! Come on!"

He grabbed her hand and began to pull her toward the exit. She gently disengaged her hand.

"I'm sorry, Misha. I don't have time to take you today."

"No!" Mikhail howled in distress.

"It's okay. I can take him," Katerina offered quickly.

Mia turned to her brother. "Would that be all right? Can Katerina take you?"

"Yes! I'll go with Katerina. Come on! It's time to go sailing!"

Mia shot her assistant a look of gratitude and mouthed, *Thank you.*

Katerina merely shrugged. As the two of them walked out hand in hand, Mia sighed in relief.

Crisis averted…

With disappointment still swirling inside her stomach, Mia made preparations for the upcoming appointment. Ample bottles of champagne and orange juice were chilling in the fridge. Clean glasses were lined up on a shelf. She chose a playlist of modern tunes, something she thought might suit the young bride who was the first client on her list that morning.

Mia thought about texting Logan an apology and letting him know she was unable to get away from the shop. After the intimacies they'd shared the night before, she didn't want him to think she was avoiding him. She also wanted to let him know she was keen to see him again. Then she thought better of it.

She had to think about Mikhail. He was her priority. Any change to her life and the people she allowed in it directly affected him. Though he seemed to have a good rapport with Logan, she didn't want to rush anything. Besides, she didn't really know how Logan felt.

He'd told her he liked her and it was obvious he was attracted to her. The passion in his kisses had been testament to that. But she needed more than passion. She needed love and respect and caring, safety and security—for both her and Mikhail. They were a team. A package deal. It was a big ask of anyone. It would take a very special person with a kind and generous heart to take them on.

Is Logan that person?

Her heart skipped a beat. *He could be… But it's really too soon to know…*

The bell above the door tinkled. She looked up in time to see her ten o'clock appointment walk into the shop with four bridesmaids in tow.

"You must be Lucy! How lovely to meet you. I'm Mia."

Mia shook the bride's hand in greeting and then introduced herself to the bridesmaids. Two of them were Lucy's sisters and two of them were friends. They were all a similar shape and size. Mia breathed a silent sigh of relief. It was always easier to dress a bridal party when the same style looked equally good on all of them.

"So, ladies. Welcome to Wishes and Dreams. It's wonderful to have you here."

The bride grinned. "We're so excited! We can't wait to start trying on dresses."

Mia smiled. "And I can't wait to help you find the perfect one. As the bride, we're going to start with you. After all, you're the most important person in the room, right?" She winked at Lucy.

The bride laughed. "Oh, I knew I was going to like you, Mia! I read that article in *Modern Bride* last month. The writer raved about you. She talked about how warm and welcoming you are and how you made her feel like a princess. I can see she wasn't exaggerating."

Mia blushed. She recalled the journalist who'd contacted her and asked to do a story on the shop. Though Mia didn't seek out publicity and preferred word of mouth over paid advertising, having a story done on her business in a magazine as reputable as *Modern Bride* was almost too good to be true. As it turned out, the journalist was also a bride-to-be. In between trying on dresses and not resting until they'd found the perfect one, Mia had shared her motivation behind starting the business.

Of course, she'd left out the bit about her drug dealer father and her adoptive mother who was an addict, but she'd shared enough to convey she'd had her fair share of sadness and challenges. Hence the yearning to spread a little sunshine where she could. What better way to do that than through a bridal wear shop? And today, after her evening with Logan, she felt even happier than usual. She beamed at the bride.

"Thank you, Lucy. That's very kind of you. I do my best. The most important thing to remember is, this is your day. No matter the well-meaning suggestions from others, including me, the decision is ultimately yours. This is one time you don't need to make a choice based on someone else's needs. Okay?"

Lucy grinned and nodded. Her eyes sparkled with excitement. "Okay."

Mia smiled back. For a lot of women, the knowledge they had complete control over the next few hours was a heady moment and one they didn't take lightly. Mia also found the knowledge usually filled her brides with confidence and that always helped when trying to choose a "happy-ever-after" dress from among the myriad of styles that lined Mia's racks.

The rest of the morning was spent surrounded by yards of silk, satin, chiffon and lace. Katerina arrived back with an exuberant Mikhail in tow. He was full of chatter about sailing and Logan, but Mia was unable to spare more than a brief moment to give her brother a quick hug. She ruthlessly pushed thoughts of Logan aside and allowed herself to be dragged back into the world of excitement and possibility that consumed her whenever she was with a bride.

Once Mia had ascertained the style of dress Lucy had her heart set on, it was a matter of finding the dress to match the fantasy. This wasn't always easy, but Mia had learned long ago the art of tact and perhaps more importantly, of gentle persuasion.

Thankfully, Lucy was easygoing and happy to accept Mia's recommendations. In between glasses of champagne and delicious canapés Mia ordered in from Joanna's café, Lucy tried one dress on after another and paraded before her bridesmaids, seeking their input. In the end, they decided on a figure-hugging, strapless satin-and-chiffon concoction that was both flattering and beautiful. The intricate beading on the bodice was particularly stunning.

"I just love it," Lucy gushed, staring at herself in the mirror. "This is the one." She turned to face Mia. There were tears in her eyes.

Mia swallowed against the lump in her throat, also close to tearing up. Finding the right dress for a bride was such an emotional journey. She was usually exhausted after a session like this one. In fact, if she were truthful, her feet hurt from standing on them for so long and her mouth was dry from talking.

Still, nothing could dampen her mood that day and the joy on Lucy's face only strengthened Mia's certainty that for some people, it was more than possible to have a happy-ever-after. She always finished a session like this one filled with hope.

As if of their own volition, her thoughts went to Logan. A smile tugged at her lips.

Katerina sidled up to her. "You look happier than usual after such a long morning. What gives?"

Mia blushed. "N-nothing. You know how it is. Being around brides always make me feel happy. Lucy was a particular joy to work with."

"True, but there's something more today. A certain sparkle in your eyes that wasn't there yesterday. If I didn't know any better, I'd guess there's a new man in your life."

Mia widened her eyes in mock amazement. "A man? Since when have I had a man in my life, new or otherwise?"

"You're right. I don't think I've ever seen you even go on a date. Still, there's only one reason a woman gets that kind of look in her eyes. What's his name?"

Mia waved her off. "Don't be silly. You're imagining things."

Katerina continued to regard her closely, a speculative gleam in her eyes. "No, there's definitely something going on. Are you sure it doesn't have anything to do with Mikhail's sailing instructor? He's awfully cute. What's his name? Logan?" Katerina winked.

Heat burned across Mia's cheeks. She turned away before Katerina could see the alarm that now flooded through her. How could it be so obvious? It had only been last night she and Logan had been together. How quickly her life had been turned upside down! How quickly her happiness revolved around him…

And then she sobered. The smiled faded from her lips.

What am I thinking? I can't get into a relationship with Logan. What about Mikhail? What would he think?

All his life, Mikhail had been the center of her attention. Her whole world. He liked Logan well enough, but as his sailing instructor. She was sure he wouldn't conceive the possibility Logan might become a more permanent fixture in their lives. Mia couldn't even guess how he might take the idea if she dared suggest it to him.

No, she needed to slow things down with Logan, for everyone's sake. After all, she barely knew him and he still didn't know about her father. She didn't think her dad being a drug dealer would matter a whole lot in the scheme of things. After all, he'd mentioned his mother had taken drugs.

Logan didn't seem the type who would blame her for the sins of her father, but what if she were wrong? Explosive passion was one thing, but it wasn't as important as trust, openness, honesty, acceptance. Until he knew everything about her and she about him, she'd best reel in her emotions and tread cautiously.

She grinned at the irony. She was the hopeless romantic, the one who believed in love and happy-ever-afters. He was the one who'd been burned. After hearing how he'd been jilted at the altar, she understood his reticence to get involved again. But here she was, the one thinking about pulling back, employing caution, slowing things down.

He appeared to be everything she'd been dreaming of, but she had Mikhail to think about. A little voice in her head warned her that nothing and no one was perfect. She barely knew Logan and she knew nothing about his family—other than the fact they were richer than Midas. She was way out of her league. If she rushed headlong into a relationship with

Logan she risked having her heart broken and Mikhail's heart as well and that wouldn't be good for anyone.

No, as much as she wanted to rush madly into the headiness that was Logan Craigdon, she owed it to her brother to take things slow. Starting now.

Chapter Seven

The traffic light turned green and Logan took off with a squeal of tires, impatient with the wait. It was early evening and the majority of peak-hour traffic had dissipated, leaving him almost alone on the road. This time the night before, he'd been eating takeaway food with Mia and Mikhail. The memory of the way he and Mia had ended their evening was still fresh. It had been all he could think about.

He'd watched eagerly for her to arrive with Mikhail that morning and had been wretchedly disappointed when the boy had arrived with a stranger. The young blond woman had been pretty enough, but she hadn't made his heart race like Mia did. She'd introduced herself as Katerina and had explained she worked for Mia. She relayed Mia's apologies and told him her boss was tied up all day.

Logan had mumbled some kind of response and had fought to hide his disappointment. He'd turned away and was immediately annoyed by his reaction. He barely knew Mia and already he was acting like a besotted idiot. It was ridiculous. Where was his cool? His pride? He, of all people, knew better than to get tangled up with a woman for longer than a night.

Still, he couldn't deny she drew him and made him forget past hurts. She was special, like no other woman he'd met.

Though he didn't know her well, there was something so good and upfront about her that seemed genuine. He couldn't imagine her being deceitful. She'd called him out for being an ass. Even better, she'd made it clear she wasn't looking for anything permanent.

He'd spent long hours lying in his bed awake the previous night, thinking about her. And then he turned his introspection on himself. Slowly he arrived at the conclusion his father was right. It was time he stepped up and took over some of the responsibility of running Craigdon Super Yachts.

The reason he'd resisted for so long was because he was resentful that CSY hadn't been his choice. Working in his father's company had been thrust upon him by reason of his accident, and while he'd come to love designing and building the luxury vessels, he'd never imagined it would be his life. His life had been on the water, the thrill of racing, the adrenaline flooding through his veins. Until that life-changing accident that had put an end to his dreams.

But since meeting Mia, his attitude had changed. He'd gained perspective. If anyone had cause to be resentful it was her. Orphaned at five and with an amputated leg after being involved in a tragic accident that had killed her biological mother. Adopted to somewhat dubious parents who had also died, leaving her with the responsibility of looking after her teenage brother who might never develop past the mental age of ten.

She'd been tested more than most and yet still managed to see the best in life and everyone around her. He'd meant it when he'd told her he admired her. And now it was time for him to grow up and quit blaming the accident and his ex on everything he wasn't happy with in his life.

Now he pressed down on the accelerator and the powerful car leaped forward as he left the city far behind. He was headed for his father's house on the outskirts of Richmond.

It was the same home where Logan had grown up. They'd moved there not long after Uncle Henry had. Their houses were close enough to be easily accessible on a pushbike.

It had been fun when they were all kids. He could remember spending many a weekend with his cousins. They'd come to his house or he'd gone to theirs. It was probably why he and his cousins were all so close. They'd spent a lot of time together while they were growing up. Their fathers might not have always gotten along, but that hadn't affected the relationship between their kids, which was a good thing. Logan couldn't imagine not having his cousins in his life.

He hadn't phoned ahead to let his father know he was coming. The truth was, he'd only just firmed up his decision. It would be one his father would be pleased about. That's why Logan was paying him a visit. To tell him in person. To watch his father's reaction. To bask in the warm feeling and closer connections his announcement would create.

He pulled into the long paved driveway that led to his father's house. The house was ablaze with light, reassuring him his father was home. As he drew closer, his headlights caught on a silver Audi parked in the circular drive. He frowned in surprise. He hadn't expected to find Elizabeth here this late at night. The two had admitted to having an affair that produced Sophia, but that had been twenty-two years ago. Surely it wasn't still going on? For the first time, he wondered if they still had feelings for each other.

Climbing out of his Mercedes, he pushed the thought aside and went up the wide steps that led to the front entryway. After a cursory knock, he opened the front door.

"Dad? Are you there?"

"Logan? Is that you?"

He heard the surprise in his father's voice. "Yes, Dad. It's me."

"Come in. We're in the living room."

Logan crossed the short hallway and walked into the room off the kitchen. Once upon a time, back when his mother was still alive, it had been the place where they'd all hung out after dinner—talking, reading, playing card games, watching TV. Now his father had made it his own. Apart from two comfortable leather couches, there was also a well-stocked bar, a small fridge and a widescreen TV. A pool table had been added a few Christmases past.

Archie stood as he entered. "Logan. It's good to see you, son."

Logan nodded in Elizabeth's direction. He and his father hugged a little awkwardly. The last time Logan had spoken to his father, they'd argued over Archie's continued insistence that Logan step up and take over more responsibility in the family company. It had been a familiar argument, one that had been going on for more than a year.

"How are things?" he asked.

Archie nodded. "Good. Your ears must have been burning. Elizabeth and I were just talking about you."

Logan raised an eyebrow and once again looked in his aunt's direction. She was seated on the couch, knitting.

He looked back at his father. "Really? About what?"

"Your father was telling me how much he'd like for you to take over the reins from him at CSY. He appreciates the time you've spent on the factory floor, but he wants you at the helm, helping to make the day-to-day decisions."

Logan braced himself for the familiar tightening in his gut. This time it didn't come. Instead, he smiled. "I see. And did you draw any conclusions?"

Elizabeth regarded him solemnly. "You might be surprised to discover I took your side, Logan. No one should be forced to give up their dreams. If your passion is boatbuilding, then that is what you should do."

She spoke with such determination, Logan couldn't help

but feel surprised. "You sound as though you speak from personal experience."

Elizabeth bowed her head. In the soft glow of the lamplight, her thick white hair created a halo around her face. Even at sixty, she was still an attractive woman. It was obvious what Henry had seen in her. And Archie, for that matter. Then she raised her face and looked at him, her gaze clear and direct.

"As a matter of fact, I do."

Once again, Logan started with surprise. "Really?"

"Yes. When I was young, I wanted to be a concert pianist. My parents didn't think it was suitable for a girl like me to have a career. I was meant to find a husband, marry well and make him a good wife. Which I did as best I could."

The melancholy in her tone made Logan feel inexplicably sad for her. It was obvious she still yearned after the loss of her dream. He welcomed her support and felt a rush of gratitude.

He moved to take the seat beside her. "I appreciate you taking my side in this, Aunt Elizabeth. Dad and I have been at odds about it for a while."

"Yes, so I understand."

"The thing is, it doesn't matter anymore." He glanced at his father. Archie's forehead furrowed in confusion. Logan hurried to explain.

"I've been thinking and I agree. It's time for me to take on more responsibility at CYS. You're not getting any younger and someone needs to be able to stand in when you're ready to retire."

Archie's eyes widened in surprise. "You mean, you're going to give up working on the factory floor and start taking an interest in the day-to-day running of the company?"

"Yes."

Archie reeled back, his mouth agape. "Wow. That's... That's great."

"Of course, I'm not going to give up designing. We're going to have to work around that."

"Of course," Archie readily agreed. "I'm just thrilled you're finally willing to become more involved. Do you mind me asking what brought about this sudden change of heart?"

"Let's just say I met someone and she managed to give me some perspective."

"Does she have a name? I'd like to meet her," Archie said. "Mia. Mia Ivanov."

Archie and Elizabeth exchanged a glance. "Ivanov? She isn't Alexander's daughter, is she?" Archie asked.

Logan started in surprise. "Yes, as a matter of fact, I think that's her father's name. He died about a year ago."

"Right. A gangland shooting. I remember."

Now it was time for Logan's mouth to gape. "A gangland shooting? No. I think you have the wrong Alexander Ivanov. Mia said her father was in construction, like Uncle Henry. He had his own company."

His father merely shrugged. "No matter. Perhaps I'm mistaken." He paused. "Tell us more about her. What does she do?"

"She owns a bridal wear shop in Mosman."

Archie's eyebrows flew up in surprise. Elizabeth looked equally shocked.

"A bridal wear shop?" Archie asked, incredulous.

Feeling defensive, Logan stared back at them. "Yes. What's so wrong about that?"

"Nothing, nothing," Elizabeth smoothed over.

"It's just that, after the fiasco with Virginia, we didn't think you'd ever get in cahoots with anyone or anything remotely connected with weddings... Yet here you are telling us about a girl you obviously care about and she owns a bridal wear shop." Archie shrugged, looking nonplussed.

"Who says I care about her?" Logan muttered. "I've only mentioned her name. I didn't say I'd proposed to her."

"You're right, son. But she's managed to change your attitude toward something that's been a bone of contention between the two of us for a long time. I don't know how she did it, but you wouldn't have paid her suggestion a second's heed if she didn't mean something to you."

Logan nodded reluctantly. "It wasn't so much a suggestion as a change of perspective, but you're right," he conceded. "She's like no other woman I've ever met. She's… She's amazing. So brave, so smart, so beautiful. But she's not looking for anything long term and that suits me just fine."

Once again, his father and Elizabeth exchanged a look, but the two of them remained silent.

"Where does she live?" Archie eventually asked.

"In Mosman, with her younger brother. Mikhail. He's fourteen."

"Fourteen? How old is this woman?"

"It's all right, Dad. She's twenty-four. She was actually adopted by Marina and Alexander Ivanov when she was five. She never knew her biological father. Her biological mother died in a car accident. Mikhail came along later. He's her step-brother."

"I see," his father replied.

"Anyway," Logan continued, "enough about Mia. I just wanted you to be the first one to know about my change of heart. I'll still be involved in the designing phase, but I'm going to hand over the reins of building them to Jeffery."

"Your foreman?" Elizabeth asked.

"He's more than capable," Archie agreed.

"I think so too," Logan replied.

"So, when do we get to meet your Mia?" Archie asked.

Logan grinned. He liked the way his father referred to her as "his Mia." It made him feel warm inside. "Soon, I hope.

I'm thinking of inviting her to Nick and Isabella's joint engagement party."

"That sounds like a good plan," Archie said. "There will be plenty of family for her to meet, if you want her to."

"Of course I do. That's the idea."

"Okay, well, good then. I'll let Isabella and Nicholas know. The party's being held in the gardens at Craigdon Manor. Saturday week. I hope Mia can make it," Elizabeth said.

Logan stood. "I'll extend an invitation to her. What's the dress code?"

Elizabeth looked a bit put out. "Formal, of course. It's an engagement party, Logan. How else would you dress?"

He merely smiled. His aunt had always been big on formal events. He was sure it must be because she loved to frock up. In all these years, he didn't think he'd ever seen her in the same outfit twice.

"Of course, Aunt Elizabeth. I'll make sure my tuxedo's clean."

She smiled and patted him on the arm. "You do that."

Logan stood. "Well, I should get going. It's getting late."

"Yes," Elizabeth replied. "I should get going, too." She glanced in Archie's direction. "I just popped in to catch up with your father."

Logan pecked her on the cheek. "Would you like me to walk you out?"

Elizabeth blushed and looked away. "No, no. I'm fine. You go ahead. I'm sure Archie will see me out."

Logan hugged his father. "Goodnight, Dad."

"Goodnight, son. I look forward to seeing you in the office."

Logan nodded. "Me too, Dad."

With that, Logan took his leave.

Archie heard the front door open and close behind Logan and began to pace the floor in front of the fireplace, his gut swirling with unease. He turned to face Elizabeth who looked equally concerned.

"What do you think about this Mia girl? She must be Alexander's daughter. How could she not? He had a house in Mosman and a daughter that age. I'm sure her name was Amelia, but it could be Mia for short."

Elizabeth nodded. "Yes, and I know for certain he had a younger son. I remember Henry talking about him once. I think the boy had some kind of problem. Maybe autism? I'm not sure, but there was something."

"Why do you think she's latched onto Logan? She must know he's a Craigdon. It can't be a coincidence that they met. I mean, it's not like he'd have any reason to visit a bridal wear shop."

"You're right. I don't like this. There's something going on. We need to find out what she's up to. Alexander might be dead, but that doesn't mean she hasn't taken over the reins of his business. Her father was a kingpin in the drug trade. I refuse to believe she didn't know about his dealings."

Archie pursed his lips. "Maybe. But let's not be too hasty. After all, your children knew nothing of their father's drug business. At least not while he was alive. It's only been since Nicholas discovered anomalies in the company books that it was uncovered."

Elizabeth nodded grimly. "Yes. At least Henry, for all his lack of morals, didn't involve his children in that business, for which I'm eternally grateful."

Archie scowled. "I wish we'd gone to the police when we first discovered what he was up to."

Elizabeth sighed. "With what, Archie? We had no evidence."

"You heard him so many times on the phone. It was obvious what he was up to."

"Unfortunately that wasn't enough to get him arrested. And even if it was, there was always the risk he had the police on the payroll. Now we know the police covered up Henry's culpability in Janelle's death, it's more than likely that was the case, even back then."

Archie sighed. "You're right. But I still don't like the fact the adopted daughter of one of the kingpins in the Russian mafia is romancing my son. I haven't heard any whispers on the street, but no doubt she's taken over from where her father left off. What does she want with my son? Surely she knows Logan never had anything to do with Henry's drug business."

"Who knows? Maybe she's scoping out the competition? I agree; there's definitely something fishy going on here. I don't believe for an instant she's merely an innocent young woman running a bridal wear shop. She's Alex Ivanov's daughter. Give me a break. It's my guess the shop's just a front. A convenient place to launder drug money."

"We need to watch her closely," Archie added.

"Yes. I'm glad Logan's inviting her to the engagement party. Let's hope she shows. That would give us the perfect opportunity to observe her."

"You don't think Nicholas and Isabella and their partners will mind an extra guest?"

Elizabeth shook her head and laughed. "Goodness gracious, no. I thought having a joint engagement party would be one way to keep the guest list under control—what with Nick and Isabella being siblings, I thought they'd have some mutual guests—but last count we were over five hundred people. At least one hundred of them are Raine's guests. They're flying in from Queensland. Do you know he has nine siblings? Five brothers and four sisters. And his parents. Then there are grandparents, cousins and friends." She laughed again. "No. I don't think one more guest is going to matter to anyone."

Chapter Eight

Katerina Popov tucked a loose strand of blond hair behind her ear and made her way through the crowded tables until she reached her brother in the busy food court. The moment he spied her, he frowned.

"So, what were you able to find out? Who is he?" Dimitri demanded.

Katerina rolled her eyes and offered him a dry smile as she took the seat opposite. "Well hello to you too, brother."

Dimitri's frown deepened. Irritation flooded his pinched face. "I don't have time for games, Katerina. This is important."

She held up her hand to pacify him. "I know, I know, I know."

"So, who is he?"

"She wouldn't tell me, but she was definitely acting strangely."

"How do you mean?"

"Like, more than once I caught her with a silly grin on her face, like she was daydreaming. Women only get like that when there's a man around. Especially women like Amelia Ivanov."

"Oh, he's around all right. I saw him go into her house the other night. He arrived moments after I called her. She had no idea I was right outside. What I want to know is who he is and why he was there."

"So you're spying on my boss now?"

"You haven't left me any choice. How else am I to get enough dirt on her to convince her to join us? *You* don't seem to be making much progress in that regard." He gave her a hard look. "We need that shop, Katerina. It's perfect. No one would suspect a bridal shop being used for money laundering. And we need to move quickly, before one of our competitors moves in and claims her for their own. It's only a matter of time before someone else makes a move. Besides, Igor is getting impatient and neither of us want to poke *that* bear."

Katerina looked at him mutinously. "Tell Igor to calm down. Just because he's the oldest of us doesn't mean he gets to push me around. The thing is, I need more time. Mia doesn't seem interested in her father's business. I've had plenty of conversations with her over the past few months. She says very little about him and when she does, she speaks of him with distaste. I don't think she held him in very high esteem."

"So? What does that have to do with anything?"

"Well, it might mean she disparaged his career in the trade. Maybe even disapproved. I don't know, but she runs her shop above board. She even accounts for cash transactions. Everything she does is done by the book. I just can't see her wanting to be part of what you do."

"What *we* do, Katerina. Don't forget that comfortable apartment of yours overlooking the harbor. We both know you couldn't afford the mortgage payments on your shop assistant salary."

She narrowed her eyes at him in a show of bravado, but her heart clenched in fear. "Are you threatening me, Dimitri?"

His laughter sounded forced. "Of course not, little sister. I'm just reminding you of how it is. The reality is, the income

Igor and I generate from our little family business helps support your lifestyle. Don't forget that. It can easily be taken away."

Katerina lowered her gaze and tried to tell herself she was overreacting. He was her brother. He'd never carry through on his threats. At least, she hoped not. Igor, on the other hand, was another matter. Despite being her brother, he'd always frightened her.

Resigning herself, she breathed out a defeated sigh. "All right. What do you want me to do?"

Dimitri sat forward. His gaze grew intense. "I want you to find out who that man is and why he was visiting Amelia. There's something about him that looked familiar. I can't put my finger on it. I need a name."

"Okay. I'll get you a name."

"Good. And be quick about it. Call me as soon as you have news." With that, Dimitri sat back and pushed away from the table. Within moments, he'd blended in with the crowds that lined the street, leaving Katerina to shake her head over his rudeness and ponder her next steps. She liked Mia but Katerina's lifestyle was important to her. And while she might be able to manage Dimitri, her oldest brother was another matter. Igor was downright terrifying. No one messed with him.

Mia was even more nervous than she'd been a couple of nights earlier, when Logan had come over to dinner. As she picked her way carefully down the grassy bank that led to the beach below, she scanned the crowd of people for Logan. She hadn't seen him since the night at her house and her belly was twisted with nerves and anticipation.

She was a bit disappointed he hadn't phoned her. Katerina said she'd explained why she'd been there with Mikhail instead of Mia and she thought he might have called. Then again, she hadn't called him, either.

"Logan! Logan!"

Her brother's excited cries snapped Mia out of her reverie. Mikhail took off at a run and hurtled toward the sand. Mia followed at a more sedate pace, her heart fluttering. She was glad for the oversized sunglasses that helped disguise the delight she was sure was plastered all over her face. As she reached Logan, she smiled at Mikhail's exuberant chattering. He was thrilled to be there for another day of sailing.

"H-hi," she stammered. Heat exploded across her cheeks. She ducked her head for a second.

"Hi." Logan smiled. His eyes crinkled in that sexy way of his. He gave her a slow once over that left fire trailing in its wake.

"I'm sorry about yesterday…" she began.

He waved her apology away. "It's fine. You're a busy woman. I understand."

She was grateful he didn't make a fuss, but a part of her wished he'd give her some indication he'd missed her.

"That doesn't mean I didn't miss you," he added, as if he read her mind.

She blushed again. "I missed you, too."

His eyes flared with emotion. Heat raced through her veins and centered in her core. It was all she could do not to throw herself in his arms and kiss him senseless.

Careful. I want to take things slowly, remember?

Mikhail hopped from one foot to the other, impatient for the adults to finish talking.

"Come on, Logan! Let's go sailing! Come on!"

Logan half-turned toward Mikhail and ruffled his hair with affection. "Give me two minutes, buddy. I'm just talking with your sister." He faced back toward Mia. "What are you doing afterwards? Do you have time for a coffee?"

Warmth rushed through her at the eagerness in his eyes. She smiled. At the same time, she shook her head.

"I wish I could, but I have another client due at the shop very shortly. In fact, I'm going to have to send my assistant to collect Mikhail after his lesson. Perhaps another time?" she added with a hopeful look.

Disappointment registered on Logan's face. "Sure. How about tomorrow? We could do dinner again. Your house, my house. Either way is fine."

Once again, she shook her head, feeling genuinely regretful. "I'm sorry. Mikhail has a tennis lesson tomorrow afternoon and he's always beat afterwards. Probably not the best night for a dinner date."

Logan began to look desperate. "Too bad. What about after Mikhail's final sailing lesson? There'll be a short ceremony where we hand out certificates and then we're throwing a little party for the kids, to celebrate their achievements. What do you think?"

Mia smiled. "That's very sweet of you. I'll clear my schedule."

Logan's answering grin lit up his face. His eyes sparkled, shining like rare green diamonds. A quiver of desire fluttered through her stomach. Bidding her brother goodbye with a hasty hug, she turned away, flustered, and made her way back up the hill to the street. Her pulse raced at the thought of spending more time with Logan. She couldn't get the smile off her face.

On the short drive back to the shop, she made a conscious effort to school her features into her normal placid expression. She didn't want to give Katerina even more reason to question her. But that was difficult when excitement and anticipation danced along her veins and sent her heart beating a staccato against the walls of her chest.

Her budding relationship with Logan—if that's what she

could call it—was still too new, too fragile to risk sharing the details with someone else. Especially her assistant. Katerina had only been working with her for a few months. She barely knew the woman. And though she was tempted to shout her happiness to the whole world, it would be best to err on the side of caution.

This was her first serious adult relationship. How did she know if these giddy feelings she felt for Logan were the real deal? She'd never been in love. She was completely without experience as far as that went and though she'd lost her virginity when she was sixteen to a boy she barely knew, it had been more a matter of curiosity and physical attraction than love.

Then there was Logan himself. For all his eagerness to spend time with her, she hadn't forgotten the hurt and rejection he'd experienced at the hands of his ex-fiancée. He still felt antsy about commitment and was very nervous when he found out she owned a bridal wear shop. Though she'd attempted to set him at ease, she worried she'd given him the wrong idea when she'd assured him she wasn't in the market for a husband.

Is that why he's now so eager? Because he thinks this is nothing more than a casual fling? A no-strings-attached, mutually beneficial arrangement where both parties get to walk away without a second glance when it's over?

The possibility gave her pause. Though she'd been honest with Logan when she'd told him she wasn't angling for a proposal, that didn't mean she never wanted to get married. In fact, that was something she'd always dreamed about—a husband and family of her own. It troubled her to think he might never feel that way himself.

And then she brushed the disconcerting thoughts aside and concentrated on thinking positive. It was early days. They'd known each other less than a week. Logan had been prepared to commit himself once. Okay, so it hadn't worked out for him and he'd been burned by the experience, but that didn't mean he wouldn't be willing to give it another go, if the timing and the woman were right. She had to believe that.

In the meantime, she'd enjoy whatever time they spent together and get to know him and let him get to know her. The physical attraction between them was undeniable. She was sure it wouldn't take too much effort for them to move from that to an emotional connection that might just last the distance. She certainly hoped it would be so.

"Hey, lover boy! It looks like your girl is here."

At Flynn's teasing comment, Logan looked up from where he was stowing away the last of the dinghies and spied Mia walking toward him. His heart skipped a beat. She wore another pair of loose cotton pants, this time in snowy white. Her hot pink blouse complimented the tones of her skin. She looked fresh and wholesome and beautiful.

He couldn't believe how much she'd come to mean to him in such a short time. It would have concerned him if it had been anyone other than Mia. Lucky for him, she'd made it clear right from the outset she wasn't looking for a husband and that suited him just fine. If anything, it made her even more attractive to him. They could enjoy whatever this was between them without fear of one of them reading more into it than it was.

Today was the final day of the sailing classes. It was the fastest five days he'd ever spent. With a pang, Logan realized he was going to miss the camaraderie he'd struck up with his students. The kids were polite, respectful and enthusiastic. Though they'd had a couple of slight mishaps, everyone and everything—including the borrowed dinghies—had come through the course with no serious damage. Most of all, he was going to miss Mikhail's unadulterated joy and absolute fearlessness when faced with the excitement and challenges that came with sailing.

Logan had enjoyed the week so much more than he'd imagined. He'd been too engaged with teaching first-timers to give much thought to the loss of his promising sailing career and the injuries that had brought it to a crashing end. Next time he saw Callum, he'd thank him for pushing him to take the opportunity. He could now appreciate what it had meant and how it had helped. A lot of it had to do with meeting Mia, but not all of it. Now she stood a few feet away from him with a soft smile of greeting on her lips.

Closing the doors on the storage shed, he turned to greet her. "Hi," he said, flashing her a grin.

"Hi." She looked down at her feet, as if suddenly struck with a bout of shyness. His heart kicked up a beat.

"I'm glad you made it back in time for the ceremony," he said.

She grinned. "Actually, it was the promise of party food that had me coming back."

Her teasing sense of humor made his heart trip over. From the corner of his eye, he saw Flynn coming toward them with a handful of lines.

"Don't forget these," Flynn said.

Logan muttered his thanks and took the lines from his brother. Flynn opened one of the doors of the shed. Logan tossed the lines onto a shelf inside and closed the door once again. "Is that it?" he asked.

"Yep." Flynn's gaze slid to Mia and then back to Logan. "Are you going to introduce me to your friend?"

Logan blushed and was immediately annoyed at himself. "Of course," he mumbled. He indicated Mia with his hand. "Flynn, this is Mia Ivanov. Mia, this is my oldest brother, Flynn."

Flynn stuck out his hand toward Mia. "It's nice to meet you, Mia. Which one of our young sailors is yours?"

Mia smiled. "Mikhail. My brother."

Flynn nodded. "Ah, Mikhail. A natural. He's been a blast. I bet you're fun, too."

Flynn shot her a cheeky look. Mia flushed, but Logan could tell she was enjoying the banter. He frowned. He didn't care for the way his brother was flirting. Besides, Flynn was already spoken for.

"How's Noah going with the party food?" Logan asked, his voice brusque. "How about you get over there and help him out."

Flynn shot Logan a knowing look and Mia another teasing grin, but ambled away without argument. Logan gritted his teeth and counted to five. Flynn meant no harm and he definitely meant nothing by his flirty behavior. Logan was the one with the problem. He had no right to feel so possessive about a woman he barely knew. Talk about overreacting.

He drew in a deep breath and eased it out. "Sorry. I—"

She squeezed his arm. "It's okay, Logan. Don't stress."

Not for the first time, her calm demeanor worked wonders on his psyche and he breathed a sigh of relief. She was so easy going. Nothing seemed to faze her. The only time he'd seen her lose her temper was when he'd been wallowing in self-pity over his leg and her reaction had been completely justified. He'd never have believed he would decide to step up in his father's company when he had felt so adamant a week ago about not doing so. She had a way of making him want to be a better person.

He almost rolled his eyes at his sappy thoughts. Instead, he linked his arm with hers and started walking back across the beach to where the certificate ceremony and party were being held. As they walked side by side he tried not to notice the warmth of her skin where it touched his arm, or the smell of her perfume as it drifted toward him on the slight breeze. Her chestnut hair, which was loose, lifted and feathered about her face. His fingers itched to brush it out of her eyes and follow the movement with a kiss.

But then they arrived and they were surrounded by the students, along with their siblings, parents and caregivers and a madly waving Mikhail who called out happily. Callum briefly addressed the group, thanking Logan and his brothers for giving up their time to run the course. There were murmurs of appreciation. Then Mikhail broke ranks and ran toward him. He threw his arms around Logan's waist.

"Thanks, Logan! You're the best!"

Logan didn't feel the least bit embarrassed. He hugged Mikhail back and ruffled the boy's blond hair with genuine affection.

"You did well, Mikhail. In fact, if you give me a minute, I'd like to make a special presentation to you."

Mikhail looked up at him with amazement. "To *me*?"

Logan grinned. "Yes, buddy. To you."

Logan looked across at Mia who stood a few yards away with the rest of the adults.

Thank you, she mouthed.

Together, Logan, Flynn and Noah handed out certificates to their students. There was much cheering and clapping and laughter all round. It wasn't only Mia who had tears in their eyes. Then Logan handed out the special awards. Each brother had selected a student who'd excelled during the course. For Logan, it had been an easy decision.

"I'd like to present Mikhail Ivanov with an award for most improved. Mikhail, get yourself over here."

Mikhail looked at his sister, a question on his face. Mia nodded her encouragement.

"Go on, Misha. Go on."

Mikhail let out a yelp of delight and galloped barefoot

across the sand, spraying it every which way. The crowd laughed. Logan shook Mikhail's hand and gave him the small trophy. Mikhail's eyes gleamed with pride. He turned toward the crowd and held it up for all to see. There was a loud cheer.

"Yay for Mikhail!" he cried, his eyes sparkling with excitement.

Logan swallowed past the lump in his throat. He saw Mia wipe tears from her eyes. Her brother faced so many challenges and yet that didn't slow him down. He'd deserved the award. Logan was filled with admiration, both for Mikhail and for the woman who'd raised him with such a positive attitude.

She must have sensed his thoughts because Mia came toward him. As if it were the most natural thing in the world, he opened his arms and she stepped into them. He held her tight against him, breathing in the sweetness of her soft hair. After a few moments, she slowly pulled back.

"Thank you," she said. Tears still glinted in her eyes.

"You're welcome," he replied, his voice husky with emotion. "He's a great kid."

She sniffed. "Yes. Yes he is."

"Three cheers for our instructors!" Jackson cried.

"Hip hip hooray! Hip hip hooray! Hip hip hooray!" the children cried in unison. Amid yelps of excitement, they swarmed around the three brothers and dragged them into the water, splashing and shouting the whole time. By the time everyone made back to the beach, they were dripping.

"Who's ready to party?" Flynn shouted.

There was a loud chorus of agreement. Both instructors and kids dried off with towels and then piled around Flynn as he handed out chocolate cake. There were also bowls of potato chips, lollies, flavored popcorn and an abundance of icy cold soft drinks stacked in coolers. The party had been thrown together with little finesse, but it seemed the kids didn't mind. Within moments they were filling their hands and mouths, laughing and talking over the top of each other.

Logan drew Mia aside. "Thanks again for coming, Mia. I know how busy you are."

She waved his comment away. "I wouldn't have missed that for the world. I'm sure it will be all Misha talks about for weeks. Maybe months."

"He deserved it. You ought to look into continuing his lessons with a proper instructor. He has natural talent and he really enjoyed it."

She smiled. "Yes. That sounds like a good idea. Are you available for private lessons?"

He opened his mouth to turn her down and then stopped. Teaching the sailing course hadn't been as painful as he'd imagined it would be. In fact, he'd enjoyed it. Agreeing to give Mikhail some private lessons would not only help the boy, it would also extend the time Logan got to spend with Mikhail's sister. It would be a win for both of them. He found himself nodding.

"Of course. When would you like to start?"

"How about next week? We still have another week of summer holidays. That would mean Misha could come down here every day. Would that work for you?"

"I'll make sure it does. But only on the condition you stay and watch. He loves having you here. It gives him further incentive to try hard. He wants to please you. He wants you to be proud of him."

She blushed and ducked her head. "I know he does. And I am. So proud. He faces every challenge with good humor and a smile." She paused and then added, "I love him very much."

She stared up at him. Logan couldn't look away. "I'm sure the feeling's mutual," he said huskily.

Before he could stop himself, he reached up and touched her face. Her skin felt as soft as silk and smelled as sweet as toffee. He cupped his hand around her cheek and then leaned in and touched his lips to hers. She immediately responded, opening her mouth beneath his. Fire ignited along his nerve endings. He was drowning in her liquid heat, oblivious to everyone and everything. There was no one and nothing but Mia.

The loud clearing of a throat finally penetrated the fog of desire that enveloped him. He broke off the kiss and stood breathing hard, staring at Flynn who stood right behind Mia.

"Logan. For God's sake, control yourself. There are kids around. Surely there's somewhere more private you can do that."

Chapter Nine

Mia's cheeks flamed with embarrassment. She lowered her head and momentarily stared at the ground. It seemed Logan felt much less repentant. He gazed at Flynn, his jaw set at a stubborn angle.

"Sure, bro. No worries."

Logan glanced in her direction and noticed her reaction. She was grateful when he took her by the hand and drew her in close against his side. He squeezed her hand in a silent act of reassurance.

"We're sorry. You're right." Mia said, finding her voice. "This isn't the place."

"Flynn's just jealous," Logan quipped. "Aren't you Flynn?"

Flynn's mouth twisted. "Hardly."

"Good. I'm glad to hear it. Now, clear out. I haven't finished…talking to Mia."

With a baleful look, Flynn left them. Logan immediately drew her close. "I don't know what the hell's got into my brother. He isn't usually so protective."

Mia laughed. "He's just looking out for you. I take it he knows about your ex-fiancée?"

"Yes, of course."

"Maybe he's a bit suspicious of my motives. Maybe he thinks I have designs on you." She winked.

He laughed much too hard. She hid a grimace behind another smile. He hugged her to him and then released her.

"I love your sense of humor, Mia. You're like no other woman I've met. I enjoy being with you. What are you doing next weekend?"

She forced a nonchalant shrug, even as her heart skipped a beat and then went racing away. "Nothing special, as far as I know. Why?"

"I have a family thing. A double engagement party for two of my cousins. I'd like you to come."

Surprise widened her eyes. She stared up at him. "A family double engagement party? That sounds…overwhelming."

He looked impatient. "I know we haven't known each other long, but I like you, Mia. I really like you. I'd like to bring you as my date to the engagement party. Introduce you to my family."

She shot him a dubious look. "As what?"

His gaze was steady on hers. "My girlfriend. Are you all right with that?"

She chewed at her lip with indecision. She wasn't sure she was ready to be introduced to the Craigdon family *en masse*. Then again, it felt kind of thrilling to hear Logan say he wanted to introduce her as his girlfriend. She wanted to say yes, but there was Mikhail to consider.

"When is it?"

"Next Saturday night."

"Tomorrow?"

"No, not tomorrow. The Saturday after that."

"All right. But only on the condition I can get a sitter for my brother."

"Of course. Better still, bring him along."

She felt a rush of warmth. "Thank you. I really appreciate your offer. It's very sweet. But I don't think a family engagement party is quite the occasion to introduce everyone to Mikhail. He gets a bit overwhelmed in large crowds. Particularly when he's among people he doesn't know."

Logan inclined his head. "I understand. Perhaps I can help you out with a sitting service? I'm sure one of my cousins can recommend one."

She smiled. "Thank you, but I'm afraid it doesn't quite work like that. Misha's very particular about who he spends time with, especially on his own. My friend from the café, Joanna, is one such person on a very short list. She's minded him before. I'll see if she's free."

Logan nodded. "Great. And before then, I'm going to give your brother some more sailing lessons. Right?"

She grinned. "Right."

Not far away, Flynn stood watching the couple, his mind awhirl. It was clear Logan was taken with the woman. Flynn had noticed from the very first day how his brother paid particular attention to her, looking for her in the crowd of arrivals each day. Flynn had also noticed how disappointed Logan was on those occasions when the woman had sent someone else in her place. It was alarming how quickly she seemed to have become important to him.

Okay, she appeared to be nice and she was certainly easy on the eye, but Logan was rushing into this way too fast. He barely knew the woman. And now Flynn had just overheard his brother inviting her to the Craigdon engagement party, a do that promised to be a large and glamorous family affair.

Logan, of all people, knew what it was like to have his heart broken. He'd been devastated when Virginia had jilted him. They'd all felt his pain. Logan had dated up a frenzy since the break-up, going home with a different girl every other night. His brothers understood his need to do that. They hadn't judged him. Instead, they'd seen it for what it was. Part of the healing.

At least none of those women were a risk to Logan's heart.

Mia Ivanov was a different matter. It was obvious she wasn't the type of woman who allowed herself to be picked up in a bar and taken home for the night. There was an innocent air about her, a youthful freshness, unjaded and almost pure. She was the kind of woman a man took home to his family and that, in Flynn's mind, made her all the more dangerous.

Flynn had seen firsthand Logan's devastation at the hands of a perfidious woman. He knew nothing about Mia and that was part of the problem, but he wasn't going to stand by and risk having Logan be hurt all over again. As the oldest brother, it was Flynn's responsibility to look out for his younger siblings. That was a responsibility he'd always taken seriously. Including now.

Noah nudged him in the side with his elbow, dragging him out of his dark thoughts.

"We're at a party, Flynn. The kids are watching. Lighten up! You look like someone stole the last piece of chocolate cake."

Flynn didn't even bother to force a smile. He continued to glare in Logan's direction. He and Mia were still standing close, talking. Noah followed the direction of Flynn's gaze.

"Whoever she is, she certainly has Logan enthralled," Noah commented dryly.

Flynn's expression darkened. "Her name is Mia Ivanov. Logan's falling for her fast. Too fast."

Noah raised an eyebrow. "I take it they've moved beyond mere talking?"

"I don't know anything about that, but I just caught them kissing and I overheard our brother inviting the woman to the engagement party."

Noah whistled. "Now I see where you're coming from. She must really mean something for Logan to invite her to a family do. He's got to know he'll be drilled by everyone from the time he arrives until the time he leaves."

"Yeah. That's what's got me worried. He only met the woman five days ago." Flynn shook his head in concern. "I don't like it. Something's off."

"What do we know about her?"

"Nothing. Yet. I'll speak to Jayde about her," he said, referring to his cop wife. "Get her to do some digging."

"I'd offer to run her name through the system, but you know that's against the rules," Noah said with an edge to his voice.

Flynn grimaced. "I wouldn't dream of asking you to break the rules! I don't want Jayde to do anything underhanded, either. I just want to know who she is and where she comes from." He looked around them. "Most of these kids came through the patrons of Callum's soup kitchen. I'd bet my last dollar she wasn't one of them. It seems odd a woman like her would even know about this sailing course."

Noah eyed Mia's designer clothes and sunglasses. "You're right. She's not the typical patron of Jennifer's Kitchen. We should ask Callum about her."

"I don't need to ask Callum to know she didn't come from that part of town. I'm going to talk to her," Flynn said, coming to a sudden decision. "Ask her myself."

With that, Flynn started toward Mia, intent on pinning her down for information.

"Hey! Flynn!" Noah called.

Flynn stopped and turned around. "Yeah?"

Noah grimaced. "Just... Go easy, okay. You're not in a courtroom now."

Flynn just glared at his brother and then slowly turned back around. Mia was now headed for the car park, her brother in tow. Logan was nowhere in sight. Flynn hurried to catch up with them.

"Mia!" he called out.

She turned around in surprise and waited for him to catch

up. "Is there something the matter? Did we forget something?"

"No," Flynn said. Mikhail stood only a few feet away, swaying from foot to foot. He looked at Flynn, grinning widely, his eyes full of curiosity.

"Logan's promised to take me sailing next week," Mikhail told him, smiling.

Flynn hid his surprise. Logan had been dragged to the beach kicking and screaming, so reluctant was he to take part in the sailing course. Now it was over and he was free to go and hide somewhere and continue to lick his wounds. But according to Mikhail, that wasn't to be the case.

Flynn turned to Mia. He kept his tone conversational. "Is that right?"

She gave him a tight smile. "Yes. He's agreed to give my brother some private lessons. Is that all right?"

"Of course. He doesn't answer to me. He's free to do whatever he wants."

"I'm glad." She paused and then gave him a pointed look. "Is there something I can help you with?"

Flynn held her steady gaze. "As a matter of fact, there is. I want to talk to you about Logan. It's obvious he likes you. I'm concerned he's moving too fast."

Mia's short bark of laughter was devoid of humor. "What business is that of yours?"

Flynn tensed. "He's my brother. I care about him. I don't want you breaking his heart."

She continued to glare at him. "And why would I do that?"

"I'm not saying you'd do it deliberately, but intentional or not, the effect would be the same. He still hasn't gotten over the last woman who did that to him."

"Oh, you mean the woman who jilted him?"

Flynn started in surprise. He couldn't believe Logan had shared that information with this woman. They'd obviously gotten a whole lot closer in the five days they'd known each other than he'd guessed. That made it all the more imperative he warn her off.

Moving into her personal space, he pointed a finger at her to emphasize his point. "Just be careful about what you're doing. Logan doesn't need another deceitful woman who says all the right things, makes him think he's hung the stars and moon and then leaves him in the dust."

Flynn kept his hard gaze on hers. "Logan thought Virginia was the love of his life. He thought they'd be married forever. She left him before they could say the vows. It devastated him. We were all helpless to do anything about it. If you know anything about that time, you'll know he's still hurting over it. I won't let it happen again. Understand?"

Though he'd kept his tone even, in deference to her brother, the look Flynn gave her made it clear he meant business. To her credit, she held his gaze without flinching.

"Are you done?"

He gave her a tight nod.

"I understand you love your brother and I'm sure your words come from a good place. But here's the thing: If I choose to spend time with Logan, then that's none of your business. Whether we fall in love or not… Again, none of your business." Her gaze suddenly narrowed. "Have you ever been in love, Flynn?"

He nodded. "Yes. In fact, I'm engaged to be married."

"Congratulations." Her tone was dry.

"What's your point?" he said a little belligerently.

"My point is, you don't get to choose who you fall in love with. It's not something that can be looked at, analyzed from all angles, discussed, debated, weighing up the pros and cons. Falling in love just happens, sometimes when we least expect it. It's not something we *plan* to do. Am I right?"

He gave a reluctant nod. "Yeah. You're right."

"So listen here, Flynn and listen well. I like your brother. I really do. He says he likes me, too. Whether that leads to love for one or both us, who knows? Not me, not Logan and certainly not you. What I will say is, it's not my intention to hurt your brother and I'm definitely not setting out to break his heart. I know how devastated he was about his almost-marriage. I don't plan to inflict any more pain on him. And this is the last time we're going to speak of this."

With that, she grabbed her brother's hand and stalked away, leaving Flynn to stare after her, baffled.

What the hell just happened and how did she turn the tables on me so completely and with such ease?

Reluctant admiration seeped through him. She sure as hell wasn't afraid to stand up for herself. That much was clear. He hoped like hell she didn't hurt his brother, but in the meantime, they were all in for a hell of an interesting ride.

Hours later, Flynn lay on his back on the mattress, listening to the waves outside his window while he caught his breath. His fiancée, Jayde Hassad, lay next to him. Both of them were covered in perspiration after enjoying a particularly enthusiastic bout of lovemaking. Flynn pulled her close against him and pressed a kiss against her hair.

"How did your last day of sailing go?" Jayde asked, her voice husky with a need to sleep.

"It was good. I think the kids enjoyed it. Logan was the real surprise. I didn't think Callum had a hope in hell in getting him to sign on for it, but he did. And he enjoyed it. It was just so good to see him out there on the water again, even in the capacity of an instructor."

"It was good of you to take time off work to help him."

"It wasn't just me. Noah came along too."

"The Craigdon brothers. A formidable team."

Flynn heard the smile in her voice. There was also pride. It made him feel good, knowing how supportive she was, not only of him, but of his entire family. It seemed Noah had also gotten lucky in love. From all accounts, Ayla was a keeper. Flynn was glad. Now they only had to get Logan over the line…

Flynn sighed.

"That sounds heavy," Jayde teased.

Flynn sighed again. "Yeah."

"What is it?"

"I was thinking about Logan."

"I thought you said he surprised himself by enjoying sailing again."

"Yeah. It's not that." Flynn paused. "He's met a woman."

Jayde's tone was neutral. "Okay."

"No, this one's different. This time it looks serious."

"Who is she?"

"She's the sister of one of the kids who signed up for the course."

"How old is she?"

He could hear the wryness in her tone. He hurried to set her straight.

"She's not a teenager, if that's what you're thinking. Her brother's fourteen. She looks about ten years older."

"So what's the problem?"

"I just don't want him to get hurt."

She turned her face and pressed a kiss against his chest. "I'm not sure that's within your control."

"You weren't there when he was left all alone at the altar. It was terrible. The church was packed. They'd started the service. Then Virginia let out a shriek and something to the effect that she couldn't go through with it and hightailed it out of there. Logan was frozen with shock. He still hasn't gotten over it."

"I understand," Jayde said in a soothing tone. "It must have been devastating for all of you."

Flynn shuddered. "You have that right."

"But you can't prevent him from heartache in the future. That's the risk you take when you fall in love. Have you forgotten how you felt before we straightened things out between us?"

Flynn sighed again and pulled her close. "No. That's what I'm worried about. It was a hell of a rollercoaster. I don't ever want to go through that again."

"Neither do I, but you surely aren't regretting the outcome?"

His arm tightened around her. "Of course not. I just worry about Logan."

"You're a good big brother. Has this woman given you any reason for concern?"

"No. Only that things between them seem to be moving at the speed of light. They only met on Monday. He invited her to the engagement party."

"Wow."

"Yeah."

"What do you know about her?"

"Nothing, apart from the fact she has a younger brother. I assume Logan has a bit more information on her. She would have filled in an application for her brother to attend the course." He paused and then added, "I was hoping you might be able to run her name through the system."

Jayde came up on one elbow and looked down at him. She slowly shook her head. "You know I can't do that. Not even for you."

He pulled a face and dragged her back in his arms. "You're right. I shouldn't have even suggested it."

"What's her name?"

"Mia Ivanov. Her brother's name is Mikhail."

"Ivanov. It's a common Russian name. It's also the name of one of the biggest operatives in the Russian mafia.

Alexander Ivanov. A big-time drug supplier and dealer. He died about a year ago. Around the same time as your uncle. A gangland shooting, I seem to recall. No one was charged with his murder."

Flynn absorbed the information. He had no way of knowing if this Alexander fellow was related to Mia. The odds were he wasn't. As Jayde said, there were plenty of Ivanovs living in Sydney and though Flynn was suspicious about how quickly she'd attached herself to Logan, she didn't seem the type to have ties to the mafia.

He sighed again. "I guess I'll just have to trust that Logan knows what he's doing."

Jayde smiled. "You can't interfere in someone else's affairs of the heart. It just won't work. If Logan had even a clue about this discussion, he'd be livid, and rightly so. He's an intelligent adult in full control of his faculties. He's entitled to choose who he falls in love with. All you can do is support him and be there to pick up the pieces. If it comes to that."

Flynn groaned. "Let's hope it doesn't come to that." He pulled her in for a kiss. "You're right, of course," he mumbled.

"Say that again, only louder this time."

He swatted her bare ass. "Brat."

She yelped in indignation. Flynn rolled her onto her back and pinned her to the bed with his weight. His cock stirred. Desire flickered in her eyes. That's all it took. He bent to capture her lips in a searing kiss. Her arms came up around his neck and held him close.

He nudged her thighs. Her legs fell open. He probed her entrance with his cock. In one sure thrust, he plunged inside her. They both groaned.

He was home.

Chapter Ten

It was the first day of the last week of the school holidays and Mikhail had pestered Mia all morning about leaving for his second week of sailing lessons. She'd assured him they would get there, but first she needed to do a few things at the shop. The most important task was to arrange for Katerina to cover the next five mornings while Mia took her brother sailing.

"Wow, he's really taken to it, hasn't he?" Katerina said when Mia told her they were extending the lessons another week.

"Yes. The instructor told me he had natural talent. I thought it would be good to foster that. And Mikhail's definitely looking forward to it. He can hardly contain his excitement."

Katerina shot her a sly look. "The instructor wouldn't happen to be the same hot guy I met last week, would it?"

Mia fought back a blush. She busied herself straightening dresses, giving her an excuse to turn her back.

"His looks are irrelevant. I'm doing this for Misha."

"Of course."

Mia gritted her teeth against Katerina's disbelieving tone. Mia didn't know why she felt the need to keep her budding romance with Logan a secret from her assistant. All she knew was that she wasn't ready to share that information yet. It was still early days and after the warning she'd received from Flynn, she was even more determined to act cautiously. She'd meant it when she'd told Logan's brother she had no intention of hurting the guy. She didn't relish the idea of suffering from a broken heart herself.

No, she'd take things slowly, get to know him, let him get to know her. And then they could see where they were at. Starting now.

"Mikhail! Are you ready? It's time to go sailing!"

"Yay!" her brother cried, tearing out of her office. "Sailing! Sailing!"

Mia smiled indulgently, her heart swelling with love. Together, they left the shop and headed toward her car. Minutes later, she pulled into the car park above Balmoral Beach. As they made their way across the grass and down onto the sand, Logan materialized from the boat shed. She could tell the moment he spotted them. His face lit up with a smile.

Mia's heart skipped a beat. She felt the warmth of his gaze all the way down to her feet. Heat crept across her cheeks and her pulse picked up its pace. In deference to the beautiful summer day, she wore a maxi dress that fell to her ankles. It was a sunny yellow color and the cotton fabric was printed with huge white-and-yellow frangipanis. The spaghetti straps showed off her toned shoulders and the fitted bodice emphasized her slim waist. On her feet were a pair of custom-made, and stylish sandals.

"Hi. Welcome back. It's great to see you both," Logan said.

"Can we go sailing?" Mikhail asked.

Logan laughed. "Of course we can! And the best thing is, we don't need to wait for anyone else to arrive. It's just you and me today, buddy."

"Yay!" Mikhail cheered.

Logan shot a cheeky look in Mia's direction. "Unless your sister would care to join us?"

Mia shook her head. "Oh, no. I don't think I'm up for sailing."

Logan's grin widened. "Why not? It might do you good to widen your horizons."

Mikhail tugged her arm. "Come on, Mia! Come sailing with us! Please!"

Mia laughed and disentangled herself from her brother. "No, Misha. For one, I'm not dressed for sailing. I need to go back to work after this."

Mikhail pouted. Logan ruffled his hair. "Not to worry, buddy. We have a whole week of lessons. Who knows? By the end of it we might just be able to convince her to come with us. For now, let's go sailing!"

"Yay!"

As the two of them walked away, Mia heard her brother chatting excitedly to Logan and his slow and measured replies. She sighed happily. He was so good with her brother. So patient and kind.

She found a comfortable spot to sit, high up on the grassy knoll, and pulled out her iPad. She intended to spend the time chasing up orders, checking her inventory and perusing the latest styles and collections online. She worked hard at providing one-off dresses so that no bride need worry her dress would appear in the media on someone else. It was a small, but important detail and one her brides appreciated.

The excited shouts and laughter down below kept interrupting her concentration. Mikhail would yelp with triumph when he managed to catch the wind with his sail and then would shout just as loudly when the wind changed and the boat wobbled and tossed him over the side. Each time he climbed back in and tried again, never once losing his temper.

A lot of that could be credited to Logan. He seemed to have a bottomless well of patience and repeated his instructions over and over again until Mikhail understood. He never once criticized, only offered endless encouragement. Mia had seen her brother attempt many challenges and some of them got the better of him. She'd seen him throw temper tantrums like a three-year-old when things didn't go his way.

But with Logan he was different. Perhaps he sensed that Logan wouldn't pander to his moods or accept excuses. Mia tried hard to treat her brother in a similar manner, but it wasn't always easy. Logan was patient but persistent and he wasn't even related to Mikhail. Mia's admiration for the man rose another notch.

The hour flew past and before she knew it, Mikhail was scrambling up the hill toward her.

"Did you see me, Mia? Did you see?"

"Of course I did! You were great!"

Mikhail beamed. "That's what Logan said, too. Logan's the best!"

Mia silently agreed.

As Logan headed toward them, she tried not to notice the play of muscle across his bare shoulders and broad chest. His skin was bronzed and shiny. Droplets of water clung to the light scattering of dark blond chest hair. Her gaze dropped lower and followed the thin line of darker hair that disappeared beneath the waistband of his boardshorts. She stared at the place between his legs where she imagined his cock lay. Desire shivered across her skin.

She tore her gaze away and it landed on his face. The knowing look in his eyes sent flames of embarrassment across her cheeks. She looked away, wishing the ground would open up and swallow her. To his credit, he made no comment.

"We had a good lesson today, didn't we Mikhail?"

"Yes! A good lesson! Can I come back tomorrow?"

"Of course. That's the deal." He turned back to Mia. "Do you have time to grab a coffee?"

She shook her head, genuinely regretful. "I'm sorry. I need to get back to work."

Logan nodded. "I understand." He chucked Misha under the chin. "Well, buddy. I guess that means I'll see you tomorrow. Maybe we can persuade your sister to stay longer next time."

"Yay! See you tomorrow, Logan!"

Mia murmured her goodbyes. With her brother in tow, she started up toward the car park. She heard Logan call out to her and turned around.

"How did you do with that sitter?"

Mia pretended surprise. "For what?"

"For Saturday night. The engagement party. Remember?"

"Oh, yes. Sorry. It slipped my mind," she lied.

The truth was, she wasn't certain she should go. A big fancy affair, one where all of Logan's family would be present and no doubt curious enough about her to ply her with all sorts of questions… She wasn't sure she was ready for that. After all, what if this turned out to be nothing more than a short-lived affair? At this point, the less people who knew about it the better.

Still, she couldn't deny a part of her longed to get to know Logan better and one way to do that was to mix and mingle with his family. From what she'd seen of him so far, she'd forged a favorable impression, but most people had skeletons lurking in the closet—secrets family members were only too willing to reveal.

Logan closed the distance between them. His gaze was open and sincere. "It would be lovely to bring you along as my date. I'd be honored, if you can make it."

At the warmth in his gaze, her insides melted like marshmallows held over an open fire.

How can I resist him? He's everything I want in a man. Everything I want for Mikhail...

"I'll get in touch with Joanna and see if she's free," she promised. "I'll let you know tomorrow."

Logan's answering smile snatched her breath away. And then he leaned in and claimed a kiss. It lasted only a few seconds, but the feel of his lips pressed against hers stayed with her for the rest of the day.

The next day, having ascertained over breakfast that Joanna was free to babysit Mikhail the night of the Craigdon engagement party, Mia headed to her bedroom and dressed for the beach. Beneath her light summer dress—this one a floral pattern of blue and orange and white—she wore a pair of bright pink-and-black boardshorts and a matching bikini top. She was nervous about Logan seeing so much of her bare skin and even more nervous about him seeing her prosthetic leg.

Though he'd caught a glimpse of it the night she'd revealed it to him in her kitchen, that wasn't quite the same thing as seeing it in the bright light of day. She'd lived with her prosthetic leg for so long she barely noticed it anymore, but that wasn't how it was for most people.

Logan had told her about his own leg. Scarred from numerous operations, he'd said. It was obvious he'd been embarrassed when he'd mentioned it. But it was still a flesh-and-blood leg, not one made of hard plastic. Though the technology had come a long way since the first leg she'd been fitted with when she was five, they still hadn't managed to replicate the feel of a human leg. She could only hope it didn't matter to him, just like the scars on his leg didn't matter to her.

"Mikhail? Are you ready?"

Her brother bounded down the hallway and filled the open doorway. A wide grin filled his face.

"Of course I am! I've been ready for *hours!*"

She laughed and rolled her eyes at him. "Hours. Right. I think it was only twenty-five minutes ago that I pulled you out of bed, but we won't dwell on that."

He giggled. Walking into her bedroom, he put his arms around her waist and hugged her. "I love you, Mia."

Her heart stuttered with emotion. Tears burned behind her eyes. She hugged him back. "I love you too, Misha. Very much."

"Very much," he agreed, looking up at her with his big blue eyes that never failed to touch her heart.

They arrived at Balmoral Beach with a couple of minutes to spare. They could see Logan down on the sand, near a dinghy. He carried two life jackets in his hand.

"Logan! Logan! We're here!" Mikhail took off at a gallop down the hill.

Mia followed at a more sedate pace, picking her way carefully over the uneven ground. She reached Logan slightly out of breath. She tried to blame it on the fact she was out of shape, but the truth was, her heart had been beating up a storm the instant she caught sight of him.

"H-hi," she stammered.

His warm gaze was filled with appreciation. "Hi, yourself. You look beautiful. I love the dress."

She blushed in embarrassment and looked away. "Thanks."

Mikhail tugged on Logan's arm. "Mia said she'd go sailing with us today. Can we go now?"

Logan's eyebrows rose in surprise. He looked at her with a grin. "Is it true? Are you coming out on the water today?"

She nodded. "Is that okay?"

His eyes sparkled in delight. "Of course it is. I can't wait to show you the ropes. Pardon the pun."

She laughed and some of her nervousness eased. He handed her one of the lifejackets and gave Mikhail the other one. "Put them on. I'll go and get another one."

With that, he turned and headed back to the boatshed. Mia took the opportunity to tug her dress over her head. She stowed it in her oversize handbag and then pulled the lifejacket over her shoulders. She was tightening the straps around her waist when Logan returned. He also wore a lifejacket and now he dragged another, larger dinghy, behind him. At the sight of it, her nervousness and apprehension returned.

As if sensing her uncertainty, Logan smiled softly. "Are you still keen to do this?"

She gave him a quick nod, but something in her expression must have given her away.

"Have you ever been sailing before?"

"No."

"I can teach her!" Mikhail cried.

Logan winked at him. "You sure can. We both can, right Mikhail?"

"Right!"

Mia looked down at her prosthesis. Logan followed the direction of her gaze. "I assume you can't get your prosthesis wet?"

She nodded. "You're right. I need to sit down to remove it."

"I'll grab you a seat." Logan hurried back to the boatshed. He returned a few moments later with a small wooden bench that looked like it was about a hundred years old. She gazed at it dubiously.

"Is it safe?"

"I think so. Definitely strong enough to take someone as slight as you."

He set the bench down beside her and she took a seat. She was relieved when the bench remained stationery. Logan was right. It was sturdier than it looked. Acutely aware of him standing a few feet away, she took a deep breath and pulled off her prosthesis. She set it on the bench beside her.

"Right," Logan said matter-of-factly. "Now we're good to go." He turned to her brother. "Mikhail, grab your dinghy and push it into the water. Not too far in. And hold on to it, okay?"

"Okay, Logan."

After waiting a moment to make sure Mikhail had followed his instructions, Logan turned back to Mia. "Okay. Now it's your turn."

She blushed. "I'm not sure I can hop that far."

He smiled. "You won't have to. I'm going to carry you."

Amid protests, Logan bent and lifted her in his arms. True to his word, he carried her to the larger sailing boat and set her gently down inside.

"You good?" he asked and followed it with a wink.

She smiled at the teasing light in his eyes. "I'm good."

And she was. He'd dealt with the fact she couldn't walk without her prosthesis without a qualm. It hadn't seemed to bother him at all. As he pushed them off the beach and into the deeper water and jumped in the boat behind her, her apprehension of minutes before, disappeared.

She looked around for Mikhail and found him a short distance away. His white sail was billowing in the wind.

"Mikhail!" she shouted over the wind.

He looked over to her and grinned. "Mia! You're sailing!"

And he was right. Logan had quietly and efficiently done whatever needed to be done so that their sail was filled with wind. The little boat skimmed over the crystal blue water, going faster than Mia imagined such a small boat could.

"Having fun?" Logan shouted.

She grinned and gave him a thumbs up. He gave her a wink.

The sheer sexiness of the man behind her had her heart

thumping with desire. As he stretched out his legs, she saw the faint white markings and some deeper purple ones of old scars crisscrossing his right leg. There were so many and she could tell how painful the wounds must have been to leave that many permanent reminders behind, but as far as she was concerned, he was beautiful.

His legs were tanned and covered in curly hair. Though the muscles were less prominent in his injured leg, they were shapely just the same. But more than that was the person he was. Considerate and easygoing. Sweet and kind. He was more than she could have ever imagined. She'd cautioned herself over falling too fast, but also recognized those feelings were out of her control.

His goodness, his patience, his sense of humor. She marveled at his willingness to accept people—she and Mikhail—and others, as they were. She wanted to know him better. She only hoped he felt the same.

Logan saw the warm emotions shining from Mia's eyes and felt a frisson of dismay. He knew she was developing feelings for him and that filled him with mixed emotions. Elation, yeah. But it also filled him with dread—fear really. If she'd been any other woman he'd dated, they would have already been to bed. It was obvious she was attracted to him and he sure as hell wanted her.

But Mia wasn't like the women he usually slept with. She had a sweet innocence about her. He didn't know if she was a virgin, but even if she weren't, she sure as hell wasn't as experienced as him. Not that it mattered. In fact, he liked that she likely didn't have a long list of ex-lovers. But it meant he couldn't follow his usual play.

Logan freely admitted to anyone who asked that he enjoyed women like some men enjoyed fine wines. He loved to be around them. He loved the way they looked. The way they smelled. The way they tasted. But he also loved his solitude and after the debacle with Virginia, he'd vowed never to get seriously involved with a woman again. His ability to trust had taken a serious beating. Not to mention the hit to his heart. It still hurt but not as much as it once had.

To that end, he deliberately chose to be with women who well and truly knew the score. Like him, they were looking for a good time, not a long time. And until now, that had worked just fine.

But Mia wasn't like those women and though she'd told him she wasn't on the lookout for a husband, he could tell she was the kind of woman who'd want to be a wife, maybe even a mother, someday. And she deserved to find someone she could love and who could love her in return. As much as he wished he could be that someone, he didn't think that man was him. His heart had been broken. He was damaged beyond repair. She deserved someone who could give her his whole heart, and the trust that came with it.

No, for both of their sakes, he needed to lay off on the charm and definitely no more kissing. It wasn't right to build up her hopes, only to dash them sometime down the track. There was no way he'd inflict that pain on her.

Unfortunately, it was too late to withdraw his invitation to the engagement party. She'd texted him early that morning to confirm she'd found a sitter for Mikhail. But that didn't mean she couldn't attend as his friend. People took friends to functions all the time. All he had to do was remember to keep his mouth and hands off her.

Hell, who am I kidding?

That would be easier said than done.

Chapter Eleven

Friday rolled around. The last day of the sailing lessons. It had been a wonderful week. Mia had enjoyed the last few days out on the water, but she'd enjoyed her time with Logan even more. She was falling in love with him and there was nothing she could do about it. She only wished he'd give her a sign as to how he felt. They hadn't kissed again since that first day.

From the corner of her eye, she watched him stow the boats and other equipment away. He'd been sweet and attentive during their last lesson, but the cheeky teasing she'd gotten used to over the past couple of weeks had disappeared. She wasn't sure why.

She took the opportunity to slip her prosthetic leg back on and then pulled her dress back over her head. She finger combed her damp hair and then pulled it back into a band. Mikhail was chattering non-stop about the waves and how they'd splashed over the boat. He'd jumped into the water to help Logan bring the boats back to shore and the water still glinted off his hair.

Her gaze drifted over him. The hours in the sun had further tanned his skin and lightened the blond of his hair. He looked like a true-blue surfer dude. He looked like Logan.

Her stomach quivered with need. After spending so much time together in the boat, only feet apart, she yearned to touch him. She wanted to trace the well-defined muscles in his chest. Run her fingers through his hair. She wanted to bend her head and taste his salty skin and flick the small nubs of his nipples. She wanted to feel every inch of his hard body and have him touch her all over, too. The only problem was, she wasn't quite sure how to go about it. She wasn't exactly experienced in the ways of seduction. In fact, she'd never seduced a man in her life. But she'd read plenty and imagined more. She was quietly confident she could pull it off.

The sailing lessons had come to an end. She supposed she could always ask him to extend them, though she wasn't sure what he'd say. She knew he worked at the family company and no doubt he had a responsible position. Surely there were other calls on his time.

He couldn't spend all of it giving sailing lessons. Nor could she afford to keep spending more than an hour every morning away from her shop. Katerina was more than capable, but it wasn't fair to expect her to keep things running for so long. This was supposed to be over within the week.

No, she'd have to think of another way to get him alone.

Maybe the night of the engagement party? Mikhail's sleeping over at Joanna's. We'll have the house to ourselves…

Once the thought took hold, she couldn't let it go. Her heart skipped a beat and then took off at a gallop.

Can I do it? Can I seduce Logan Craigdon?

She was filled with a surge of eagerness and anticipation. The night of the engagement party would be the perfect opportunity to test her seductive powers. She couldn't wait.

Logan returned. With the sun at his back it formed a halo behind his head, gilding the blond with gold. He smiled and the whiteness of his teeth against his tanned skin was almost blinding. Everything about him turned her on.

"So, what's on for the rest of the day?" she asked.

Logan grimaced. "I have a couple of meetings at the office and a project that's falling behind. What about you?"

"Stock take. The scourge of all business owners."

"Sounds like fun."

"Yeah. About as fun as getting a root canal."

A thoughtful look crossed his face. She raised an eyebrow and smiled. "What is it?"

His smile was slow in coming, but when it did, it lit up his face. She was prompted to ask him again what he was thinking about.

"How would you feel about playing hooky?"

She grinned. "What do you mean?"

"Let's ditch our work commitments and go and have lunch." He winked.

It was the wink that did it. Her insides turned to mush. She gave about ten seconds thought to the work that waited for her at the shop and then looked up at him and laughed.

"Yes! Let's do it!"

His smile widened. "Really?"

She turned to Mikhail. "Would you like to go to lunch with Logan?"

"Yay!" Mikhail cheered. "Lunch!"

Logan grinned. "I guess that settles it."

At Logan's suggestion, they agreed to eat at Beaches bar in Balmoral. He'd assured her the food was good and the views of the harbor were sensational. The lure of outdoor dining on such a spectacular summer day was hard to beat. Traveling in separate cars, Logan spent the time second-guessing himself over extending the invitation.

What the hell am I thinking? I'm supposed to be keeping my distance. We're meant to be in the friend zone. That's it.

Just try telling that to his libido. Every time he got near her, he got aroused. There was nothing he could do about it. The more he denied himself, the more he wanted her. It was crazy. He hadn't meant to extend their time together—he'd actually planned the opposite to keep things on an even keel. It had been hard enough getting through the past five days in particular.

Though she hadn't spent every day in the boat with him, each time she did he'd gone a little insane. He'd never wanted a woman the way he wanted her. He tried to tell himself it was because he'd put her out of reach that she'd become so utterly desirable, but he knew that was a lie. He wanted her because she was Mia. Unique. Special. Beautiful. Being so close to her and not touching her was driving him slowly mad.

So what the hell just happened?

Right when he should have been bidding her farewell and feeling grateful he'd survived the week, he'd asked her out to lunch.

What sort of idiot am I?

A happy one. The truth was, he couldn't get the smile off his face. As Mia pulled into the Beaches car park behind him, he watched her say something to Mikhail. The boy grinned. Mia smiled affectionately and ruffled her brother's hair. They both climbed out of her car.

Logan did the same. Using the remote to lock the Mercedes, he joined them.

"Have you been here before?" he asked.

"No. But I've heard great things about the place."

"Everything you've heard is true. The place is owned by my brother's fiancée, Jayde Hassad. Well, technically it's owned by her father, but given he's currently sitting in Long Bay Correctional Center awaiting trial on serious drug charges, I'd say it's a fair bet the place is hers. From what I heard, he won't be seeing freedom for a long time."

Mia's eyes widened in surprise. "So your brother's fiancée is involved in illegal drugs?"

"No. Only her father. In fact, Jayde's at the opposite end of that scenario. She's a detective with the DEA. She was working undercover at the time, gathering evidence against her father, among other people. She was instrumental in his arrest. Apparently he was a pretty big player in the drug business."

Mia looked slightly shocked. Logan wondered whether it was too soon to share this kind of stuff. He didn't want to send her running.

"It sounds a bit more hectic than it is," he added quickly. "Jayde hadn't seen her father for twenty years."

Mia only looked at him with more questions in her eyes. Logan shook his head. "It's a long story and I don't have all the details. You're probably best to go directly to the source. Flynn and Jayde recently got engaged. I guess that means she intends to hang around for a while."

He half-grinned. Their gazes caught and held. Emotion flared in Mia's eyes. Logan's heart skipped a beat and took off at a gallop. She continued to stare at him, her eyes now dark with desire.

His chest tightened with nerves and anticipation. Though a voice in the back of his head told him not to do it, Logan was helpless against the magnetic pull between them. It was like he no longer had control over his emotions or his actions. Oblivious to Mikhail, Logan reached for her hand.

He drew her close and planted a kiss on her mouth. She gasped in surprise, but didn't pull way, so he did it again. This time, he put more effort into it and molded his lips to hers. So soft, so sweet, so delicious. The scent and taste of her filled his head. He could kiss her all day...

With a groan of capitulation, her arms stole up and tightened around his neck. He deepened the kiss, pressing against her lips. She opened her mouth and his tongue slipped inside, learning the taste and feel of her heat.

He was in heaven… He was in hell…

"Logan and Mia are kissing. Logan and Mia are kissing. Logan and Mia are kissing."

Mikhail's cheerful chorus suddenly registered in Logan's passion-fogged brain. He broke the kiss off with a gasp. Breathing hard, he stared at Mia. She looked equally dazed.

"I-I'm sorry," he stammered.

Her cheeks were flushed from passion and maybe embarrassment. She touched a finger to his lips.

"*Shh*. Don't apologize. That would spoil everything."

Logan looked into her eyes and wondered what the hell he'd done. So much for keeping his distance. What a joke. And he'd kissed her in front of Mikhail. How would he explain to the boy it wasn't meant to be serious? How would he explain to Mia?

He'd known from the outset she wasn't the kind of woman who went in for one night stands. Though she'd never said anything, he'd been around long enough to tell. And now he'd gone and ruined everything by kissing her.

But she felt so good in his arms… She tasted so sweet, so warm, so passionate…

His cock was hard and throbbing and his blood coursed hotly through his body. All he wanted was to draw her close and kiss her like that again. Despite what his head kept telling him, his heart had different ideas and right now, with the taste and feel of her fresh in his mind, he couldn't bring himself to regret it.

With their fingers entwined, he threw an arm around Mikhail's shoulders and led the way inside Beaches. They ordered fish and chips and shared them at a table on the balcony that overlooked the harbor.

"You were right about the food," Mia commented, swallowing another piece of tender crumbed fish.

"Yes, and from where I sit, the view's pretty special, too." He shot her a meaningful look and winked.

She blushed adorably. Mikhail stuffed a handful of crispy golden chips into his mouth. He spoke around the mouthful. "Good chips."

They all laughed. Logan was flooded with warmth. Less than two weeks earlier he hadn't even known Mia and Mikhail. Now it was hard to imagine spending any length of time without them. It scared him how quickly he was falling for her—and how fast he'd come to care for her brother.

After the pain and humiliation Virginia had inflicted upon him not so long ago, he was certain he'd never feel deeply for a woman again. He sure as hell hadn't imagined he'd be contemplating another serious relationship. And yet that's exactly what he suddenly was doing.

"Do you have time for coffee and a milkshake?" he asked as they finished eating.

"Milkshake! Yay!" Mikhail exclaimed.

Mia regarded her brother affectionately and then looked at Logan. "I guess inventory can wait just a little while longer."

"We could go to my apartment. It's not far from here and I make a mean chocolate milkshake."

A flash of surprise crossed Mia's face and then she smiled. "Sounds great."

Once again, Mia and Mikhail climbed into her car and followed Logan. The invitation to visit his home surprised her. Until he invited her to his apartment she hadn't been sure he wanted more from her than a quick-and-easy relationship, one they could enjoy while it lasted and then leave with no regrets. After all, he'd been straightforward: He wasn't looking for anything long term and she assured him she felt the same.

But extending their time together by inviting them out to

lunch and now to his apartment made her wonder if something had changed for him. She certainly hoped so.

Logan turned into the paved driveway of a small apartment complex. The off-white rendered walls and sparkling silver window frames looked new. The gardens were well-maintained. The grass was a brilliant green. They were close enough to Balmoral Beach that Mia guessed a spectacular water view lurked on the other side of the building. Logan pulled up outside a lock-up garage. Mia came to a halt beside him.

"Nice digs," she said.

"I like it," he replied modestly.

The three of them were whisked up to the top floor in a shiny silver lift. They stepped out onto carpet and walked halfway down the corridor.

"This is me," Logan said and inserted a key into the lock.

He opened the door and stood back for Mia and Mikhail to enter. The apartment was pristine, with shiny marble tiles and off-white walls. Splashes of contemporary artwork gave the open plan living room and kitchen some color, but the most magnificent thing was the view of the harbor that was perfectly framed between floor-to-ceiling glass.

"Wow! I can see why you like this place. Unobstructed views," she said with a tinge of envy.

"Yeah. I can't complain."

She grinned. "Your father must pay you well."

He flushed. "Yeah, I guess. I paid for this with part of my inheritance. My uncle was very generous on his death. At least with me."

"Wow," she repeated, her gaze returning to the view. "That sounds like my kind of uncle."

Logan merely smiled. Mikhail dashed around the room, looking at this and that. The bookshelves were filled with books, along with a collection of expensive-looking sculptures.

He picked up one after the other, studying them closely, before placing them back down again. An anxious Mia cautioned him to slow down and be careful. And then he spied a motorbike helmet that sat on the coffee table.

His eyes went wide with excitement. "Is that *yours*?"

Logan shook his head. "No, sorry. It belongs to my brother."

"Flynn?" Mia asked, curious.

"No. Noah. He's into motorbikes."

"I love motorbikes!" Mikhail said.

"Do you?" Logan asked.

"Yes!"

"Have you ever been on one?"

"No. At least, I don't think so." He turned to Mia. "Have I, Mia?"

Mia laughed and ruffled her brother's hair. "You've watched them on TV plenty of times, but no, you've never been on one."

Mikhail turned to face Logan. "Could I ride Noah's? Could I?"

"Well..." Logan shrugged helplessly.

"Please..."

"It depends on your sister."

Mikhail immediately turned his attention to her. He grabbed the side of her dress and tugged. "Please, Mia? Please..."

She grinned. "I guess so. If it's okay with Noah."

"Yay! Motorbike! Motorbike! Motorbike! When can we go, Logan? Can we go now? Can we go now?"

Logan laughed. "Whoa! Steady on, buddy. Noah's probably at work right now. But I promise to call and ask him, okay?"

"Do it now! Do it now!" Mikhail demanded.

"Misha, you know better than that," Mia quietly admonished.

Mikhail was immediately contrite. "Sorry, Logan."

Logan smiled and squeezed her brother's shoulder. "No harm done, Mikhail. I promise to call Noah as soon as I can. You might have to wait until the weekend or maybe even past that to go for a ride, but I promise I'll make it happen. Okay?"

"What day is tomorrow?" Mikhail asked.

"Saturday," Mia supplied.

He turned back to Logan. "That's the weekend. Can I go tomorrow?"

"Maybe. Or Sunday. Or maybe next week. It depends on Noah. He's a police officer. He does shiftwork. We'll have to find a time he's free."

Mikhail nodded happily. "Okay."

"What do you say, Misha?" Mia asked.

"Thank you, Logan."

"No worries, mate. It's all good."

Mia looked up. Their gazes caught and held. He was so generous and kind. She was falling in love. She just hoped he felt the same way. Flynn had been so concerned about her breaking his brother's heart. But now, she was more and more concerned that it would be her heart that would be broken and that she might never be able to put it back together again.

She looked at Logan again and saw the sincerity in his eyes. He was the real deal. The stakes were high, but if winning meant she came out with Logan's love, she was prepared to take the risk.

She knew all about life throwing curve balls, but how she reacted to those circumstances was completely within her control. She could have blamed the world for her misfortunes—orphaned at a young age with the added tragedies of losing her leg, living with a drug dealer and having a drug-affected parent. Instead she refused to let those misfortunes define her. She was determined to take control of her life and run her own race, including looking out for her brother.

Falling in love with Logan came with considerable risk. He'd been hurt in love and was now a self-declared commitment phobe. But she also knew how he looked at her, how it felt when they kissed. How he treated Mikhail.

She couldn't believe under all that bluff and bravado, Logan didn't feel something for her, a deep connection that was worth fighting for. And if she was living in some fantasy world and he didn't feel that way at all… Well, she'd deal with that in the same way she'd dealt with all the other challenges and disappointments that had come her way. With her shoulders back and head held high.

Chapter Twelve

It had been a great day. Logan had entertained Mia and Mikhail with various tales from his childhood, including the many sailing races he'd participated in and the fun he'd had with his brothers out on the water. They enjoyed cappuccinos from his state-of-the-art coffee machine and he'd been more than generous with the ice cream and chocolate sauce he dropped into Mikhail's milkshake. They'd parted early afternoon with Logan promising to arrange Mikhail's bike ride with Noah as soon as he could.

With a contented sigh, Logan flicked on the indicator of his Mercedes and turned into the wide driveway that led to the Craigdon Super Yachts premises. The production yard and offices were all contained on the same site, which made it convenient for Logan to move between the two. He'd been expected there right after the sailing lesson, but he hadn't been able to bring himself to end his time with Mia so soon. They'd been having such a great day. He wished it could have lasted forever.

What ridiculousness is this? She's just a woman. Why am I so tied up in knots?

A voice in the back of his head reminded himself how treacherous women could be and how he needed to take a step back, slow down, get to know Mia before it was too late.

Before he was hopelessly in love with her. Yet after the day he'd just spent with her and Mikhail, he pushed the voice away. Nothing was going to spoil his mood. Nothing.

His phone began to ring. He grimaced, assuming the call was from his father wondering where the hell he was. He glanced at the screen and his heart lightened.

Flynn.

He pressed the button to answer the call.

"Flynn. How're you doing?"

"I'm fine. I'm sitting outside the courtroom waiting for my next case to be called. What are you up to?"

"On my way to CSY. Dad's been expecting me since this morning."

"Ouch. What did you do? Sleep through your alarm?"

Logan laughed. "No. I was giving Mikhail a private sailing lesson. He's really showing promise."

"Your generosity wouldn't have anything to do with the boy's hot-looking sister, would it?" Flynn replied in a dry voice.

"Of course not!" Logan joked.

Flynn laughed. "No, of course not! Listen. I was just wondering how much you know about Mia's family?"

"A little. Why?"

"I got curious about her. I mentioned her to Jayde."

Logan felt a stab of irritation. "Why would you discuss my girlfriend with Jayde?"

"Don't be like that. I can see how much this woman means to you. She's not like all the others who've come in and out of your life in the past year. I want to make sure she's legit. That she's not going to turn around and break your heart. I'm just looking out for you, that's all."

"I'm a big boy, Flynn. I don't need you looking out for me."

"I know, I know! But I can't help it." There was a pause

and then Flynn asked, "Do you know anything about her parents?"

"Yes." Logan sighed. "Her mother died when she was five. She was adopted sometime after by Marina and Alexander Ivanov. Mikhail came along five years later. He's their biological child."

"I see."

Logan frowned. Something in Flynn's somber tone sparked another stab of annoyance. "What is it, Flynn? I can tell you're holding something back. For God's sake, spit it out!"

"Well… It's just that… Alexander Ivanov was a big-time drug dealer and a highly placed operative within the Russian mafia."

Laughter exploded out of Logan's mouth. He shook his head in disbelief. "Right. And you think he's the same Alexander Ivanov who went to an orphanage and adopted Mia as a child. The same Alexander Ivanov who started a construction company and was responsible for many of the apartment buildings on the lower north shore. *That* Alexander Ivanov."

"Jayde said—"

"Look, Flynn. I get that Jayde's a hotshot detective with the DEA, but you're trying to tell me she knows Mia's father is the same Alexander Ivanov you're talking about? There must be hundreds of Alexander Ivanovs in this city. *Puhlease*, Flynn! Give me a break!"

"I didn't say she knew anything for certain. It's not like she's run your girlfriend's name through a police database," Flynn muttered.

"I should hope not!"

"Look, just forget about it, okay? I shouldn't have said anything. The thing is, you're my little brother and you've been hurt pretty badly by a woman before. I couldn't bear to see it again."

Logan sighed, his anger dissipating. For all his meddling in Logan's affairs, Flynn's heart was in the right place. On some level Logan was grateful for the show of love and support. When he spoke again, his voice was rough with emotion.

"I get it, Flynn. You're just looking out for me, like you said. And I'm grateful that you care, even if I don't approve of where you went with it."

"Thanks. Well, you take care of yourself. And say hello to Mia. She seems like a nice girl."

"You can talk to her yourself at the engagement party. Ask her all the questions you like. She's agreed to come along as my date."

Flynn's laughter was slightly strained. "Is she crazy? I hope you've given her fair warning about what she's in for."

Logan chuckled. "Of course not. That's part of the fun," he joked.

"Well, I guess I'll see you there."

"You can count on it."

Mia came awake on Saturday morning with a smile on her face. She stretched her arms above her head and thought about the time she and Mikhail had spent with Logan the previous day. It had been perfect in every way. Logan was funny, attentive, generous. She was sure he had plenty to keep him occupied in his father's business and yet he'd chosen to spend his time with them. And though she'd protested, he'd paid for their lunch, had taken them to his apartment for coffee and milkshakes and had even offered to arrange for Mikhail to take a ride on a motorbike. She'd never met a man quite so wonderful.

Life couldn't be this good, could it? I keep waiting for the hammer to fall. There must be a flaw. No one's that perfect.

And yet she couldn't think of one. Perhaps she'd have an

opportunity to quiz the people closest to him at the family function she was attending with Logan that night. Maybe they'd share a secret or two from Logan's past. Something to take the shine off his perfection.

She couldn't imagine anything changing the way she felt about him. She'd fallen in love with him. Head over heels. Ridiculous-silly-grin-all-over-her-face in love. It should have been embarrassing, but all she felt was joy. After all the misfortune she'd suffered in her life, maybe the tables had finally turned. Maybe it was time for some good luck to fall her way. Whatever the reason, she'd grab it with both hands.

If only I knew for sure Logan feels the same way…

He'd certainly given every indication he was falling for her. *But what if I've misread the signals? What if I'm wrong?*

No, she wouldn't allow her thoughts to drift in that direction. Not today. Not when she was feeling so wonderful about the future and what might lie in store.

Her phone beeped, indicating an incoming text. Reaching over, she picked it up from where she'd left it plugged into a charger on her bedside table. Her heart turned over. A smile lifted her lips. It was from Logan.

Thx 4 a g8 day yesterday.
Looking forward 2 the party
2 nite. Pick u up @ 7

She hurriedly texted back.

Sounds g8. Can't wait.

With excitement and anticipation and more than a little trepidation surging through her veins, Mia threw off the covers and climbed out of bed. She hopped into the bathroom. After a quick shower, she fitted her prosthesis to her stump and after throwing on some clothes, padded down the hall to Mikhail's room to check on him. He was awake, watching a movie on his iPad.

"Hey, buddy. How did you sleep?"

"Fine."

"Only a few more days of holidays and then you'll be back at school. You're going to be a big Year Nine student. Fancy that!"

He smiled cautiously. "Yeah."

She moved further into the room and sat down on the edge of his bed. "Are you looking forward to returning to school?"

He shrugged and kept his gaze fixed on the screen.

"Is there anything you're worried about?"

"No."

"Are you sure?"

"Yes."

"Have you been chatting to Jason and Max over the holidays?" she asked, mentioning Mikhail's two closest friends.

"Yeah. A bit."

"What have they been up to?"

"Not much." And then he grinned. "I told them I'd been sailing. Might go on a motorbike ride… And about Logan and how cool he is. They were so jealous."

Mia's heart turned over at the mention of Logan. She was so glad Mikhail liked him. If she and Logan were ever going to make it as a couple, it was imperative Mikhail be completely comfortable with the idea.

She looked at her brother. "Logan *is* pretty cool, isn't he?"

"Yeah! Logan's the best!" And then Mikhail added, "What happened to his leg?"

"What do you mean?"

"The scars and stuff. And he limps."

Mia explained about the accident and how one of the bones hadn't mended so well.

"Why doesn't he just get a fake leg, like you? There's no scars on your leg and you walk just fine."

Once again, her heart turned over with emotion. She shuffled up the bed and gave Mikhail a hug.

"You're such a sweet boy. The best brother in the world! I love you so much."

He looked up at her, his blue eyes clear and innocent. "I love you, too."

She kissed him on the forehead and then pulled back when he scrunched up his face in distaste.

"Why do you like kissing people? I saw you kissing Logan. Yuck."

Mia smiled. "People who love each other kiss. It's a way of expressing your love."

"Do you love Logan?"

Mia stared at Mikhail, completely taken aback. It took a few moments for his words to fully register. "Why would you ask that?"

"Well, you were kissing him. You just said—"

"Yes, I know what I just said," she interrupted, feeling flustered.

"So, do you love Logan?" Mikhail persisted.

Mia prevaricated. "Would it upset you if I did?"

"No," Mikhail replied without hesitation.

"You really like Logan, don't you?" she said.

"Yes. He's cool."

It was a relief to know how Mikhail felt. He was the most important person in the world. Any relationship she had would always include him. It was comforting to know if things between her and Logan developed into something serious, she had Mikhail's support.

"Logan has invited me to a party tonight."

Mikhail's face lit up. "A party? Can I come?"

"No, buddy. It's just for grown-ups. But I have a special surprise. Joanna's going to look after you."

"Joanna from the café?"

"Yes. Is that all right?"

"Yes! I like Joanna. She's nice. And she makes the *best* milkshakes."

Mia smiled. "Yes she does."

She stood and picked up the dirty clothes on Mikhail's floor. She'd do the laundry later. Right now, she needed to sort through her wardrobe and find something suitable to wear to the party. No doubt it would be a posh do with plenty of beautiful people dressed in the latest fashions. Lucky for her, she owned a dress shop. Not all the dresses were for brides. If she couldn't find what she wanted in her wardrobe, she could always go to the shop.

"Okay, buddy. As soon as your movie finishes, I want you to get up and take a shower. Don't forget to brush your teeth and make your bed. After breakfast, you need to decide what you're taking to Joanna's."

"Am I having a sleepover?"

"Yes. Is that all right?"

"Yes! I love sleepovers! Can I watch movies at Joanna's?"

"I'm sure you can, but don't forget your manners. It's polite to ask Joanna first if that's all right. She might have some other fun things planned for you."

Mikhail's sweet face lit up with excitement. He jumped out of bed and started enthusiastically taking off his pajamas. Mia smiled and quietly left the room, pulling the door closed behind her. She headed back to her bedroom, anticipation filling her veins.

Opening the door to her wardrobe, she studied the array of evening gowns that hung on the rack. The black satin sheath was gorgeous and it always made her feel good. But black was a bit somber for an engagement party.

She pulled out a long-sleeved crimson number that fit her like a glove. It clung to her curves and with its plunging neckline, left little to the imagination. No, that one was probably too risqué to wear to a family function. She didn't want Logan's family talking about her for all the wrong reasons.

She moved clothes around, selecting this dress and that, holding them up for inspection and then discarded them one by one. On the far end of the rack hung an off-the-shoulder, electric blue, satin and chiffon creation. The color had caught her attention the first time she'd seen it wrapped in tissue paper in the delivery box. It had come with an order of bridal dresses. She'd added a few other dresses and accessories that would be suitable for wedding guests.

She might only be attending an engagement party, but the blue number was perfect. She pulled off her clothes and tried the dress on. The soft fabric felt divine against her skin. The hem swished around her ankles. The cinched-in waist gave her shape and emphasized her breasts which were on display in the low-cut bodice. Sexy, but not trashy. That was exactly the image she was counting on. All she needed was her pair of custom made black four-inch heels to complete the look and to keep the hem of the long dress from dragging on the floor.

Twirling around in front of the mirror, she couldn't keep the grin off her face. Excitement and anticipation thrummed through her veins. She couldn't wait for Logan to see her like this. She knew he was attracted to her, but she wanted more than that. She wanted to blow his mind.

She hoped when he saw her in the dress that would be enough for him to realize he wanted more than a casual fling. She hoped it made him start to think about forever...

Chapter Thirteen

Craigdon Manor was just as elegant and impressive as Mia had imagined. Logan had told her it was built in 1927 and had remained in the hands of ancestors of the original family until his uncle had purchased the property about twenty-five years ago. The house displayed all the hallmarks of its impressive Art Deco architectural period, including rounded corners and stylized geometric detailing. The three-story house was set across an expansive six hectares, with the stately grounds incorporating a full-size tennis court, nine-hole golf course, heated pool and spa. Mia had never been anywhere so grand. And it wasn't only the house that was intimidating.

It seemed the who's who of Sydney high society had flocked to celebrate the double engagement party of members of one of the city's most reputable families. Nicholas and his fiancée, Harper, stood beside his sister Isabella and her fiancé, Raine. The women looked resplendent in full-length satin designer dresses. Isabella wore a brilliant shade of purple while Harper wore emerald green. Sparkling jewels adorned their necks. The men looked equally impressive in Armani suits. Raine had gone with black on black and Nicholas had opted for charcoal-gray. Their ties reflected the color of their respective fiancée's dress.

Mia was so excited to be there. Despite her silent urgings to take things slowly, it seemed she couldn't get enough of Logan. She thought about him all the time and wanted to be with him. Talk to him, share his day. Tell him about hers. She'd fallen in love with him. That ought to scare her, but all she could do was smile.

The only thing that really held her back was Mikhail, but after talking to him about how he felt about Logan, many of her concerns in that department had eased. She'd always known any man she invited into her life would have to accept her brother without question. That was not negotiable. She had a feeling Logan would do that. He treated Mikhail with kindness and respect and didn't make any allowances for his disabilities. He made Mikhail feel like he was just another ordinary teenager and that filled her heart with gratitude and only made her like Logan all the more.

She was flooded with nerves as she climbed the wide stone steps that led to the entryway where the engaged couples stood greeting their guests. She was about to meet Logan's family. He'd told her his mother had been killed in a car accident, but his father was still alive. In fact, his father was helping to host the party, along with the matriarch of the family, Elizabeth Craigdon.

Logan had warned her that all his extended family would be there, including Callum, Noah and Flynn. Though she hadn't been introduced to Callum, she was relieved to discover there were at least two other people at the party that she knew. Kind of.

A fresh wave of nervousness washed over her. As if sensing her apprehension, Logan reached for her hand. She clung to him, grateful for his support.

The smile of greeting offered by Isabella and Raine when Logan introduced them appeared genuine. Isabella graciously welcomed Mia to Craigdon Manor. They complimented each other about their dresses and then it was Nicholas and Harper's turn.

"You're looking sharp Nick," Logan teased.

"You too," Nick quipped and then turned his attention to Mia.

"You must be Mia. I've heard a lot about you."

She murmured a nervous response and wondered which one of the Craigdon brothers had spoken about her to their cousin. She'd met Flynn and Noah at the sailing course. Recalling Flynn's warning not to break his brother's heart, she frowned. Then again, maybe Logan had been talking about her. That thought made her feel a bit better.

"Well, it's lovely to meet you Mia," Harper added graciously. "I hope you enjoy the night."

They walked inside the house. What was impressive from the outside was even more breathtaking on the inside. Cathedral ceilings, sparkling chandeliers, travertine tiles. A sweeping staircase that led to the floor above. Everything was so tasteful, so elegant, so sophisticated. And yet, there were homey touches that told her this was a place where a family lived. Little knickknacks here and there. Personal mementoes. There were also framed photographs of family members hanging on some of the walls and standing on side tables.

Logan snagged a glass of champagne and a glass of orange juice from a passing waiter and handed the juice to her. She murmured her thanks, pleased he'd remembered she didn't drink. He leaned over and kissed her cheek.

"Have I told you how beautiful you look tonight?" he murmured.

His appreciative gaze traveled slowly over her off-the-shoulder, electric blue, satin and chiffon dress. His gaze lingered on her breasts. So far, Logan had only seen her in loose pants, shirts and boardshorts. Even in her bikini top she'd been covered with a lifejacket. There was a part of her that wanted him to see her as a sexy, desirable woman. From the look in his eyes as he gazed at her, it appeared she'd succeeded.

He bent his head. His lips teased the soft skin of her ear. He nuzzled her neck. She shivered with desire and closed her eyes against the sensual onslaught. Her nipples pebbled with need.

"Sorry to interrupt, but I believe my mother and your father are looking for you."

Mia's head snapped up. She opened her eyes on a gasp. Callum stood beside them, grinning widely. Embarrassment heated her cheeks. She glanced at Logan who appeared completely unperturbed.

"Callum. It's good to see you."

"You, too." The men hugged briefly. Callum gaze shifted to Mia. "You came along with your brother to the sailing course, right?"

Mia managed to nod. "Yes. I haven't had the chance to thank you. I understand it was your idea."

Callum nodded. "Yes, but it was this guy here who made it happen. He agreed to run the course and then cajoled his brothers into helping. Without them, we would never have gotten it past the idea stage."

"Well, I'm grateful to all of you. My brother had a wonderful time. It was so good for his confidence."

Callum smiled. "I'm glad to hear it." His gaze sidled to Logan. "It looks like your brother's not the only one who's had a boost to his confidence."

While heat exploded once again across Mia's face, Logan continued to look unruffled. In fact, he slipped his arm around her waist and drew her closer.

"Absolutely," he responded with a wink in her direction. He turned back to his cousin. "I'd like to thank you too, Callum."

Callum merely looked amused. "For what?"

"For arm wrestling me into taking on the course. If you hadn't, I would have never met Mia. She's changed my life."

Callum's gaze became more thoughtful. He looked from one to the other and finally settled back on Logan. "You're right, mate. There's something different about you. You seem more…settled. More at peace. Dare I say, even happier?"

Logan grinned and tightened his hold on Mia. "I *am* happier. Happier than I thought possible."

Callum's answering smile appeared genuine. "I'm glad," he said softly. "I'm so glad." And then he cleared his throat. "If you're willing, I'd like to put together another sailing course sometime. God knows, there are plenty of kids who'd benefit."

Logan nodded. "Yeah. That sounds good. Count me in."

Callum smiled. He patted Logan on the shoulder and went to turn away. "Don't forget to say hello to Mom and Uncle Archie. They heard you arrived. They're looking for you. Apparently they're dying to meet Mia."

With that, Callum gave them a cheeky grin and took his leave.

⌒

With fingers entwined, Mia and Logan made their way through the partygoers in search of his father and aunt. Every now and then someone would greet Logan with affection and he would stop and introduce Mia. Each time he did it, he drew her close. She heard the pride and possession in his voice as he spoke her name and it only made her feel more special. Whether he knew it or not, Logan gave every indication he was falling just as hard and fast as she had. That was a heady feeling.

Then Logan came to a halt before an older couple she guessed was his father and Elizabeth Craigdon.

"Dad. Aunt Elizabeth. It's good to see you. I'd like you to meet Mia Ivanov."

Archie Craigdon had the same tall, broad-shouldered appeal as the other Craigdon men. Though his hair was liberally speckled with gray, she could see it had once been a dark blond, similar to Logan's, but instead of green eyes, Logan's father had brown. They now regarded her with avid curiosity.

"Mia. It's lovely to meet you. We've heard so much about you," he said.

She smiled. "Thank you. It's nice to meet you, too."

She turned to Elizabeth. Logan had told Mia his aunt had turned sixty last birthday, but Elizabeth looked ten years younger. Her clear blue eyes sparkled. Her translucent skin was barely wrinkled. Her thick, snowy white hair was swept off her forehead and framed her face in an elegant bob. Rings sparkled on her fingers, matching the diamonds that glinted at her ears and around her neck. She wore a frock from a designer Mia recognized as being among the world's best. And while the look she bestowed on Mia was filled with caution, there was a warmth in her smile that eased some of Mia's tension.

Mia extended her hand in Elizabeth's direction. The woman took it. Her grip was surprisingly firm.

"Mia. It's lovely to meet you."

Though the words were polite enough, Mia sensed an undertone. Elizabeth's gaze had sharpened on hers, become almost pointed. Mia frowned in confusion, not sure what was going on. The four of them indulged in general chit chat, including relaying the story of how Logan and Mia met, but she couldn't help feeling the older Craigdons were assessing her character with a razor-sharp awareness, weighing up the truth of her words and the authenticity of her feelings for the man who stood by her side.

She understood how they might feel protective toward Logan, given what had gone on before with his ex-fiancée. For that reason, Mia took it upon herself to assure them she was genuine about Logan, even going so far as to tell them she was aware of his painful past.

"I care deeply for your son and nephew," she said. "I promise I won't be cavalier with his heart."

They regarded her dubiously and there was nothing she could do but accept that they knew nothing about her and it would take time for them to trust her and accept her word. After a few more moments of strained conversation, to Mia's relief Logan muttered about catching up with them later. Archie regarded them solemnly. Elizabeth merely nodded.

"Enjoy the party," she said.

Mia murmured her thanks and left with Logan, grateful to make her escape. Logan snagged another champagne and a glass of orange juice from a passing waiter and both of them moved away from the crowd to a quieter spot in the shadows. Mia took a healthy sip of her juice. Logan followed suit.

"So. That's my father and my Aunt Elizabeth. Now we have that over with, we can relax."

She regarded him curiously. "It sounds as though you were as nervous about the meeting as I was."

He chuckled. "Yeah. You're right. I already told them about you and they were keen to meet you, but… It's always a bit nerve-racking, right?"

She smiled softly. She reached up and cupped his cheek with her hand. It was freshly shaven. The skin was soft and the smell of his cologne was driving her crazy.

"Thank you," she whispered. She pressed a gentle kiss against his lips.

At the touch of her lips, his eyes flared wide. Desire swirled in their depths. "For what?" he asked, his voice husky.

"For being so wonderful."

He took a breath. "Did you mean it when you said you cared for me?"

She held his gaze, hoping to convey her sincerity. "Yes."

Emotion flared once again in his eyes. "Good. Because I feel the same way."

Joy crept slowly through her veins and then exploded into a grin. "You do?"

Logan reached for their glasses and set them on a low table nearby. Heedless of where they were, he picked her up and spun her around. "Yes!"

Sliding her slowly down the length of him, her feet had barely touched the ground when his lips came down on hers. Though they were mostly concealed in the shadows, she was surprised and overjoyed that he felt comfortable kissing her so passionately so close to his family and the other guests.

As his mouth moved over hers with increasing heat, she opened to him. His tongue immediately stole inside. At the same time, his hand moved up and cupped her breast, sending hot shards of need exploding inside her.

Slowly, the kiss came to an end. Logan lifted his head and smiled down at her. "That was amazing."

Too overwhelmed to speak, she merely smiled and nodded. She'd never felt so happy. Every dream she'd ever had of finding her soul mate was coming true. The man she'd been waiting for stood inches away from her, looking as happy as she felt. Logan retrieved their glasses and clinked his glass to hers.

"Here's cheers," he said.

"To what?"

The look he gave her was intense. "To us."

She felt the heat of his gaze on her bare skin. It sent delicious feelings of desire coursing along her veins. "To us," she repeated. She took a sip from her juice.

They shared another kiss and then Logan leaned back

against the wall and drew her against him. She stood with her back to him, his arms wrapped around her waist. She sighed softly.

"What is it?" he asked, nuzzling her neck.

"This. It's all so wonderful. Like something out of a dream."

She turned to look at him. His green eyes were alight with emotion.

"You're right," he said huskily. "It *is* like a dream. But if this is a dream, please don't wake me up."

She laughed. Her gaze roamed around the room and fell on a tall, broad-shouldered man with dark hair and angry eyes. Though he was dressed as superbly as the other guests, he appeared to be set apart from the rest of the partygoers. As if he was there, but only on the periphery. An onlooker, rather than a participant. His expression was dark and brooding. He certainly didn't appear to be enjoying himself.

"Who's that?" she asked, surreptitiously pointing in the man's direction.

Logan sighed. "That's Christopher Barrington. Henry Craigdon's illegitimate son."

Mia blinked in surprise. She didn't know Henry had fathered a son outside of his marriage. Obviously the man was accepted by the family. Mia assumed he hadn't gate-crashed the party.

As if sensing the direction of her thoughts, Logan added, "He was born before my uncle married my aunt. He's the oldest of Henry's children."

"He looks…upset. What's the matter with him?"

Logan sighed again. "Don't pay him any heed. He's angry at the world. My uncle never recognized him as his biological son. Not even in his will. Christopher took it hard. I guess he had good reason. It must have been tough growing up knowing your father didn't want to have anything to do with you. Least of all, to give you his name."

"Poor guy. He looks like he's in need of a friend."

"You're probably right. But tonight I'm not sharing you with anyone." With that, he turned her around to face him and kissed her again. Mia kissed him back, putting everything she felt for him into it. When the kiss came to an end, they were both breathing hard.

Mia smiled. "I'm all yours."

Chapter Fourteen

sabella Craigdon draped her arms around her fiancé's neck and moved to the slow beat of the music. With her cheek pressed against Raine's and breathing in the scent of his woodsy cologne, there was no place she'd rather be. The engagement party was in full swing and even though she was sharing hostess duties with her brother and Harper, she was starting to wear out. Her face was sore from smiling. Her stilettoes were killing her feet. She'd be glad when the evening drew to a close and she could take off her glad rags and slip into something more comfortable.

"What are you thinking?" Raine murmured.

She gave him a small smile. "Would it be terrible if I said I can't wait for the night to be over?"

Raine merely chuckled. "Your feet are hurting, right? What did I tell you? I don't know how the hell you walk in those things. They look like instruments of torture."

"Yeah, yeah, yeah," she replied, rolling her eyes. "The lengths we go to for fashion."

Raine twirled her around and then they came back together, cheek to cheek. They danced a few more bars in silence.

"What did you get up to today?" she asked. "I barely saw you this afternoon."

"I was out looking at office space in the city."

She frowned. "Why would you be doing that?"

"Because I know how much you love living in Sydney, being close to your family."

Isabella stopped dancing. She looked up at Raine in confusion. "Are you thinking about moving down here from Brisbane?"

He nodded. "Yes."

"But what about your business? What about all the contacts you've built up over the years?"

He shrugged. "I can always start again."

Isabella's stared at him incredulously. "You love me enough to do that?"

Raine regarded her steadily, a somber expression on his face. "I love you more than life itself. You're my world. My everything. There's nothing I wouldn't do for you." He bent his head and kissed her softly. "All I want is to see you happy."

She shook her head, overwhelmed by the strength of his love. "Raine. Wow. I… I don't know what to say."

"You don't have to say anything."

She looked at him. "Yes. Yes, I do. See, I always knew if I wanted to be with you I'd have to leave Sydney. Brisbane is your home, the place where you have your business. I love that you're willing to give up all that to be with me, to make me happy, but the thing is, knowing you're prepared to make that sacrifice is all that matters."

She stared at him with all the love she felt inside. "The thing is, I'm happiest when I'm with you. Where we live doesn't matter. Yes, I'll miss my family, but you're my family now. Wherever you are is where I want to be. Always."

He looked down at her, his eyes wide with surprise. A smile tugged at his lips. "Are you sure?"

She framed his beloved face with her hands and kissed him soundly on the lips. "Yes. I'm sure. No more talk of office space and moving to Sydney. I can't wait to start our life together in Brisbane. Now, how soon can we get out of here? My feet are killing me!"

Mia and Logan continued to do the rounds of the party guests. At one point the speeches were made and the two happy couples cut identical, three-tiered cakes. Both Nick and Raine gave a speech about their future wives. Their love was palpable.

Mia yearned to know that kind of love. Someone to wipe away life's disappointments. To be there through the good and the bad. Someone she could rely on to always have her back. And for her to do the same for her partner. She looked at Logan who stood beside Callum a short distance away.

As if sensing her gaze, Logan looked up at her and smiled tenderly, saluting her with his champagne flute. She lifted her glass and smiled back, filled with hope.

With the speeches done and the cake cut and after a quick word to Mia, Logan headed inside to find a bathroom. Listening to the joy and happiness in his cousins' voices as they spoke about their future wives filled Logan with an overwhelming sense of yearning.

After the debacle of his almost-marriage to Virginia, he'd firmly believed he'd never allow himself to get swept up in the emotions of love again. He continued to enjoy women, but he was determined never to give one his heart. He didn't think he could bear the pain of ever going through what he had with Virginia.

But then he met Mia and everything was turned on its head. His previously held conviction to never again allow himself to fall in love faltered each time he was with her. She was sweet, giving. Smart, hard-working, resilient. Not to mention she was the sexiest woman he'd set eyes on. His heart felt under siege every time she smiled.

Am I falling in love?

He could scarcely believe it. It had been more than a year since Virginia jilted him. He'd been certain the pain and humiliation would be with him forever. For so long, he'd wallowed in self-pity. Along with his devastation at losing his promising career in sailing, it had consumed him.

But lately he'd been looking at the world differently and he had Mia and Callum to thank for that. He realized life had gone in a different direction to the one he planned, but was that such a big deal? Life threw up challenges all the time. It was how one reacted to those challenges that revealed a person's true measure.

He'd never pegged himself as a coward, but he could see now that's exactly the way he'd been acting. He'd been running scared from life, from disappointment, from feeling emotion. He hadn't wanted to feel anything. Being numb was good.

But it hadn't made him happy. He knew that now. The way he felt when he was with Mia—and even her little brother—that's what life was all about. That's what made him happy. He smiled.

"Logan. I'm glad I caught you. Do you mind stepping into the study?"

Logan blinked at his father and then slowly registered his words. "Um, sure. I'll be there in a minute."

Archie nodded and turned away in the direction of Uncle Henry's study. Logan found a bathroom and after washing his hands, he followed after his father. Opening the door, he was surprised to find his Aunt Elizabeth was also there.

"I asked Elizabeth to meet us here," Archie said, noting Logan's reaction.

Logan shrugged nonchalantly, but a feeling of foreboding crept into his gut. "What's this all about?"

Archie crossed the room and sat down behind Henry's impressive, hand-carved cedar desk. He indicated that Logan take a seat opposite, beside his aunt. Logan hadn't been in the room since the reading of the will. The memory of the somber occasion sent another wave of nervousness through his gut.

"What's going on?" he asked, pleased his voice didn't reflect his apprehension.

"Mia seems nice," his aunt responded.

Logan looked at her and kept his tone neutral. "She is."

His father stacked his fingers together and regarded him solemnly. Logan's belly took a nosedive.

"The thing is, son. We have some concerns about her."

Logan frowned. "Concerns? What the hell does that mean?"

Archie looked uncomfortable. He cleared his throat. "The thing is, your aunt and I have reason to believe she's not who she says she is."

Logan sat forward in his seat. "What are you talking about? You've only just met her."

"She's Amelia Ivanov, right? You call her Mia."

"Yes," Logan replied warily.

"And her father was Alexander Ivanov."

"Yes."

"She has a brother, Mikhail."

Logan twisted in his chair impatiently. "Yes. So what? What is this all about, Dad?"

"Your father believes Mia Ivanov's father was one of the bosses of the Russian mafia. Deeply involved in the illegal drug trade, prostitution and a raft of other criminal activities."

Logan felt the color drain from his face. "*What?*"

Once again, Archie cleared his throat. "Your aunt is right. That's exactly who this woman is. Given your uncle's involvement in illegal drugs, we can only wonder why she's chosen to become friendly with you."

Logan's bark of incredulous laughter sounded loud in the silence of the room. "You have to be joking! Mia? A drug dealer? She abhors everything to do with illegal drugs! Her adoptive mother died from an overdose. She wants nothing to do with the stuff. She once told me it would be a deal breaker in our relationship if I'd ever used illegal drugs." He shook his head. "I'm sorry. But you have the wrong person."

"We don't think so."

The gravity of his father's tone gave Logan pause. Archie took advantage by handing him a sheaf of 8 x 10 colored photos. Logan glanced at the one on top.

"That's Alexander Ivanov," Archie explained. "Mia's adoptive father."

Logan shook his head. First Flynn, now their father. "How do you know so much about him?" he asked.

Archie compressed his lips. "I've known him from years ago. He came by here late one night, looking for your uncle. Henry was out. Ivanov was agitated. He kept saying he needed to see Henry. It was important. I didn't know what was going on. He began demanding that I give him some shit." Archie grimaced. "His words, not mine. It didn't take a genius to work out he was referring to illegal drugs."

"What did you say?" Logan asked.

"I told him if he didn't get off the property, I'd call the police. He eventually left." Archie sighed. "After that I hired a private investigator and made some inquiries. I discovered the late-night visitor was heavily involved in the Russian mafia." Archie indicated the photographs in Logan's hand. "Those are some of the pictures the PI took during the course of his investigation."

Logan frowned. "Why didn't you go to the police?"

"With what? I had no evidence. Ivanov could have simply denied the whole conversation. Hell, he could have denied even being here. I had no proof."

"Is that why Uncle Henry beefed up security around this place?" Logan asked.

"Yes. Ivanov's unexpected visit shook him up. Though he wouldn't admit it. He installed CCTV cameras, starting at the front gate. He also installed metal detectors and security guards at Craigdon Enterprises. He was determined no one would come onto his property again without his knowledge."

"What did he say when you asked him about Ivanov?"

"He denied everything. Said he'd never heard of Ivanov and didn't have a clue why the man had thought Henry could supply him with drugs. But of course, that didn't stop my brother from spending a fortune on additional security measures. His actions weren't consistent with his words, and though I had my suspicions about how my brother managed to finance his extraordinary lavish lifestyle, I had no proof."

Logan turned to his aunt. "What about you? You lived in the same household. Surely you had an inkling about what was going on?"

Elizabeth shook her head. "Your uncle and I might have lived under the same roof, but for all intents and purposes we lived separate lives. We stayed together for the sake of our children and because our faith forbade divorce. It had been that way for years."

Logan stared at the Persian rug that lined the polished floor of his uncle's study. "I wish I'd said something."

Both Archie and Elizabeth sat forward in alarm. "What do you mean?" Archie asked.

Logan drew in a deep breath and blew it out. He'd come clean with his brothers. It was time his father learned the truth.

"I used to work for Uncle Henry, dealing drugs."

"What?"

The shock and outrage was mirrored on the faces of both his father and his aunt. Logan refused to back down. Now that the truth was out there, he wanted to be done with it.

"Uncle Henry approached me when I was ten or eleven. He asked me if I wanted to make some pocket money. That's how it started." Logan went on to detail how he'd begun as a lookout while Henry took deliveries off the wharf and later graduated to selling speed to his school mates. He kept Noah out of it. It wasn't his place to tell them he wasn't the only family member Henry had recruited.

Afterwards, there was a shocked silence. Logan used the time to flip through the photographs. There were several of the man Archie was certain was Mia's father. Some on his own and some with other people. There was no one Logan recognized. Until he got to the last couple of pictures. Both of them were of Mia. The last one included Mikhail.

They both looked several years younger. Mia's hair was shorter and Mikhail still had a pudginess about him that suggested he was a little kid. They were at a park. Mikhail was on the swing and Mia was behind him, pushing him. Both of them were laughing. It was a nice picture, but it was all a lie.

Realization slowly set in. Alexander Ivanov was Mia's father. He'd adopted her as a child. Raised her as his own. There was no way she couldn't have been aware of his occupation. She'd told Logan her father was in construction. Had even mentioned several apartment blocks he'd constructed on the lower north shore.

Yeah, right. Construction, my ass…

Either that or she was just as much a pawn in her father's illegal drug business as he had been in his uncle's. And then another thought occurred to him. There was a third possibility. Maybe she was as oblivious to what had been going on as Archie and Elizabeth had been? While they'd suspected

Henry of illegal activities, they'd both been clueless about Logan's involvement. He could only guess they were just as oblivious to what Noah had done.

Scrubbing his hands through his hair, Logan groaned in frustration. He didn't know what to believe. Was Mia an innocent victim? A consummate liar? Or something in between?

His aunt was the first to break the silence. "I'm so sorry, Logan. I had no idea Henry had used you in that way. If I'd known about it, I would have forbidden it."

Archie snarled, his expression furious. "I would have beaten him to within an inch of his life." Tears of anger glimmered in his eyes. "Why didn't you ever come to me, son? Why didn't you tell me what was going on?"

Logan kept his gaze fixed on the rug. "At first I thought it was all a bit of fun. When I got old enough to realize the seriousness of it, I was ashamed."

Archie pushed away from his desk and began to pace the length of his study. "I can't believe he involved you! It makes me sick! What if you'd been arrested? Your life would have been destroyed!"

Logan's shoulders slumped on a heavy sigh. "Let's just be thankful that never happened, Dad. The fact is, Uncle Henry is dead. There'll be no justice from that quarter."

Archie's pacing slowed. When he returned to his seat behind the desk, he looked like he'd aged a decade.

"I'm so sorry, son. I should have known. I should have done something!"

"Forget it, Dad. I have. It's over with." With another sigh, he got to his feet. "I'd better get back to the party. Mia will be wondering what happened to me. Thanks for telling me about…everything."

Archie stepped forward and enveloped Logan in a hug. "I love you, son. Don't you ever forget that."

"I love you too, Dad."

"What are you going to do about Mia?" Elizabeth asked.

Logan compressed his lips, feeling grim. "I'm not sure yet. I guess I'm going to talk to her and see if I can get to the truth. There's a possibility she's an innocent pawn in all of this and was oblivious to who and what her father was."

"Of course. Well, good luck," Elizabeth replied. Standing on her tiptoes, she kissed him on the cheek. "We're always here if you need us. Anytime."

Chapter Fifteen

Mia was looking for Logan. He'd told her he was going to the bathroom, but that had been half an hour ago. Though she went into all of the rooms occupied by party goers, it seemed he'd disappeared. She was just about to start her search out by the pool when she spied him coming out of a room adjacent to the foyer. The serious expression on his face gave her pause.

"There you are! What happened to your party mood?" she teased.

He barely acknowledged her. His expression remained bleak. A frisson of alarm arced through her. "Logan? What's wrong?"

"We need to talk. Let's get out here."

With the revelations of the past thirty minutes creating havoc inside him, Logan held open the door for Mia while she climbed into his Mercedes, then limped around to the driver's side. He'd limited himself to a few glasses of champagne over the course of the past several hours and was well capable of driving them home. His mind was clear, which was a good thing. At least he could give his full attention to the turmoil that churned in his guts.

He desperately wanted to believe Mia was oblivious to who her father really was and what he'd done for a living, but there was evidence that pointed to the contrary. He'd seen firsthand the proof of Mia's lavish lifestyle—the expensive car, the luxury home, a private school for Mikhail—it must be one hell of a successful bridal wear shop. It wasn't the first time the thought had crossed his mind, but he'd been too invested in getting to know her and he'd thrust his curiosity away. Now it came rushing back to him like a category-five cyclone, tossing his thoughts around like flotsam, loose and unmoored.

Mia shot him a worried glance. A frown marred the smooth skin of her forehead. He could understand her confusion. Prior to him disappearing from the party, he'd been in a playful mood. He'd been dancing with her, moving to the beat, doing his best to show up Noah. Of course, there was no chance of that. Noah and his girlfriend, Ayla, were almost professional-level tango dancers. No one else attending came even close.

Eventually he and Mia had stopped dancing and had moved off to one side and simply stared at the happy couple, mesmerized like all the other guests. On the floor the couple moved with such grace and style, anticipating each other's moves, in perfect rhythm to the music.

Fast forward to now and Logan was taut with anger and confusion, hardly able to speak.

"Are you going to tell me what's going on, Logan?"

Her tone was calm and measured and went some distance toward dousing his anger. He believed in innocent until proven guilty. She deserved a chance to be heard.

"You didn't tell me your father was *the* Alexander Ivanov."

Still, her voice remained calm. "What's that supposed to mean?"

"Your father was a member of the Russian mafia. He was involved in drug dealing, prostitution and God knows what else. Don't tell me you don't know about any of this."

His words were met with stunned silence. At last she sighed quietly. "You're right. My father was a criminal of the worst kind. I didn't lie to you when I told you he was in construction—that was true. But that was a front for his more unsavory ventures."

He glanced at her in shock. "So you *did* know!"

"Yes."

"Why didn't you tell me?"

She laughed without humor. "Oh, right. When was I supposed to introduce that into our conversation? The afternoon we went for coffee? The night you brought over dinner? Perhaps I should have slipped it in there between the spring rolls and the curry?"

"That's not fair, Mia."

"Of course it's not fair! You of all people should know by now that life isn't fair! I hated everything my father represented. I hated it from the first moment I learned the truth. I think I was about eight.

"Thanks to my father, my mother had easy access to drugs and alcohol. It seemed like no time at all and she was hooked. My little brother was born with Fetal Alcohol Syndrome. Things will be difficult for him for the rest of his life. My mother died with a needle in her arm. Mikhail was just seven. My father was riddled with guilt over her death, but not enough to give up his lucrative business.

"The very day after her funeral, I caught him on the phone talking to one of his associates. They were arranging for the delivery of an incoming shipment of drugs. I ran to the bathroom and vomited."

Her breath came fast. Her cheeks were flushed. Her eyes flashed with a fierce anger. Her reaction was too real, too raw to be fraudulent. Compassion moved inside him. He wanted to take her in his arms and hold her tight, but this wasn't over yet.

"When he died," she continued in a calmer tone, "I'm ashamed to admit the overwhelming feeling I had was relief. Though it upset me to learn he was gunned down in the street like a dog and I was sad we'd lost our father, for the most part I accepted that for someone like him, it was probably what he deserved. He'd destroyed the life of my mother and made Mikhail's life far more challenging than it ever should have been. He loved us, but he loved the money and power he gained by being a drug lord more than he did anything or anyone else. Including his family."

She choked on a sob and Logan bit his lip against a surge of emotion. With his free hand, he reached for hers and squeezed her fingers. "It's all right, Mia. I didn't mean to upset you."

She dashed at the tears on her cheek. "I'm fine. I'm glad it's out in the open. You have every right to be angry. I gave you such a hard time when I thought you might have been a drug user and all along, I kept my shameful past hidden."

He bit down on a surge of guilt. He still hadn't told her about his involvement in his uncle's business. Maybe it was time to come clean and hope for the best? Or perhaps he should just keep his mouth shut. After all, it had happened such a long time ago and it wasn't like he'd ever get involved in that kind of thing again.

She let out another quiet sob and he was moved to speak. "It wasn't *your* shame, Mia. You're not responsible for your father's sins."

The tears now rolled down her face in earnest. "I know that!" she cried. "In my head I know that. But try telling that to my heart! I knew what he was doing and yet I did nothing. I *said* nothing.

"I could have gone to the police. I could have told them everything. And yet I stayed quiet. I stayed quiet because I was scared of what would become of Mikhail if Dad was taken away. Or worse, if somehow the courts didn't convict him and Dad tossed me out on my ear. I couldn't take the risk that Mikhail's life would be turned upside down, no matter what happened. So I did nothing.

"I continued to live in that beautiful house and drive my beautiful car. They'd been paid for with drug money, but I chose to set that aside. After my father died, I thought about selling the place and moving, but Mikhail was settled there and in a good school nearby. And I had my business.

"I told myself we were entitled to live comfortably, after all we'd put up with. But I felt guilty. I still feel guilty. Every single day. The only way I've been able to live with myself is knowing that I now support myself and Mikhail through my business. My legitimate business, where I abide by the law, pay my taxes and try hard to focus on happy moments. After all, it doesn't get happier than finding the perfect dress for a bride."

Her voice cracked. Burying her face in her hands, she sobbed like her heart was broken. Logan changed lanes and pulled up to the curb. Unclipping his seatbelt, he reached across the console and took her in his arms. She collapsed against him and was overwhelmed by a fresh tumult of tears.

Her tears tore at his heart. He held her close and whispered words of comfort in her ear. Relieved that she was as good and kind as he'd always thought, his heart flooded with love and compassion. There was no way he didn't believe her. No one could be that good at lying.

As her tears subsided to the occasional hiccup, he slowly lifted her head off his chest. She stared up at him, her eyelashes wet with tears. As if in slow motion, their lips met and with gentle sighs they melded to one another.

Sometime later, he pulled back. The muscles in his side protested the awkward position he'd been in for too long. There had to be a better way to make out with the girl he was falling in love with.

"I want to make love with you, Mia."

She regarded him solemnly. "Yes."

A surge of blood rushed to his groin. They were nearly back at Mosman. Balmoral was right down the hill. "Your place or mine?"

"Mikhail's spending the night at Joanna's."

"Your place is closer."

Her smile filled his heart. "Agreed."

Nerves swirled in Mia's stomach, making her feel slightly ill. Though she wanted to make love with Logan, she was worried about what he'd think about her leg. She was scared he might be turned off—or worse, filled with revulsion. It was a natural reaction. Being confronted with the reality of someone missing part of their leg wasn't for the faint of heart. Mia had lived with it for so long she often forgot about it. But for Logan, it was completely new.

Then there was her lack of experience in the bedroom. While she wasn't a virgin, she might as well be. She'd had sex once with a guy she barely knew. She'd met him at a party when she was sixteen. He was keen to get to know her better. She was flattered by the attention. They'd done it standing up against a wall outside the house where the party was held. They'd both been drinking. He didn't even notice her prosthesis. It was over in only a few minutes. She was left to wonder what all the fuss was about. It had been brief and it had been uncomfortable. At least he'd worn a condom.

But with Logan, she instinctively knew things would be different. For one, he was nowhere near drunk. He wasn't even tipsy. Secondly, he knew about her leg. Thirdly, she cared deeply for him. Though she'd never been in love, she had a sneaking suspicion this was what it felt like. The thought both exhilarated and terrified her. She wished she knew how he felt.

As if sensing her inner turmoil, Logan glanced across at her as he pulled up alongside the curb outside her house.

"We don't have to do this, Mia."

She bit her lip, embarrassed that her thoughts were so visible. "It's not that. I want to. I really do. I like you, Logan. I… I might be even falling in love with you."

His eyes flared wide with emotion. A joyous smile lit up his face. "You are?"

She met his gaze a little unsteadily. "Y-yes. At least, I think so. I've never been in love. I don't know how it's supposed to feel."

"Excited, giddy, nervous and everything in between. Thinking about you all the time. Wanting to be with you. Missing you," he added quietly. He stared at the steering wheel. "I've been in love before. That's exactly how it felt." He paused and then added, "For a long time I refused to allow myself to get close to another woman again. I wasn't brave enough to put myself through the heartache when it all fell apart."

He looked up at her. "But then I met you and you exploded in my heart. You weren't like any other woman I'd met. I found myself wanting to take the risk of another broken heart. It might all end in devastation, but there was also a chance it might work out. I was willing to take that chance. For you." Her breath hitched at the intensity in his gaze and he continued, "I'm in love with you, Mia."

She reached out and covered one of his hands with hers. "Does that scare you?"

"Yes!" He gave a strained laugh. "It terrifies me. But the thought of not giving things a go between us, not being brave enough to see where this might lead, scares me even more."

Cradling his face between her hands, she kissed him softly on the lips. "I'm scared, too. I'm scared you'll be repulsed by my leg."

Logan's expression filled with love. "I've seen it already, remember? Besides, nothing about you could repulse me. It saddens me thinking about the trauma you went through, but when I look at you, all I see is a courageous, beautiful, kind-hearted, compassionate woman.

"I feel ashamed. For so long I've wallowed in self-pity, when what happened to me couldn't even come close to what you've suffered. And yet, here you are. Strong and confident and happy. Smiling at the world. Running a business, raising a brother, getting on with life."

He pressed his forehead to hers. "You make me want to be a better person, Mia. I *want* to be that person. For you."

With that, he climbed out of the car and came around to her side. He opened the door and took her hand and drew her out. Together, they walked up the steps to Mia's front door. She fished in her purse for her key and opened the door. Though nerves still swirled in her stomach, it was more anticipation than dread.

Still, she was a novice at initiating love-making. She didn't have a clue how to go about it. She switched on lights and set her handbag on the counter and then turned to face him, feeling awkward.

Should I make the first move, or should I wait for him?

A fresh wave of uncertainty washed over her.

"Would you like a drink?" she asked for want of something to say.

"No," he said, his gaze on hers. "I don't want a drink. I want you."

With that, he stepped forward and took her in his arms. She melted against him. She tilted her head up and their lips met. The kiss started out slow and gentle, but it quickly gathered heat.

Logan's mouth devoured hers like a starving man. She met his response with equal passion. And then Logan bent and swept her off her feet. She gasped and clung to him, her arms tight around his neck.

"Which bedroom is yours?" he murmured, nuzzling the soft skin of her neck.

"Second on the left."

He turned and strode down the hallway, carrying her with ease. He nudged her door open all the way and stepped inside her bedroom. He felt along the wall for the light switch. She blinked at the sudden illumination. A part of her wished it were still dark. He was the first man she'd brought home. He was about to be the first man to see her naked. The first man to see her stump…

He slid her down the length of his body and her thoughts evaporated. There was nothing and no one but Logan. His muscular body was reassuring in its strength. Solid. Dependable. Safe. He continued kissing her, nuzzling at her ears, her throat, the top of her breasts. With a murmur of impatience, he reached around and undid the zipper of her dress.

Tugging it from her shoulders, he pushed it down until it fell in a pool of satin at her feet. She stood before him in her underwear—scraps of black lace that left nothing to the imagination. She'd chosen the lingerie on purpose, hoping he might get to see her in it. Now they were here, together in her bedroom, about to make love.

At the sight of her, his eyes flared wide with emotion. "You're so beautiful," he whispered, his voice husky with desire. He reached out and traced a finger across the soft skin of her breast. His finger rasped over her sensitive nipple. Beneath the lace of her bra, her nipple pebbled in response.

Her heart thumped. Heat rushed through her, filling her. "Logan." His name was a moan of want and need and desperation.

With his heated gaze still fixed on hers, he stepped back

and pulled off his clothes. His jacket, his tie, his shirt. His skin was bronzed. His muscles, well-defined ripples of perfection. He bent and tugged off his boots and socks. Then his hands went to his belt. He slid the leather from the loops on his pants and then released the button and undid the zip. He shucked the pants off his hips and stepped out of them, kicking them aside.

Her stomach clenched with need. He stood before her clad only in his boxers. Her gaze skimmed across his pectorals, the taut muscles in his stomach and lower. His erection strained against the silky fabric of his underwear. A shiver of desire mixed with nerves flooded through her. She moved her gaze lower. Across well-muscled thighs covered in dark blond hair and lower again.

The scars were still visible on his right leg. White, spidery ones and thick, ugly keloid scars that still bore the evidence of his pain. The muscles in his calf were slightly wasted, not quite the size of his other leg. He stood before her, stiff and straight, enduring her scrutiny in silence. When she at last lifted her eyes to his, she saw the vulnerability in his gaze. Her heart turned over with love.

He's just as scared as I am about what I'll think of his appearance… His leg.

"You're beautiful," she whispered. "So perfect."

His mouth twisted. "Hardly perfect."

"Perfect," she said more firmly.

Taking courage from him, she moved over to the bed and sat down. Taking a deep breath, she undid the straps of her prosthesis and pulled it off, along with the protective sock. He stared at her. She lowered her gaze, unable to look at him. She waited for him to respond.

He moved to sit beside her. Turning her face to his, he kissed her softly. At the same time, his hand trailed down her thigh, over her kneecap and finally came to rest on her stump.

His fingers stroked the warm flesh, traced the faint scars. His touch was gentle, filled with tenderness.

"Perfect," he said.

Tears pricked her eyes. She offered him a wobbly smile. He reached out and wiped away the moisture with the pad of his thumb. She bit her lip against a surge of emotion.

Slowly, he eased the straps of her bra off her shoulders. Like he was unveiling the greatest of treasures, he reached around and undid the clasp at her back. Released from their confines, her breasts sprang up, full and round, her nipples pert. Tossing aside the black lace, he cupped one of her breasts in his hand.

"So beautiful," he murmured. He bent his head and gently, almost reverently took her nipple in his mouth.

The most exquisite sensations arced through her, like nothing she'd ever known. Every nerve ending tingled. She felt the pull of it deep down inside. And then he gave the same loving attention to her other breast.

Gently, he pressed her back against the pillows. She lay down with a soft sigh. Kissing his way down her sternum, he nuzzled her stomach, paused to dip his tongue in her belly button before continuing his sensual exploration. His lips moved over the soft skin of her stomach. With his finger, he traced over the lace that covered her womanhood. She swallowed a gasp.

"*Shh,*" Logan whispered. "Let me love you."

With infinite gentleness, he eased her panties down her hips. She lifted her bottom to aid their descent. He tossed the scrap of lace away and lowered his face to her most sensitive flesh. At the feel of his tongue, she arched off the bed. His slow strokes sent her into a frenzy of need. She'd never wanted anyone like this, or felt anything like it.

Long and slow and deep, Logan continued to love her with his mouth, his tongue, his lips.

And then he slipped a finger along her wet slit and eased it inside her. The feelings that overwhelmed her were excruciating and a little frightening. His finger moved along with the rhythm of his tongue, long and slow and deep. She squirmed against him, panting with her building desire. She yearned for something that was just out of reach.

"Logan," she moaned, burying her hands in his hair. He continued his onslaught, stoking the fire that burned inside her until it was almost more than she could bear.

"So soft, so sweet, so beautiful," he murmured. And then he moved even lower still and kissed his way down her thigh.

When he got to her stump, she tensed beneath him. His hands were gentle as they stroked her skin. And then his mouth replaced his fingers and he kissed the faded scars.

"Did it hurt a lot?"

"Yes. I think I've blocked out the worst of it."

"My poor baby."

"I learned not to think about it. After all, nothing was going to bring my leg back. Or my mother."

"So much pain. I wish I could have been there to ease it from you."

She was filled with warmth at his compassion. "I could say the same thing about you."

He sat up and moved until he lay down beside her. He gathered her in his arms. "My suffering was nothing compared to what you went through."

She gave him a tiny smile. "Are we comparing our suffering now?"

He smiled softly. "No. I'm just glad you survived your ordeal. That you've now come into my life."

This time when he kissed her, she felt the full force of his passion. Her arms crept up around his neck. She held him to her and kissed him back like she couldn't get enough.

The desire in her rekindled into a flaming roar. She moved restlessly against him, eager to get as close to him as she could.

As if sensing she was ready, he released her and moved away enough to shuck off his underwear. He knelt on the bed, gloriously naked, and let her look her fill. He was magnificent. Every inch of bronzed, muscled male. Unable to help herself, she reached out and touched him.

Chapter Sixteen

Logan groaned as Mia's hand encircled his cock. He was so hard he thought he might explode. Blood pounded through his veins. His balls were full and tight. And now, with her small, soft hand touching him, it was all he could not to press her back against the mattress and take what she was so willing to give. He'd promised her hours of pleasure, but he wasn't sure he could hold out that long. Not their first time, anyway.

And then she released him and the breath eased out between his taut lips. But the torture wasn't over. Her fingernails scraped over his nipples, sending pleasure spiraling to his groin. She pressed her palm against his pectorals, learning their feel and shape. Her hand trailed lower, across his belly that was tight with need. She skimmed past his groin and concentrated on stroking his legs. First one, then the other, from the top of his thigh all the way down to his feet.

When she got to his scars, she paused. He held his breath. Her lips replaced her fingers. She kissed the ugly reminders of all that he'd lost. And then he thought of all she'd endured and he made a vow there and then never again to feel sorry about what had happened to him. In many aspects, she had lost more. She'd faced life's challenges front on, with courage and determination and a generosity of spirit he deeply admired.

She kissed her way back up his injured leg and finally reached his cock. Once again, she encircled his hardness with her fingers and then leaned forward and took him into her mouth.

Hot, wet silk surrounded him. He was in heaven. He was in hell. Her lips and tongue drove him crazy. Need thundered through his veins. He suffered the delicious torture for as long as he could, but eventually he twisted his hips away from her.

"Enough," he rasped.

She looked momentarily startled. "Did I hurt you?"

"God, no. But if you don't stop now it will be all over before it's begun."

"Does that matter?" she asked.

"It does to me."

She shrugged as if it were of no consequence. He looked at her, suddenly curious. "Mia, you've…done this…before… Haven't you?"

She blushed, but nodded. "Of course."

"I mean, it doesn't matter to me if you haven't."

"I'm not a virgin, Logan. But I've only done it once before, when I was younger."

"Once…okay. I'll try to take it slow but I want you so much it might not be possible the first time."

He kissed her until she was once again writhing with need beneath him. He straddled her hips and nudged apart her thighs. His cock probed her slick entrance.

And then she froze, her eyes suddenly flaring with panic. Logan tensed and pulled back. "What is it? What's wrong? I'll go as slow as I can, sweetheart. Relax."

Embarrassment flamed across her cheeks. "That's not it. I… I don't have any condoms."

He swallowed a sigh of relief and gave her a reassuring wink. "Then I guess it's lucky I came prepared." With that, he climbed off the bed and fished in his pants for his wallet.

A moment later, grinning widely he brandished a condom. "Crisis averted."

She watched as he sheathed himself. He found her curiosity endearing. So sweet, so fresh, so innocent. The thought filled him with warmth. He settled himself beside her once again.

"Now, where were we?"

Kissing and stroking her, he reignited the fire that burned in her eyes. Unable to take the sweet torture a moment longer, he once again positioned himself between her thighs. He watched her reaction while he eased himself into her tight heat. Her eyes were closed. Her chest rose and fell in time with her rapid breaths. As he slid deeper inside her, she opened her eyes and reached for him, pulling him down flush against her.

Skin to skin, he breathed in the sweet scent of her hair. His cock was deep inside her, but she was so snug he gave her a moment to adjust. When she moved restlessly beneath him, he slowly withdrew and then plunged into her again. Over and over, he loved her with his body.

He heard the sweet murmurs of her desire as it built to a crescendo. Her fingers dug into his back. She clung to him, her breath coming fast. He encouraged her with quiet murmurs.

"You feel so good, Mia. So hot and tight and wonderful. Yes, can you feel me? Do you like that?"

And then she tensed beneath him and cried out. He felt her spasm around his cock. His mouth captured her groans of delight and release. Slowly, she quieted and relaxed against the sheets. Her body went limp beneath him.

She looked up at him, her eyes wide and incredulous. "That was... That was amazing."

The look on her face told him everything he needed to know. "That was your first climax."

A delightful pink colored her cheeks, but she nodded. "Yes."

He chuckled. "The first of many, I promise."

Her eyes flared with emotion. She reached up and pinched his nipples, a cheeky glint in her eyes. He groaned, suddenly filled with the need for his own satisfaction. Moving once again, he concentrated on the exquisite feeling of being inside her. His hips thrust harder, faster, blood crashed through his veins. And then he was there—free-falling. He shouted his release.

It was a long time later that his breathing slowed enough for him speak. With her cradled against his side, he pressed a soft kiss against her lips. "Thank you."

She twisted her head to look at him, a tender look on her face. "For what?"

"For making me realize what it means to make love. Until now, I didn't have a clue."

Mia frowned. "You mean, you and your ex-fiancée never…?"

His lips twisted in a grimace. "No. We'd agreed to save ourselves for marriage." He drew her closer. "Now I know why my brothers are walking around with goofy looks on their faces. Being in love with the woman in your bed makes all the difference. I wish someone had told me that earlier."

Mia nodded, her eyes wide and luminous. "What we did can't compare to anything else I've ever felt. It was magical." And then her expression turned impish. "You promised me hours of pleasure. How soon can we do that again?"

Mia walked into her shop the following Monday morning feeling like she was floating on air. She and Logan had spent the rest of the weekend together. They'd collected Mikhail from Joanna's after breakfast and had taken him down to the beach. Logan had borrowed a couple of surfboards from the local surf club and had spent the next few hours teaching

Mikhail to surf. The smaller waves at Balmoral made it the perfect training ground.

Mia stayed up on the grassy knoll, watching them. She continued to marvel at how good Logan was with her brother. Though most of the time Mikhail was happy and easy going, every now and then he got into a mood. Mia knew from firsthand experience it often took a lot of patience and perseverance to shake him from it.

And yet Logan seemed to take the mood swings in hand. Even from a distance, she heard him use repeated words of encouragement and when things didn't work out Mikhail's way and his frustration got the better of him, Logan's calm voice managed to ease the tension and it wasn't long before Mikhail was laughing again.

It was a joy to watch the two of them together and in many ways, a relief. It was nice to have someone to share the challenges Mikhail presented. Someone to help carry the load. Mia never regretted her decision to become Mikhail's legal guardian and he'd always have a home with her, no matter what. But she'd be lying if she didn't admit that sometimes he plain wore her out. Especially during the six weeks of summer holidays.

She was grateful he'd returned to class for the beginning of the school year. She could get back into her normal routine and devote more attention to her business. Thank goodness for her assistant. Mia didn't know how she would have kept everything running these past couple of months without Katerina. The woman really was a godsend. Hardworking, courteous and bright. What more could Mia want?

As she opened the door and came through the back entrance to the shop, she saw Katerina was already there.

"Hi," Mia greeted her in surprise. "What are you doing here? You don't start until nine."

Katerina smiled. "I thought I'd get a head start on some of

those orders." With her head, she indicated the computer screen which displayed the spreadsheet Mia had been working on last week.

"That's great," Mia said, surprised. She'd never asked Katerina to take on those extra duties, but she appreciated the girl's initiative. "You're worth more money."

They both laughed. Mia asked her if she wanted a coffee. "I'm running next door to Joanna's."

"A flat white with one sugar would be heavenly," Katerina replied.

Mia winked. "Coming right up."

Katerina gave her a curious look. "Someone had a good weekend."

Mia blushed. All she could picture was Logan, bronzed and naked and magnificent, as he made love to her over and over again.

Katerina shot her a knowing look. "Ah, like that, is it? Okay, so this time I'm simply not going to believe you if you tell me you don't have a man in your life," she teased. "Or maybe you have a woman? Is that how it is?"

A fresh wave of heat burned Mia's cheeks. "No, no. I... I like men just fine." Katerina continued to look at her knowingly. Mia closed her eyes briefly and then opened them again on a sudden decision.

"Okay, you're right. I've met someone. A man. He's...wonderful."

Katerina's eyes gleamed. "I knew it! Who is it? Tell me his name! I want all the details."

Mia shot her an enigmatic grin. "Surely not *all* the details."

"Okay, well let's start with his name."

"You already know him. Logan Craigdon. Mikhail's sailing instructor."

Katerina pounced. "I *knew* it! I could tell you were into him. You never leave the shop for anything more than a coffee and yet you were spending hours down at the beach. Now it all makes sense."

Mia squirmed a little. "Yes, well… Anyway, Logan and I are…dating."

Katerina squealed in delight. She threw her arms around Mia in a spontaneous hug. "Oooh! I'm so happy for you, Mia!"

Mia ducked her head. "Thank you."

"It's about time you found someone to love. After all, what good is there in owning a bridal wear shop if you never get to be a bride?"

Despite protesting Katerina's assumption, to which she merely smiled, Mia silently agreed. As Katerina returned to the computer, Mia headed toward the exit in search of caffeine. She might even share her good news with Joanna.

The moment Mia pulled the door to the shop closed behind her and disappeared up the street, Katerina pulled out her phone. For too long she'd been looking for an opportunity to grill Mia about her so-called man, but she hadn't known how to approach it. Earlier she didn't have any personal knowledge of a gentleman caller. She had no idea how to steer the conversation in that direction.

But now Mia had spared her the trouble. The woman had dumped the information in Katerina's lap. Now at last she could get Dimitri and more importantly, Igor off her back. Quickly, she called Dimitri's number. He answered on the third ring.

"What have you got for me?"

"Well, hello to you too brother," she said in a sarcastic tone.

"Save it, Kat. I hope you're calling with news. Igor's getting impatient."

"Then you're in luck. I have a name."

"The guy I saw at Amelia's house?"

"Yes. His name's Logan Craigdon."

"Craigdon? You mean, Henry's son?"

"How the hell am I supposed to know who his father is? You asked for a name, not a family history."

"Henry was part of our network. He ran his own show in the eastern suburbs. We could always rely on him to pay big for the best gear. Our profits dropped significantly after his death. And now with John Hassad in the can… It's been rough. Lucky there's always someone else willing to step up. I wonder if this Logan guy has taken over from Henry?"

"I don't know about any of that. But you wanted a name and I got you one."

"Yeah. You did well. Thanks, sis. Maybe you'll get to keep that sweet apartment after all."

Katerina could see Mia outside the front door, negotiating the handle while balancing the tray of coffees. Quickly she ended the call and dropped her phone back into her bag. With a smile fixed carefully on her face she hurried over to help her boss.

That night, Logan came over for dinner. As much as they both wanted to end the evening in each other's arms, they'd decided for Mikhail's sake, they'd take things slowly. They wanted to ease Mikhail into the idea of the two of them being in love, including the time when they hoped to move in together, although discussions were yet to be had on that front.

Mia hoped Logan would be willing to move in with her and Mikhail. It would be easier on her brother if things remained the same, as much as possible. Having Logan around every day and every night would be change enough for him to come to terms with, but she hoped he'd be happy to have him there.

Right now the three of them were in the kitchen making beef tacos. The mince was cooked and the tomatoes diced. Mikhail was mashing avocado. Logan was slicing lettuce. Mia excused herself to go to the bathroom. She was halfway down the hall when she heard her phone ring.

"Mia! It's for you!" Mikhail called out.

"Who is it? Tell them I'll call them back."

"He says his name's Dimitri. He says it's urgent."

At the mention of Dimitri's name, Mia went cold all over. Knowing Logan had overheard everything, made it even worse. The last thing she needed was her boyfriend asking questions. Through gritted teeth, she gave Logan a tight smile and took the phone off Mikhail. Not wanting Logan to think she didn't want him to listen in, she turned her back and greeted Dimitri in Russian.

Dimitri's harsh voice sounded in her ear. "You did the right thing by taking my call, Amelia. Good girl."

"Why are you calling me, Dimitri? How many times do I have to tell you? This has got to stop. I'm never going to change my mind. Why can't you get that through your thick head?"

"*Tut, tut*, Ameila. You're such a hypocrite. I know all about your boyfriend. Logan Craigdon. Interesting, Amelia. You say you don't want anything to do with your father's legacy, yet you spread your legs for the nephew of one of the city's biggest drug bosses."

Mia gasped in shocked. She edged her way out of the kitchen. "What are you talking about?"

"Don't tell me you never heard your father talk about Henry Craigdon? Craigdon was one of your father's biggest clients. He paid your father big money for top quality drugs. He ran his own show over in the eastern suburbs before he dropped dead of a heart attack last year.

"Now it seems his nephew's taken over the reins. Didn't

you know your lover boy inherited his uncle's company? He's meant to be a property developer, but you and I know all about that. It wouldn't be the first time a legitimate business was set up as a front. You need to start being a bit more amiable with me, Amelia, or Mikhail and I might have to have a little chat."

Mia froze. "You keep my brother out of this! Stay away from him! He has nothing to do with this!" From over her shoulder, Mia saw Mikhail edging toward her. Logan wasn't far behind.

"I have to go, Dimitri. I have visitors. I'll phone you back." She ended the call though she felt sick to her stomach and trembled all over, she plastered a smile on her face. She was only thankful Logan didn't understand Russian.

"So, who's ready for tacos?"

Logan stared at Mia's pale face and frowned. *What the hell was that all about? Why is she acting so weird?* And why was she speaking Russian? At least, he assumed it was Russian.

From the tone of her voice and the tension in her spine it was obvious it hadn't been a social call. It was also obvious she didn't want him to overhear. Is that why she'd chosen to speak in Russian, or was the person on the other end of the phone someone who didn't speak English? He hated that he felt suspicious, but he couldn't help it.

Something about her demeanor set him on edge. Even now, he could see the strain around her eyes and the tension in her body. She was smiling and talking like she didn't have a care in the world, but it all felt forced. He sure as hell wasn't convinced.

When she turned suddenly and headed for the bathroom, Logan sidled up to the counter where she'd left her phone. Hating himself, he touched the screen, pleased to discover it hadn't switched itself off. Tapping the phone icon, he checked the call log. The most recent call had come from a man by the name of Dimitri Petrov.

The name meant nothing to him, but it was possible someone else might recognize it. Someone like his cop brother, Noah. Pulling out his phone, he sent Noah a quick text. To his relief, his brother replied straight away.

Why do u want 2 know?

Logan swallowed a groan.

Rather not say.

True to form, Noah replied.

I guess that's 2 bad.

Logan shook his head. Sometimes his brother was unbelievable. Why did he have to be such a cop?

Oh, btw. I need a favor.

The reply came back just as fast.

Another 1?

Smart ass…

Yes. This 1's 4 Mia.

Noah's reply made Logan smile.

Anything 4 Mia.

Logan typed a quick reply.

Gr8. Her brother would love a ride on ur Fireblade. Can u spare the time?

As he thought he would, Noah came through for him.

Of course. When?

How about 2morrow after school?

A moment later, Noah responded.

I can probably swing that. Where at?

Logan grinned.

I'll text u the address. C u @ 4pm.

Mia came out of the bathroom feeling only slightly better. She'd splashed cold water on her face and had managed to get the trembling under control, but there was a hard knot of fear in her stomach that would make it impossible to eat. She just hoped no one was paying too much attention.

Logan was on his phone as she emerged into the kitchen. He quickly set it aside and came toward her.

"Are you okay?"

The concern on his face filled her with warmth. For so long she'd had no one to look out for her, to worry about how she was. It was nice knowing Logan cared enough to want to know.

She forced a smile. "Yes, of course. Just a little tummy upset."

Logan frowned. "Is there anything I can get for you? Some antacid? Something else?"

She shook her head. "No, thank you. I'll be fine. But I might skip the tacos, if that's all right."

"Of course. Would you rather I leave?"

"No, no. I'm okay. You and Mikhail go ahead and eat."

"Okay. If you're certain."

"I am."

She helped set out the dishes of food on the counter and handed both Mikhail and Logan a plate. She sipped from a glass of soda water while they made their tacos.

Logan turned back to her with a smile on his face. "Oh, I have good news. I just got a text from Noah. He's free tomorrow afternoon to take Mikhail for a bike ride."

Mia managed a genuine smile. Once again, Logan had proved how kind and thoughtful he was.

"That's great! Did you hear that, Mikhail? Tomorrow you're going for a ride on Noah's motorbike!"

The smile of excitement on her brother's face filled her with emotion. "Yay! Motorbike!"

Over Mikhail's head, she looked at Logan. *Thank you,* she mouthed.

He sent her a wink. Her heart filled with love. Could this guy be any more perfect?

Chapter Seventeen

The next day passed in a blur. Every time the phone rang, Mia jumped, expecting it to be Dimitri. She still hadn't called him back. There was no way she was ever going to give in to his demands, but she'd be lying if she said he didn't frighten her. And there wasn't only him. His brother, Igor, was downright terrifying. It was only a matter of time before he joined forces with Dimitri to get her to capitulate. She only wished there was someone she could talk to about it.

Logan immediately came to mind. Her spirits lifted, but just as quickly plummeted again. There was no way she could drag Logan into her mess. What if the Petrov brothers turned their anger on him? No, it was her father who was responsible for this. This was her fight. It wasn't fair to involve Logan, no matter how much she wanted to.

She thought about what Dimitri had told her the previous night. She refused to believe his vicious lies. There was no way Logan Craigdon was involved in drugs. He'd been angry and upset when he'd found out the truth about her father. She'd opened her heart to him, bared her soul, cried her eyes out while she told him about her past. If he'd been involved in his uncle's drug business, he would have said something then. She was sure of it. Logan Craigdon was a good and decent man.

The day seemed to drag on forever, but eventually it was

time to collect Mikhail from school. On the way over, she received a text from Logan confirming they were still good to go. She gave him a thumbs up emoji, followed by two love hearts.

Mikhail came bounding out of the school gate, a wide grin splitting his face. "Mia! Mia! You're here! Are we still going for a motorbike ride?"

"Of course, buddy. Logan and his brother are on their way over now."

"Yay!" he cheered.

She couldn't help but smile at his excitement. All the way home he chattered non-stop about the bike and what it might look like and how fast it might go. By the time they turned into their driveway, he was almost hoarse. Logan and Noah were already there. Standing near the curb was a shiny red motorbike.

Mikhail screamed in excitement and dashed out of the car. "Logan! Logan! You're here! Wow! Look at that bike!"

"Mikhail, you remember my brother, Noah?"

Mikhail nodded. "Hi, Noah."

"This is Noah's bike. He's agreed to let you go for a ride with him."

"What do you say, Mikhail?" Mia said, coming up beside him.

"Thank you Noah," Mikhail dutifully replied.

"That's okay, mate. I'm pleased to offer you a ride. Us motorbike men need to stick together, right?"

Mikhail beamed. "Right!"

"Well, how about we get going? Are you ready?" Noah asked.

"Yay!" Mikhail shouted.

"I should probably get you into some jeans and a long-sleeved shirt first," Mia suggested.

"Absolutely," Noah agreed. He looked at Mikhail. "You

should always wear protective clothing when you're riding a motorbike."

Quickly, Mia took Mikhail upstairs and waited while he changed his clothes. In addition to the jeans and jacket, he'd also pulled on some boots.

"Can we go now, Mia? Can we go?"

She ruffled his hair affectionately. "Of course."

Back down on the street, Mia helped her brother pull on a helmet and tightened up the strap. Noah climbed on the bike and held it steady while Logan helped Mikhail swing his leg over the side and get himself seated in position. Logan pointed out the footrests and told him to put his arms around Noah's waist.

"Hold on tight, Mikhail!" Mia shouted over the sudden roar of the engine.

The look of delight in Mikhail's eyes was clear to see. Mia looked at Logan and her heart filled with love. This whole experience was happening because of him.

What an incredibly special man. How did I get so lucky?

While they waited for Noah and Mikhail to return, Logan asked her about her day. She offered him vague responses, doing her best to keep things light. There was no way she was going to drag him into her problems. No, she'd call Dimitri and make sure he knew in no uncertain terms that she was never ever going to be part of his establishment. Somehow, she'd deal with his threats to tell Mikhail about their father. Maybe she'd tell Mikhail herself. Give him a watered-down version. Something he could accept. Then Dimitri's threat would be worthless.

The roar of a motorbike drowned out their conversation. They both turned toward the street as Noah drove up the road and came to a stop beside them. Noah held the bike steady while Mikhail climbed off the back. He pulled off his helmet, grinning.

"That was sick, Mia! That was so sick! You should go! You should go for a ride!" He turned to Noah. "Can my sister go for a ride, too?"

Mia laughed and held up her hand. "Whoa! Mikhail! Slow down, buddy. It's all right. I don't want to go for a ride. At least, not today. Maybe some other time."

From the corner of her eye, she saw a black sedan with dark tinted windows slow to a stop opposite her house. She watched while Dimitri opened the door and got out. He looked straight at her and smiled. Goosebumps pebbled her skin. Her blood turned to ice.

Frantic, she looked at Logan and Noah who were talking to Mikhail. They were pointing out various things on the bike and explaining to Mikhail what they were. Mia sent a silent prayer Dimitri would see the men and stay where he was—or better still, leave. Instead, and to her horror, he crossed the street and came toward her, his arms opened wide.

He greeted her in Russian. "Amelia! How lovely to see you!"

Avoiding his embrace, she dragged him to one side. "What are you doing here?" she hissed.

"Come now, Mia. You know why I'm here."

"I've said all I have to say to you, Dimitri." She threw a panicked look over her shoulder. To her relief, the men remained engrossed in the motorbike. She turned back to Dimitri. "You need to leave."

"Come now, Mia. There's no need to be like that. We could be so good together. Why are you so against it? It would make your father so proud."

At the mention of her father, Mia tensed. "Go. Now. Before I scream." Her tone brooked no argument.

He shot her a wry smile. "Scream? No, I think not. If you were going to scream you would have done it the moment you set eyes on me."

Dimitri moved closer and took hold of her arm. His grip was tight enough to be uncomfortable. She bit back a cry of alarm.

"Let go of me," she managed, pleased her voice remained calm.

"You're not listening to me, Mia. We want that shop."

"You can't have it. It's mine."

Anger flared in Dimitri's eyes. His hold on her tightened. "If you don't give us that shop, you're going to regret it. Don't forget that brother of yours. Remember how much you love him? I can make life very difficult for you, Mia. For both of you. Whatever would become of your beloved brother if you were to disappear?"

Fear iced her veins. She stared at Dimitri, too terrified to speak.

"Ah, I see you understand me. Good. That's very good. Now perhaps you'll listen. There's something else I want. Your father kept a book of all of his contacts. I saw it once myself. You must have it. And you're going to hand it over to me."

"I don't know what you're talking about," she lied.

Dimitri's gaze narrowed. Anger flashed in his eyes. He raised his arm and for a minute she thought he might strike her. She let out a cry of fear. But then he seemed to remember where he was and the witnesses who stood close by. His arm slowly lowered.

"Don't cross me, Mia. You'll regret it if you do. You and Mikhail."

Logan kept glancing behind him to where Mia and the man she'd called Dimitri stood in conversation. They were too far away for him to hear what they were saying. Besides, they spoke in a foreign tongue. Russian, he assumed. Logan's gaze returned to Noah.

"You didn't happen to think about that name I gave you last night, did you?"

"Dimitri Petrov?"

"Yes."

"As a matter of fact, no. You still haven't told me why."

"Does there have to be a reason?"

"Yes."

Logan sighed. He glanced once again behind him and then returned his attention to his brother.

"Last night Mia got a call from this guy. Dimitri Petrov. They spoke in a foreign language. I'm guessing it was Russian. The thing is, I think that's the same guy she's talking to now. Last night, she looked scared. About as scared as she looks now. What do you think?"

Noah looked over to where Mia and the stranger stood in conversation and then turned back to Logan.

"Yeah. Maybe. It's hard to tell from here."

"Does the name mean anything to you?"

Noah sighed. "The name Petrov is well known in the Russian mafia. In fact, two of the most notorious drug dealers in Sydney are Dimitri and Igor Petrov. They're brothers. Igor is the beef, Dimitri is the brains. It's hard to tell which one is more dangerous."

"You've got to be kidding! The mafia?"

"Don't get too worked up. 'Dimitri' and 'Petrov' are both very common Russian names. It doesn't mean she was talking to *the* Dimitri Petrov. She could have been talking to anyone."

Noah pulled out his phone and pointed it in the direction of Mia and her friend. He snapped a few quick shots and then tucked the phone back in his pocket.

"What did you do that for?" Logan asked, curious.

"There's something about that guy that's bugging me. Call it cop intuition. I wouldn't mind running his picture through a database or two."

Logan thought about what his father and Aunt Elizabeth had said. Dread filled his gut. "What are you thinking?"

"I don't know."

Mia let out a small cry. Both men looked immediately in her direction. Dimitri had her by the arm, his expression dark and threatening. Both Craigdons took off at a run and crossed to where Mia stood. They got between her and the man she'd called Dimitri just as the man raised his arm as if to strike.

Logan stared the man down with a steely glare. "I think it's time for you to leave. The lady's done with you."

Dimitri looked like he was about to argue, then Noah took a step forward. Dimitri looked from one to another and wisely decided it was time to retreat. He turned his back on them with an angry huff and headed back to his car. Logan turned toward Mia.

"Are you all right?"

She nodded shakily.

"Who the hell was that?"

She bit her lip and closed her eyes and then opened them again. "He's…an old friend of my late father. He…took my father's death hard."

Logan frowned. "Are you sure that's all it's about?"

She nodded again. "Yes."

Though Logan didn't know whether to believe her, he wasn't going to pry it out of her. At least, not now. He'd try and get her to talk about it later. Forcing a smile, he kissed her on the mouth.

"I'll just say good-bye to Noah, okay?"

"Sure."

Noah had moved to stand by his bike. Logan told Mikhail to go and check on his sister. When the boy had gone, Logan turned back to his brother.

"I don't like anything about that man."

"I agree. What did Mia say about him?"

"That he was a friend of her late father's."

Noah looked grim. "I see."

"What's that supposed to mean?"

"Did you believe her?"

Logan bristled. "What the hell are you implying?"

Noah sighed. "Nothing. But… The thing is, things have been moving so fast with you and Mia. You barely know her. You're rushing headlong into this relationship without fear of the consequences."

Logan tensed. "I'm a big boy, Noah. I can take care of myself."

"I'm worried about you, Logan. Don't you remember how it was when Virginia abandoned you? Do you want to go through that again?"

"Mia's not like that," Logan insisted. "She's kind and sweet and generous. Innocent, good and true. She doesn't have a deceitful bone in her body. She's nothing like Virginia!"

"How do you know? You've only known her a couple of weeks."

Logan set his jaw at a stubborn angle. "Sometimes you just know."

Noah sighed. "Hey, I'm not trying to give you a hard time. I'm only looking out for you. I don't want to see you get hurt again."

"You and Flynn both," Logan muttered sourly.

Noah looked at him in surprise. "So Flynn has some concerns, too?"

Logan merely shrugged and stared at the ground.

"You should listen to us, Logan. At least take a step back, slow things down. There's no need to rush. If she's who she says she is and if she feels as strongly as you do, she'll understand."

Logan shot his brother a defiant glare. "What do you mean, *if* she is who she says she is? Yes, she's Alexander

Ivanov's daughter. Yes, the daughter of a drug lord. But she had nothing to do with that dirty business. She abhors everything to do with it. Besides, I'm twenty-five years old. I don't need advice from my brother who, until recently, had never even slept with a woman."

Noah looked hurt. Logan immediately felt terrible. "I'm sorry, Noah. I'm an asshole. That was a low blow."

Noah punched Logan half-heartedly on the arm. "You're right. You are an asshole. And I'm sorry you don't want my advice. It's just that I care about you."

"Yeah, yeah, yeah. I get it. Flynn's the same. Everyone's looking out for poor old Logan. It might tip him over the edge if he gets his heart broken again."

"That's not what I mean!" Noah protested.

Logan waved him away. "I know. I get it. I appreciate your concern. I really do. But I've got this, Noah. Maybe things won't work out between me and Mia, but I have to give it a try. I've never felt this way about a woman. Not even with Virginia. I owe it to myself to see if it's the real deal. I don't want to spend my life regretting anything. Not anymore. I'm done with that crap."

"Fair enough. Well, if there's anything I can do, let me know. I'm always here for you, bro."

Logan was filled with a rush of emotion. His voice turned rough. "Thank you, Noah. That means a lot. And thanks for taking Mikhail out. You've made his day."

Noah glanced across to where Mikhail was still busy filling his sister in on all the intricate details of their ride. She smiled and murmured and asked questions… Noah looked back at Logan.

"She seems nice. She really does. I wish you all the best."

"Thanks, bro."

"I might do a little digging on our friend. Run his picture by some colleagues. See if he looks familiar to anyone."

Logan smiled with gratitude. "Thanks, Noah. I really appreciate that."

Noah winked. "No worries. What are brothers for?"

Chapter Eighteen

Christopher Barrington sipped from his scotch. He'd indulged in a few more than he normally did and right now, he was thankful for the sturdy oak bar that helped keep him upright. He was at his favorite city haunt—Harry's Bar. It was seedy and dark and a magnet for the less savory members of society, but that's why he liked it. He felt more comfortable there than he did in the glitzy ballrooms of the rich and famous, including his family. In Harry's Bar, he felt like he was among his own kind.

It was way past late. Midnight had come and gone. He squinted at the clock above the bar. Nearly two. No wonder he felt tired. Of course, it could also be attributed to the copious amounts of alcohol he'd consumed.

"Would you like another?" the heavyset barman asked as Christopher finished his drink.

Christopher looked down at the empty glass. It blurred in front of him, duplicating itself. He shook his head. "Nah. I've had enough." In fact, what he needed was a trip to the bathroom.

Easing himself off the barstool, he carefully placed one booted foot after the other and kept his gaze fixed on the back wall where the restrooms were located. He wobbled a little bit and grabbed hold of the back of an empty booth to steady himself. Two men sat in the next booth with their heads close together, talking in low overtones.

They both looked older than Christopher. One was graying and slight and spoke in a mild tone, but the cunning look in his eye took Christopher aback. The other one was a bear of a man, broad of shoulder and thick across the chest. Scars and tattoos covered his bulging biceps. With beady eyes and a large bald head, he sure was an ugly beast. They barely looked at Christopher as he approached.

"I'm telling you, Igor. I tried everything. I even threatened her brother. The thing is, she isn't interested. Alexander's brat refuses to play ball."

The other man responded with a snarl. "You didn't try hard enough, Dimitri. We need that bitch on our side. We need someone we can trust. With Craigdon dead and Hassad in the can, we need to regroup."

At the mention of the name "Craigdon" Christopher's interest was piqued. He stopped short a few yards away and glanced again at the men. They were engrossed in their conversation. Easing into the booth behind them, he pretended to be immersed in the replay of the cricket match playing on the widescreen TV. The two men continued to talk.

"Alexander kept an address book, Igor. I know he did. I saw it. He kept a record of everyone he dealt with. Suppliers. Other dealers. Runners. He even had the names of a couple of cops who were on his payroll. They were all there. She must have it."

"Did you ask her for it?"

"Of course I did! She denied any knowledge of it."

"She's lying."

"Yes. Out of respect for Alex, I've tried to keep things civil. I called her a few months after his funeral, just to sound her out, but the bitch shut me straight down. At the time,

I thought she was probably still grieving. After all, the prick was her father. Then we put Katerina into that shop of hers. Who'd have thought Alexander's daughter would own a bridal wear shop. Have you ever heard of anything so ridiculous?

"Still, it's the perfect cover. I got someone to do a background check. The shop's legit. Everything's done by the book. Katerina's confirmed that. Since she's been working there she's had a chance to look deeper behind the business structure. It's all above board. That's what makes it the perfect vehicle to launder the drug money. Only the bitch won't come to the party. When I put the suggestion to her again recently she told me to fuck off. Not in those words, of course. Amelia Ivanov has too much breeding for that."

The one called Igor snarled. With his back to the men, Christopher couldn't see their faces, but he could imagine the look on the ugly one's face. Christopher swiveled his head. From the corner of his eye, he saw Dimitri lean back, putting some distance between him and the other man.

Igor slammed his meaty fist down on the table. "Enough, Dimitri! Who the fuck does Amelia Ivanov think she is? Her father was a drug lord. Does she think she can escape that kind of past? Hardly. It's also clear she doesn't have any idea who she's dealing with. We're the Petrovs. No one fucks with us and from what I've heard, this bitch has been fucking with us for nearly a year. We've tried to play nice, but we're done," Igor said. "That bitch's going to regret refusing to do business with us."

Christopher glanced in the men's direction again. Anticipation flooded Dimitri's face, followed by a slow smile. "What are you going to do?"

"The first thing we're going to do is get that address book. I won't accept any bullshit excuses. Maybe I'll cut up that pretty face of hers. After that, she'll know we mean business.

Perhaps she'll be more willing to listen to our proposal."

The smile he gave the other man was pure evil. The one called Dimitri grinned and then took refuge in his beer. Shortly afterwards, the men left. They didn't cast so much as a glance in Christopher's direction.

Christopher needed another drink. He felt shaky and apprehensive. Though this wasn't the first time drug dealers had frequented Harry's Bar, it was the first time Christopher had come up close and personal to them. It was obvious the woman Amelia was in trouble. Concern pricked at his conscience.

I need to stay out of this. It has nothing to do with me. For all I know, this woman deserves what those men have in store for her. She's probably a dealer, too. What did they say about her father? A drug lord?

Troubled, Christopher vacillated back and forth about what to do. He went to the bathroom and then returned to the bar and was no closer to arriving at a decision. Then his phone rang, giving him a reprieve. He fished it out of his pocket and checked the screen.

Noah.

He tapped the button and answered the call.

"Noah. What are you doing, calling so late?"

"Yeah, sorry Christopher. I'm at work. Nightshift. I know you're a night owl. I didn't wake you, did I?"

"No. I'm out. Drowning my sorrows in a bar with a bottle of scotch. In fact, I think I've done a pretty good job of it. My head's spinning."

"Well, lucky for you, I've got good news. It might help draw you out of your doldrums."

"Hit me with it. I could do with some good news."

"I just got word we've got a sentencing date for Kevin Beechwood. Seeing that you were instrumental in helping to put the police commissioner away for a number of serious crimes, I thought you might like to know."

"Yeah, thanks. I only did what anyone else would have done."

"That's not true. I know cops who wouldn't have had the courage or the foresight to record such a serious crime that was happening right before their eyes. You could have simply done nothing. Or even better, you could have gotten yourself well away from there. No one would have known any different. The commissioner might very well have gotten away with attempted murder. You should be proud of yourself. I am. And so is the rest of the family. I brought them all up to speed at the last family dinner."

Christopher felt a surge of warmth at Noah's words. For years he'd been on the outside of the tightly knit circle of Craigdons, even though he was one. For the first time in his life, he felt a slight thawing of the animosity he'd held toward them.

"Thanks, Noah. You don't have to say that."

"It's true. I believe everyone deserves their fair due, you included."

Christopher thought about the two men he'd overheard, making threats against the woman.

Should I say something to Noah? Perhaps the names mean something to him? He's a cop, after all. He has access to databases no one else does. He might be able to track the woman down, warn her.

"Listen, I've come by some information. Don't ask me how and I don't even know if I heard it right. Like I said, I'm drunk…"

"What are you trying to say, Christopher?"

Noah sounded impatient. Christopher frowned and tried to think through the blur of his thoughts. Men. Right. Nasty men. Dealers. "Do the names Dimitri and Igor Petrov mean anything to you?"

Noah's tone was both shocked and grim. "What do you know about the Petrov brothers?"

Christopher smiled with relief. Perhaps he wasn't that drunk after all? "So you do know them?"

"They're on a police hit list of criminals. Drugs. Assaults. Robberies. They're big players in the Russian mafia. The DEA's been following them for years. Dimitri recently surfaced in Jayde Hassad's covert police operation. He was in cahoots with her father. The DEA could have gotten Dimitri along with John Hassad, but they decided to wait until they could net the whole ring. Dimitri's only one of a number of players." Noah paused and then added, "Tell me what you know."

Christopher relayed the conversation he'd overheard as best as he could. He cursed the gallons of scotch he'd consumed that made his memory hazy.

"Amelia Ivanov? Are you sure?" Noah sounded tense.

"Well, no. I can't be certain," Christopher slurred. "My heads pounding like shit. Too much scotch. I should be home in bed… I think that's what they said… Alexander… That's another name I heard. Sounded like he was dead."

"Shit."

The shock and disbelief in Noah's voice gave Christopher pause. "What is it?"

"I think they're talking about Logan's girlfriend. Mia Ivanov."

Christopher tensed. "Are you for real?"

"If what you say you heard is right, yes. This isn't the first time the Petrov brothers have been associated with Alexander Ivanov. That's Mia's late father. He died a year ago. I'll send it further up the line so someone can look into it. Someone with more intel on the who's who of the Russian mafia than I do. But thanks, Christopher. Once again, you've helped out. You might have let yourself down in the past, but no one should be forced to pay for their mistakes forever. I don't care what anyone else says, you're a decent bloke and I appreciate your trust in sharing the intel."

Once again, warmth surged through Christopher's veins. It felt good to be treated so well, like an equal. Especially by a Craigdon. It wasn't that long ago when Christopher would have thought such a happening impossible. He wondered if any of the others felt that way.

Probably not. Especially the ones he'd played dirty tricks on. At the time, he'd thought it was funny to make trouble for them. Now he saw that it had been nasty and malicious and entirely self-serving. Shame burned his cheeks.

Muttering his farewell to Noah, Christopher ended the call. In a few weeks, he'd be forty-one. He was getting tired of seeking revenge on the family when the main target for his anger was a man now beyond his reach. Maybe it was time to make amends, offer an olive branch…

Noah put down his phone, feeling troubled. He wasn't sure what to make of Christopher's information. He couldn't imagine Christopher actually knew the Petrov brothers, so how did he come by their first names? Even stranger, that he had connected the Russian drug dealers with Mia Ivanov. It sounded so weird, it could just be true. Then again, it was obvious Christopher was drunk. He could have imagined the whole thing…or got it totally screwed up.

What to do?

There was no harm in making a report about the alleged conversation and sending it to his boss. He could decide what, if anything, to do about it. No doubt he'd ask Noah to chase up Christopher tomorrow, after the man had been given the chance to sober up. Perhaps his memory of what he'd seen and heard would be clearer then…or not.

Noah shook his head and sighed. He was tired. The first nightshift was always a struggle. No doubt the fatigue was making it harder to think things through logically. It was funny how things looked different at two in the morning than they did in the bright light of day. He had no way of knowing if the Dimitri Petrov he'd spied talking with Mia was the same Dimitri Petrov who was on the hit list of every DEA operative. Still, there was no harm in doing a little checking. He'd promised Logan, after all.

Drawing his keyboard closer, Noah logged into the police database and typed in Dimitri's name. It took a few moments for the file to load. When it did, Noah gasped. The mugshot of Dimitri Petrov stared out at him. It looked a hell of a lot like the guy who'd been outside Mia's house a couple of days earlier.

Then Noah recalled taking a photo of the guy on his phone. Tugging it back out of his pocket, he swiped through his photos until he found it. Grabbing the screen with his fingers, he expanded the shot until Dimitri's face filled the screen. He then looked back at the mugshot. The guy had put on a bit of weight and his hair had receded since the last mugshot, but there was no doubt it was the same man.

Shit.

The Dimitri they'd seen with Mia was *the* Dimitri Petrov—the Russian drug boss.

Noah's mind went into overdrive. What did it mean? Was Mia part of a drug ring, or was she a mere pawn in their game? Was her safety under threat, like Christopher seemed to think, or was this a falling out between comrades? The afternoon Noah had seen them together the air between her and Dimitri had appeared tense, but there was no denying her late father was a notorious drug boss. Which side was she on?

I should tell Logan about the connection… That the two men are one and the same. As for the other, until I can confirm what Christopher told me, there's no sense worrying Logan unnecessarily….

Making his mind up to only tell Logan what Noah knew for sure, Noah once again picked up his phone. Then he remembered the time and stopped short. Noah's news could wait at least until the sun came up.

With his mind still in turmoil, Noah pushed away from his desk and went in search of caffeine. He needed something to get him through the night. He'd barely taken two sips out of his mug before a call came in about an armed robbery. It was suspected the perp was a dirty cop. With a sigh, Noah set his mug down, pushed away from his desk, and left.

The sun had barely peeked its head over the horizon when Logan's phone rang. He groaned. In deference to Mia's desire to ease her brother into the idea of them being together, he'd spent the night in his own bed, but they'd stayed up late on the phone talking. It felt like he'd barely closed his eyes.

Still half asleep, he reached across his bed and checked the screen.

Noah.

"*Ahh.*" Logan groaned. "I'm gonna kill him." It took him a couple attempts to tap on the right button. "Do you have any idea what time it is?"

Noah sounded apologetic. "Yeah, it's five in the morning. I'm at work. There's no easy way to say this."

Logan was instantly alert. He sat up in bed, his heart pounding. "What's happened? Is it Dad?"

"Dad? No. It's not Dad."

"Then who? What's going on?"

"I'm sorry, bro. I have some bad news."

"Spit it out, goddammit!" And then another, more awful thought occurred to him. "Please don't tell me it's Mia!"

In a low and serious tone, Noah proceeded to inform him that the Dimitri they'd seen talking with Mia outside her home and who was a friend of her late father was also a notorious drug dealer with links to the Russian mafia.

Logan couldn't disguise his shock. "You mean he's one of *those* Petrovs? The ones you talked about?"

"Yes."

A roaring sound of disbelief and anguish filled Logan's head. No! It couldn't be true! Mia wouldn't be having conversations with a drug dealer, even one who'd been her father's friend. She abhorred drugs. They'd ruined her life and the life of her brother. She'd made it clear, if Logan was into drugs she wouldn't have anything to do with him.

But what about the weird phone call she'd felt she had to conceal? Then the visit outside her house. If she were truly being coerced into something she didn't want to do, wouldn't she have called for help, when she had both Logan and Noah to come to her assistance? She'd cried out, obviously in pain, when Dimitri had grabbed her arm. But then had said she was ok. Although she hadn't looked at him when she said it. What was she hiding?

The endless questions kept running through his head until he felt like he could scream from the torment. No matter what the evidence appeared to show, he refused to believe the worst about her until he'd heard it confirmed from her mouth. Until then, he'd give her the benefit of the doubt.

I need to talk to her. I need to find out the truth…now.

With his mind already on the upcoming conversation, he rushed to get off the phone. "Noah, I've gotta go."

"Wait. There's something else. I wasn't going to say anything because I'm not sure how true it is, but Mia might—"

"No, no more!" Logan interrupted. "Please, Noah. I can't bear to listen any more. Not right now. I need some time to get my head around this. I need to talk to Mia. I'm sorry, Noah. I'll call you later."

With that, he ended the call and then switched off his phone.

Jumping out of bed, Logan pulled on a pair of shorts and a T-shirt and went in search of his sneakers. He snatched his car keys off the kitchen counter then left his apartment, determined to get some answers.

Mia heard the persistent buzzing of her front door bell and frowned. It was way early. Much too early for visitors. She thought about ignoring it, but the buzzing continued. With a sigh, she located her prosthesis and strapped it on then pulled on a robe over her pajamas. She opened the door to Mikhail's bedroom, relieved to see he was still asleep. Curious about who would be calling on them this early in the morning, she headed to the front door.

She peeked through the peephole and saw Logan. She frowned in confusion.

Why is Logan standing outside my front door?

It was too early for her brain to be working properly. Still half-asleep, she undid the deadlock and opened the door.

"Logan, do you have any idea what time it is? What are you doing here?" Then she noticed how somber he looked. Dread formed like ice in her stomach. "Logan? What is it? What's wrong?"

"Can I come in?" he asked, ignoring her questions.

She blinked and shook her head in confusion. "Yes. Yes, of course." She stood back and allowed him to enter.

He followed her down the hall and into the open plan living and kitchen. When he got to the end, he turned to face her. The look on his face sent shards of alarm arcing through her.

"Please, Logan. You're scaring me. What's wrong?"

"Dimitri. Dimitri Petrov. I know everything."

Her stomach sank. She wasn't sure what he knew, but it was obvious whatever it was had made him very unhappy. She could only guess he thought she was complicit in Dimitri's business.

"How do you know his name?" she asked, curious.

"The other night you received a phone call. I heard you speaking in Russian. Well, I just assumed it was Russian. You seemed upset afterwards. I wondered who you'd been speaking to. So when you went to the bathroom, I checked your phone. His name was listed there."

Logan stared at her defiantly. Mia looked at him, incredulous. "You checked my phone? How dare you!"

Embarrassment turned his cheeks pink. He stared at the floor. "I'm sorry. It was wrong. But I was worried about you."

"That's no excuse for breaching my privacy. You could have asked."

"Would you have told me?" he shot back.

She thought about it and then answered honestly. "No."

"Why not?"

She threw up her hands in frustration. "Because I knew how you'd react! Like this! You found out Dimitri's a drug lord and now you think I'm one, too. I can see it in your eyes."

"You're wrong. I haven't jumped to any conclusions. I'm here to ask you to explain. I want to hear your side of the story. In my experience nothing is ever black and white."

She frowned at him in confusion. "What are you talking about?"

Chapter Nineteen

Logan sighed wearily and scrubbed at his hair. "You know why I didn't care your father was a dealer?"

She shook her head, not sure where he was going with this.

"It's because I used to deal drugs, too. For my uncle. I was just a kid, but that's beside the point. I knew it was wrong."

She stared at him in shock. "You told me you'd never been into drugs! You lied to me!"

His gaze remained steady on hers. "No. I spoke the truth."

"But you just admitted you were a dealer."

"Yes. I'm not proud of that, but I never took them. I swear."

"How old were you?"

"Ten. Eleven. I can't remember for sure."

She looked at him, flabbergasted. "Ten or eleven? Who gets their nephew to sell drugs for them at that age! You were a child!"

"Yes."

She stared at him a moment longer. Slowly her shock and anger subsided. "How long has it been since you sold drugs?"

"I haven't had anything to do with them since I quit on my uncle. I was about twelve."

"And you never experimented with them yourself?"

He held her gaze. "Never."

Her shoulders slumped on a sigh. "Wow. I mean, wow."

"Yes."

She moved over to the kitchen and started the coffee machine. "I don't know about you, but I need some caffeine."

"Sounds good," he said and joined her at the counter.

"How do you take it?"

"Black, no sugar."

As she set about making coffee, he continued to speak. "Tell me about Dimitri. Who is he and why is he in your life?"

Mia carried two cups of steaming coffee over to the table that stood in the kitchen nook. She set them down and took a seat. Logan sat down opposite her.

"Dimitri and his brother Igor were in business with my father. They moved large shipments of illegal drugs, mostly cocaine, and then supplied the drugs to other dealers around the city."

"How do you know all of this?"

Mia stared at her coffee. "My father would come home and boast about his exploits. He thought I'd be proud of him. He couldn't have been further from the truth."

"Did he ever ask you to become part of it?"

"Of course he did. Many times. I always flatly refused. I didn't want to have anything to do with it. Fortunately, he didn't force me against my will."

"When did Dimitri come into it?"

"After my father died Dimitri called me and asked me to come on board, to basically take my father's place. I refused him, just like I'd refused my dad. Unfortunately, Dimitri wouldn't take no for an answer. Over the past few months, he's become more and more persistent. When you saw him the other day at my house, he… He threatened me."

Logan's fists clenched. Anger flushed his cheeks. "That bastard! Why didn't you say anything?"

"I was scared and Mikhail and you and Noah were there... He threatened Mikhail. Threatened to tell him about our father; suggesting that Mikhail would be in a deep pool of trouble were I to just disappear some day. I didn't know what to do. I didn't want to set Dimitri off. Neither did I know for sure that you'd believe me."

The last was hard for her to admit, but she had to say it. It was the truth.

Logan reached over and took her hands. "I'm sorry you felt that way, Mia. I truly am. But I understand why you felt as you did. I guess I was a bit confused about it all, too. I wasn't sure what was going on. I'd overheard that phone call... Then this guy Dimitri turns up... You told me he was a friend of your father's..." He shrugged.

"It's okay, Logan. I understand your point of view. I'm just glad we've got it all out in the open now. No more secrets."

He leaned over and kissed her gently on the mouth. "No more secrets."

She took a sip from her coffee. "So, what do we do now?"

"He threatened you and Mikhail. I think we should go to the police."

As she stared at Logan, she came to a decision. Determination, mixed with a healthy dose of fear, burned in her stomach.

"I can't live like this, in constant fear. I want to do more than lock them up. I want to bring him down. Him and his brother, their whole operation."

Logan was already shaking his head. "I can't let you do that. You'd be putting yourself in danger."

"I have an address book of my father's... It names names and outlines culpability... We could use that as bait. Dimitri already knows about it. He's asked me to hand it over."

Logan frowned. "All the more reason for you to stay the hell away from them and let the police deal with it."

Mia touched his arm. "I have faith in you and our police force. I know you'll keep me safe."

Logan muttered under his breath. Mia tightened her hold on him.

"I need to do this, Logan. Not only for me, but for Mikhail. As long as Dimitri and Igor are still out there, their threats will always be hanging over me. If not them, someone else in their gang will step up and put the pressure on. It'll never be over." She paused and added, "No, this is the only way. I want to bring the lot of them down. I want to shut down the whole operation and get the drugs off the streets. I didn't do the right thing back when my father was alive. Now's the time to come forward. With you supporting Mikhail and I, I can do it."

Logan continued to look unconvinced, but assured her he would support her decision in whatever way he could. He was concerned about possible repercussions down the track. Large-scale drug operations always had deputies ready to step up to take control and seek revenge on those who'd dared to disrupt their business.

He hugged Mia hard, needing to reassure both of them everything would be all right. "I'm going to call Noah. He was the one who told me Dimitri was part of the Russian mafia. He'll know what to do."

Mia nodded. "It's the only way, Logan. Otherwise I'll never be free."

Logan regarded her solemnly. "I'm here for you Mia. And Mikhail. Now and for always."

Noah was awoken from a deep sleep by the sound of his phone. He'd arrived home after his nightshift and had struggled to clear his mind enough to sleep. So much had happened. It seemed Dimitri and Igor Petrov were in business with Logan's girlfriend, or at least hoping to persuade her to come on board. From the tension Noah had witnessed between Mia and Dimitri, it was Noah's guess Mia was offering some resistance. Either that, or she was playing hard ball, negotiating the terms.

Getting called out to the armed robbery meant he hadn't found time to call Logan again. That was probably for the best. Noah had checked his emails before his shift ended. His boss still hadn't replied. Until he'd been given the go-ahead by his boss to escalate the matter, it was best to let things lie. Now someone was calling him. All he wanted to do was close his eyes and get some sleep.

Hopefully Ayla will answer it and deal with whoever's on the other end…

The phone continued to ring, hurting his ears. Too late he remembered Ayla would already be at work. With a curse, he rolled over in bed and padded down the hallway to the kitchen. He picked up the phone from where he'd left it on the charger. He barely looked at the screen.

"Who the hell is it?"

"Sorry to wake you, Noah. It's Logan. We need to talk."

With a groan, Noah leaned back against the kitchen counter. His eyes felt gritty and sore. Still, for Logan to call when he knew Noah would be trying to sleep, something urgent must have happened. Either that or he was paying him back for the call Noah had made to Logan in the early hours of that morning.

"What is it?"

"It's about Mia. We talked. She told me everything."

"She's in business with the Petrov brothers?" Noah asked, his voice filled with disbelief.

"No. But they've been trying to coerce her into letting them use her shop as a front to launder the drug money. She has some evidence she found after her father's death but hasn't shown anyone. The last time she talked to Dimitri he threatened her if she didn't hand over particular documents and come on board." Logan drew in a ragged breath. "Despite that, she wants to do whatever she can to bring them in. She's willing to wear a wire."

Noah blew out his breath. "Logan… Hell… Does she have any idea the kind of danger she'll be putting herself in?"

"You don't think I've had this conversation with her already?" Logan's tone was as dry as sandpaper.

Noah flushed. "Of course you have. It's just that… There's something you didn't give me a chance to tell you last night."

"What is it?"

Noah heard the fear in Logan's voice. He wished he could reassure him. "The thing is, last night before I called you, I got a call from Christopher."

"What the hell does Christopher have to do with anything?" Logan asked impatiently.

"Christopher might have overheard Dimitri and Igor talking in a bar last night. He didn't have a clue who they were, but they mentioned the name 'Craigdon' and he decided to listen in on their conversation. Then he heard them talk about Mia. Again, he didn't know who this Mia was, but the Petrov brothers appear to be plotting harm against her. He decided to do the right thing and he brought the information to me. I'm not sure how reliable his information is because I could tell he was pretty drunk. He admitted he'd been drinking heavily. I didn't want to alarm you unnecessarily until I knew if what he said was true."

There was a moment of shocked silence. "Fuck. What if it is? What if they're gunning for Mia?"

"We don't know anything for certain. It might not have even been our guys. I've put in a request for the bar's CCTV footage. That ought to at least confirm who was there. Who knows—Christopher might have imagined the whole thing.

Or perhaps this is his idea of sick joke. It's not like he hasn't played tricks before."

"But you don't think that, right?"

"Honestly? I don't know," Noah admitted. "But we can't afford to take the risk of ignoring it. Where's Mia now?"

"Right here, with me. We're at her house."

"Good. Stay with her. I need to confer with my boss, but I'll see what I can do about getting her some police protection. Although until we have Christopher's information verified, I'm not sure we'll have any luck with that."

"Don't worry, I'm not letting her out of my sight."

"Good. Be careful. We have no idea if and when these men might strike. They're incredibly dangerous."

"I'm trying to get her to call in sick today. She's insisting on going to her shop."

"I understand she might want to carry on business as usual. Perhaps she's right… We don't want the Petrov brothers getting a hint that we're onto them. I sent my boss an extensive email about all of this while I was at work last night. I'm hoping he's already taken some action on it. Leave it with me and I'll find out. In the meantime, try and keep Mia close."

"Don't worry, if that means spending the day inside a bridal shop, I'm prepared to do it."

"Poor Logan. You must really care for this girl," Noah sympathized.

"I'm in love with her," was the simple reply. "Now I know exactly what you and Flynn were on about. There's nothing I wouldn't do for her. If necessary, I'd give my life."

Noah chuckled. "Wow. Well I hope it doesn't come to that. You really do have it bad. I'm happy for you, bro. I really am. I never thought I'd see the day when you were in love again."

There was a pause. When Logan spoke again, his voice was gruff with emotion. "Yeah, well, it hasn't been easy, but Mia's the best thing to ever come into my life."

"Good on you. For now, you need to keep her safe. I'll be in touch with further details as soon as I know what's going on. Okay?"

"Thanks, Noah. I really appreciate this."

"You're welcome, little brother. Anytime."

Noah arrived for his final nightshift of the week and found a note on his desk. It was from his boss. They'd obtained CCTV footage of the bar where Christopher had allegedly overheard a conversation between two known criminals. Noah's boss had emailed the link to him.

Taking a seat before his monitor, Noah pulled his keyboard toward him and entered his login details. He opened his email and found the one from his boss. Clicking on the link, he waited impatiently for the file to load.

The grainy black-and-white footage wasn't the best, but he immediately recognized Christopher seated in a booth in the back. Directly in front of him sat Dimitri and another man Noah assumed was his brother.

"Bingo." At least that part of Christopher's recollection was right. Noah reached for his phone. It was seven in the evening. Hopefully Christopher hadn't already hit the bars.

The phone rang three times before it was answered.

"Hello?"

"Christopher. It's Noah. I want to talk to you about last night."

"Last night? What about last night?"

Noah cursed under his breath. "You called me. After two. You were in a bar. You told me you overheard a conversation between Dimitri and Igor Petrov. Don't you remember?"

There was a pause and then Christopher responded. "Oh, yeah. Right. Now I remember. Shit, I can't believe how much I drank last night. I woke up with a throbbing headache.

Serves me right, I guess."

"I need you to tell me again what you heard."

Christopher groaned. "I've spent all day trying to block out last night."

"Please, Christopher. This is important. I need you to tell me everything you can remember."

Christopher started out hesitantly, but by the time he'd finished, he'd pretty much repeated what he'd told Noah the night before. After thanking his half-cousin for his time, Noah ended the call. His boss had already left for the day, but Noah shot him an email to let him know he'd confirmed everything with Christopher and the information about the Petrov brothers was still good.

It would now be up to his boss to escalate the matter further. No doubt he'd involve the DEA. These guys were on their hit list, after all. Now it was time for him to bring Logan and Mia up to speed. If she truly wanted to be involved in getting the men arrested and charged, they had a lot of work to do.

He arranged to meet them at Mia's house. They'd just finished dinner and Mikhail was ensconced in his room, watching a movie. Soon it would be his bedtime. Then they could talk.

Mia made the three of them coffee and then excused herself to go and tuck her brother into bed. She returned a few minutes later and took a seat at the table. She folded her hands in front of her. Her expression was composed.

Noah admired her resilience. It was a brave thing she was about to do. He told her as much.

She waved away his praise. "It's like I told Logan. I have no choice. I'll never be free until those two men are in jail."

"I understand," Noah replied. "Okay, so here's where we're at. We've verified Christopher's information. By tomorrow, the DEA will be involved. They'll put together a taskforce and set about preparing a warrant to obtain a listening device." He looked at Mia. "Are you still willing to go down that path?"

"Yes."

"Good. It's my guess the taskforce will want you to set up the meeting between you and the Petrov brothers at your house. It will be much easier for the team if they can install the listening devices there. Will that be a problem?"

A flash of fear crossed Mia's face, but quickly disappeared. "No," she said firmly. "I'll do whatever I have to as long as Mikhail is somewhere else. Somewhere safe. The only thing is, I've only had contact with Dimitri. I've never spoken to Igor about this. I think it would appear strange to Dimitri if I asked to speak with both of them. Besides, I'd much rather meet with Dimitri on his own. Igor is in a different category of scary."

Noah nodded. "Fair enough. I'll pass on the information."

"How long do you think it'll take to put the plan in place?" Logan asked.

"It will take at least a couple of days to obtain the warrant, maybe longer. Then we'll have to send in a covert team to install the listening devices in Mia's house. There will be a meeting where everyone on the taskforce will be brought up to speed about how the operation's going to go down. Mia will be part of that meeting." He looked at Logan. "My guess is that it could take four or five days before we're ready to put the plan into action."

"Four or five days!" Logan exploded. "What are we supposed to do in the meantime? They threatened her, Noah! Have you forgotten that?"

Noah held onto his patience. "No, Logan. I haven't forgotten. But we can't go rushing into this. We're only going to get one chance to catch these men. They've avoided the police for a long time. They know what they're doing. If we don't take the time to formulate a plan that has the best chance of succeeding, we might as well not even try."

Mia regarded Noah steadily. "You're right. So, what do we do in the meantime?"

Noah blew out his breath on a sigh. "You do what you always do. You get up, take Mikhail to school, go to work…"

Mia looked aghast. "Take Mikhail to school? There's no way I'm letting him out of my sight!"

Noah remained calm. "I understand you might feel that way, Mia. But the most important thing here is normality. We don't want to trigger any suspicion on the part of our targets. Everything has to go on as normal until we're ready to jump. That includes sending Mikhail to school."

"Well we definitely should alert the principal and his teacher," Mia said.

Noah shook his head. "I'm afraid not. Secrecy in these types of operations is imperative. The less people who know what's going on, the better. We don't want someone inadvertently saying something and word getting back to our targets. That's the single quickest way to failure and could be fatal."

"But what about Mikhail's safety? What if they try something with him as a way to get to me?"

Noah continued in the same measured tone. "We can put together covert surveillance outside Mikhail's school. Make sure he's where he should be. As you know, there are very strict rules in our schools about letting people enter the grounds. That works both ways. Our officers wouldn't be able to come onto the grounds without being challenged and we don't want anyone knowing they're there. By the same token, the Petrov brothers or any of their henchmen will also be kept out."

He paused and added in a gentler tone. "Our schools are very safe, Mia. I'm sure you know that as well as I do. Having Mikhail attend school and keep up the appearance of normality will give this operation the best chance it has."

She continued to feel concerned. "Are you sure?"

Noah flicked a glance toward Logan who gave him an imperceptible nod.

Logan reached for Mia's hand and squeezed it. "These guys are experts," he said in a low tone. "We need to trust they know best."

Her reluctance was evident when Mia eventually nodded her agreement. "Okay. But if anything happens to Mikhail, I'm holding you responsible." She gave Noah a hard look.

Noah held her gaze. "Fair enough."

On Monday morning, when they pulled up at the curb outside Mikhail's school, he jumped out of the car and kissed Mia goodbye and gave Logan a big wave. They'd tried to avoid discussing the situation in front of Mikhail and it appeared they'd succeeded. As far as he was aware, there was nothing untoward going on. He bounded inside the school gates with a big smile on his face.

Logan glanced at Mia. He could see the concern on her face and understood how hard it was for her to leave him at school, knowing the potential threat.

"We have to trust that the police know what they're doing," he said quietly. "They're the experts."

Mia turned to him and sighed. Tears glinted in her eyes. "You're right. But it's so hard! What if something happens to him? I couldn't bear it if he was hurt!"

Logan awkwardly drew her into his arms. He murmured words of comfort against her hair. "It's going to be all right, Mia. It's going to be all right."

She took a shuddering breath and pulled away. He was relieved to see her usual grit and determination evident on her face.

"You're right. The police have this. *We* have this. I'm not going to let the Petrov brothers dictate the terms of my life. Let's go."

Next they headed for the shop. Though Logan didn't normally drive her to work, today he wanted to ensure there was no one lurking in the shadows of her shop. Mia's assistant, Katerina, was already there. Mia introduced them. Logan recognized her as the girl who'd brought Mikhail to his sailing lesson.

Katerina immediately turned to Mia and gave her an exaggerated wink. Mia blushed. It was obvious to Logan the women had been talking about him. The thought pleased him.

With her cheeks still pink, Mia sent the girl out for coffee. After she left, Logan sauntered over to Mia and shot her a knowing look.

"You seemed awfully eager to get Katerina away from here," he teased. "Are you embarrassed to introduce me as your boyfriend?"

Mia's blush deepened. "Of course not. It's just that… Okay, so you caught me out. Yes, Katerina and I have spoken about you. In fact, you were all she could talk about that day she took Mikhail to his sailing lesson. She kept talking about how good looking you were…" She grinned at him. "Of course, I'd already noticed that. How could I not? You're gorgeous."

"Aw, thanks." He chuckled. "So what did you tell Katerina about us?"

"The Monday following the weekend we spent together… Well, what can I say? It was hard for me to conceal my happiness. Katerina noticed right away. She guessed there was a man involved. We… We might have talked a little about you."

He raised a single eyebrow in silent query. "Not in any detail," she hastened to add. "I just told her…you know…that I'd had a good weekend. With a guy. With you."

By now her cheeks were scarlet. She appeared so delightfully young and innocent when she looked like that. He could barely restrain himself from taking her in his arms and kissing her senseless.

"And how did Katerina react?"

"She was pleased for me."

Logan frowned. "So what's the big deal about introducing me today? It seemed like you wanted to get her out of here."

"You're right. I wanted to give you the opportunity to check in all the dark corners, open cupboards, that sort of thing. That's what you came for, isn't it? You're looking for boogeymen?"

He laughed, glad she wasn't going to give him a hard time about wanting to know she was safe. As quickly as he could, he did a walkthrough of the shop and ascertained they were alone.

"Right. Now you can go to work. I'll be fine."

He frowned in sudden indecision. He didn't want to leave her alone. "Are you sure?"

"Yes. I'm sure. Noah told us to act as normal as possible. You being here isn't that. You should go. Besides, I don't want to spook Katerina. She knows nothing about the Petrov brothers. And that's how it's going to stay."

Still, Logan resisted. "I'm your boyfriend. Is it so strange that we might want to hang out?"

She gave him a droll look. "In case you haven't noticed, you're a guy and this is a bridal wear shop. I've owned this shop for, let's see…three years and in all that time, do you know how many men I've had in here?"

Logan grinned. "How many?"

"None. Absolutely zero. Now, Katerina's only been with me a few months, but that's long enough for her to realize this is not the kind of place guys like to hang out, even ones as besotted with their girlfriends as you are."

Unable to help himself, he settled his hands on her waist and drew her toward him until they were touching. "Is that what I am? Besotted?"

She gave him an arch look. "Aren't you?"

He loved that she was confident in the way he felt about her. It made him feel good. It gave him hope she felt the same way. And then he put it into words.

"About as besotted as you are with me, right?"

She grinned. "You got me." With that, she tilted her head and kissed him.

No doubt she meant it as no more than a quick kiss, but the moment her lips touched his, he was on fire. Pulling her hard against him, he slanted his mouth and deepened the kiss. His tongue sought entry and it was granted. Her mouth was warm and wet and silky. She tasted faintly of toothpaste. Her arms came around his neck, holding him close, kissing him as passionately as he kissed her.

His body had ignited with desire. His cock was hard and throbbing.

This is ridiculous… We're in a shop… A bridal wear shop…

Slowly, reluctantly he brought the kiss to an end. When he lifted his head, both of them were breathing hard.

"Wow," she said. "It just keeps getting better. Has anyone told you before that you're an excellent kisser?"

He gave her a lopsided grin. She wasn't the first woman to compliment him on his kissing skills, but there was no way he'd tell her that. Instead, he simply shrugged and said, "I aim to please."

Her eyes flared with desire. "Oh, you do that all right."

"I'm glad," he said softly and then gently set her aside. "You're right. I should get going." He gave her one last quick, hard kiss on the lips. "Stay safe. Call me if you're concerned. About anything. Okay?"

"Okay."

"Promise?"

She nodded. "I promise."

Chapter Twenty

As soon as Katerina cleared the shop front, she walked a few more yards and then pulled out her phone. She scrolled through her contacts until she found her brother. He answered after the sixth ring.

"Dimitri! What are you doing? Why did it take so long to answer your phone?"

"Whoa! Settle down, little sis. What's got you in such a lather?"

"Something's going on. With Mia. She has that guy with her. Logan Craigdon. He's at the shop."

"What do you mean? Did he drop in to say hello?"

"No! They arrived together. She just sent me out to get coffee. I don't know why he's here, but something seems off."

"I checked into him. He works for his father as a ship builder, or some such thing. One thing, he's not a cop."

"Still, it seems odd that he's here. Especially only a week after your visit to her home."

"You're right. Logan was there when I arrived, along with some other guy. They had a motorbike. For a minute I nearly kept driving, but then I saw her brother, Mikhail. I decided to take the opportunity and to hell with the men. My threat to bring harm to Mia and her brother was more effective with him standing only a few yards away."

"Who was the other guy?"

"I didn't know him at the time, but I've since done some research. His name's Noah Craigdon. He's Logan's older brother. And he's a cop."

Katerina gasped. "Oh no! Do you think he recognized you?"

"I don't think so. Surely he would have approached me if he had. Said something… He's with the Law Enforcement Conduct Commission. It's a fancy name for what used to be known as Internal Affairs. He investigates his own. No doubt that's why he doesn't have a clue about what's going on in the real world."

Katerina breathed out a shaky sigh of relief. "Lucky for you."

"Yeah. It was only when I got a bit rough with Mia that the Craigdons stepped forward and intervened. Even then they only told me to get lost."

"You need to be more careful, especially now we know one of them is a cop."

"Don't you worry about me, Kat. Thanks for passing on the information. Maybe we have Mia running scared. That would be good news. I'll increase the pressure. One way or another, that shop will be ours."

"Just you take care, Dimitri. You and Igor. I don't want to lose either of you."

Dimitri's laughter sounded in her ear. "I'll be around to annoy you for a long time yet, Kat. Same with Igor. We Petrovs didn't get this far without knowing how to take care of ourselves—and our enemies."

With his thoughts still firmly on Mia, Logan absently answered a call on his car kit from Noah.

"Noah. What's happening?"

"Hi, Logan. I was just calling to check on Mia. I take it she took Mikhail to school today?"

"Yes. Business as usual, isn't that what you wanted?"

"This isn't a joking matter, Logan." Noah's voice sounded tense.

"Okay, okay. I'm sorry. Don't worry, I'm concerned about all of this as much as you. That's why I drove Mia to work today. I wanted to stop by and check out her shop. Make sure there was no one with evil intent lurking nearby."

"You *what?*"

The anger and shock in Noah's voice gave Logan pause. "I went to Mia's shop and made sure there was no one suspicious hanging around. What's the problem?"

"Fuck! Logan! Didn't you listen to a word I said? Normality is the key to keeping everyone safe. How many times have you dropped Mia off at work? Gone into her shop?"

"None," Logan admitted, his gut filling with dread.

"Exactly. Fuck. You might have ruined everything. You want to hope the Petrov brothers don't have the place under surveillance because you've just given them one hell of a tip-off that something's awry."

"Oh, fuck," Logan whispered, his voice ragged with fear.

Noah sighed heavily. "Listen, don't stress about it. What's done is done. We're in the very early stages of planning. Hopefully they still don't have a clue."

Dread continued to swirl in Logan's gut. He couldn't believe he might have inadvertently caused Mia danger.

"Is there anything I can do to fix it?" he asked weakly.

"No. Just do as I say. Stick to your usual routine. She needs to stick to hers. Leave the rest to the experts. Someone from the DEA will be in touch."

With that, Noah ended the call, leaving Logan to feel sick in his gut all the way to his office. He thought about ringing

Mia and warning her to be extra cautious, but he didn't want to scare her any more than she already was. All he could do was hope Noah was right and that this early into the operation, the Petrov brothers remained completely oblivious to what was being planned.

For the next four days, Mia found herself jumping at shadows. She hated that Dimitri and his brother had her so on edge. Every now and then Katerina shot her a bemused look. Once she'd even asked her if she was all right.

"Of course," Mia responded, pasting on a bright smile. "Why wouldn't I be?"

She tried harder to regain her normal equilibrium. She was pretty sure Dimitri wouldn't try anything in plain sight. At any time, the shop could be filled with clients and apart from when she was on her break or the occasional time when she went out on an errand, Katerina was always nearby.

The hardest thing was trying to put the impending operation out of her mind. Thinking about it reminded her of the potential danger she was in. Especially since she remained adamant she was willing to do whatever the police required of her in order to get the Petrov brothers locked up, including setting up a meeting with Dimitri and having her house bugged. Until he and his brother were off the streets forever, the threat they represented to her and Mikhail would never go away. She'd live her life always looking over her shoulder. There was no way she was prepared to live like that.

But she also worried about Logan. She could tell he was worried about her and Mikhail. She could see it in the way he stared at her when he thought she wasn't looking. It had been that way all week. She was sure his own work was suffering. How could it not? She knew how distracted she was. No doubt Logan had been affected the same way.

Taking the opportunity when the shop was momentarily empty of customers and Katerina was on her lunch break, Mia picked up her phone and called him.

"Hey you," she said when he answered the phone.

"Hey yourself. How are things?"

"Not too bad. Quiet at the moment. I was thinking about you."

"That's nice. I'm always thinking about you."

"I'm worried about your work. That you might be falling behind."

"My work's fine," he replied in a firm voice. "Don't worry about me."

"I can't help it. I know how hard I'm finding it to concentrate. This waiting is driving me insane. It must be the same for you and your work requires so much more focus than mine."

"You're my number one priority, Mia. I'm allowed to worry about you. All I want is for you to be safe."

She compressed her lips. "I love that you think like that, but your career is important, too. I'm sure you have deadlines to meet. Your clients—"

"Are going to have to wait," Logan said firmly. Then his tone relaxed. "Don't worry, in between random sessions staring out the window and praying for this to be over, I've been working on some designs. I'm only a little bit behind in my schedule. It's all good."

Her shoulders slumped on a sigh of defeat. "Okay. But… This could go on for a while. It's been four days already and we haven't heard a thing from the police. Can your company afford to let you slip behind? Won't your clients get angry? Take their business elsewhere?"

"Don't you worry about my company. It'll be fine. Besides, it's my father's company and though I've agreed to take over more of the day-to-day running of it, I haven't taken over yet.

Dad will have to step back into a more active role for a bit. He's capable and has the time. As for my clients, I'll lay on some of the Craigdon charm. Find some excuse for my tardiness. They'll be fine."

She worried at her lip, still not convinced. "Are you sure?"

"Yes. I'm sure. Now, quit worrying. Hopefully we'll hear from the police soon and we can put all of this behind us." He paused and then added, "How's Mikhail?"

"He's fine. He doesn't have a clue what's going on."

"Good. That's the way it's meant to be. Tell him I'll see him tonight."

Her heart leaped in anticipation. "Can you spend the night?"

Logan sighed. "You know how much I'd love to do that, but Noah told us to continue on as normal. Unfortunately, you and I still haven't managed to wake up in each other's arms."

Tears burned behind her eyes. "I can't wait for this to be over," Mia whispered.

"I can't either."

A phone in Logan background began to ring, bringing an end to their discussion. With a soft sigh, Mia hung up the phone and started sorting through a rack of new stock. A few minutes later, her phone rang. It was Logan.

Her heart skipped a beat. She answered the call. "Did you forget something?"

"I just had a call from Jayde Hassad. She's a detective with the DEA. She's also—"

"Flynn's fiancée," Mia finished. "I met her at the party. Why did she call you?"

"She wasn't sure how secure your surroundings were. She thought I was a safer bet."

"Okay. Did she have any news?"

"Yes. They're almost ready. The police have obtained a

warrant and they have a plan in place. They want you to come to the station and go over it. They'll make sure it's done with utmost discretion. No one will know you're there. Are you sure you're still willing to go ahead with this?"

She eyed him steadily. "Yes."

Logan cursed softly under his breath. "I'm not sure if this plan is just plain stupid or if you're the bravest woman I know."

She managed a smile. "The latter, I hope."

Logan sighed softly. "You're right. Though it drives me crazy with fear knowing what kind of danger you're prepared to put yourself in, I have nothing but the greatest respect and admiration for your courage."

Warmth flooded through her. She tightened her grip on the phone and wished he was there so she could kiss him. He put her thoughts into words.

"I wish I was there. I want to kiss you so badly, to hold you close, to reassure myself you're going to be okay."

"Me too," she whispered. "And thank you for your support, Logan. That means a lot to me. *You* mean more than a lot to me."

His voice turned gruff. "Just make sure you come out of it in one piece. I haven't finished with you yet."

She managed another small smile. "Really? What do you have in mind?"

He chuckled wickedly. "You'll have to wait and see for yourself. I promise you, it'll be worth your while."

Desire leaped inside her, sending her nerve endings tingling. Her smile widened. "I'm counting on it."

It took another day to put everything in place. Mia went through the plan and listened hard to all the head of the taskforce had to say. It helped that Jayde was part of the team.

At least Mia had a familiar face to focus on.

She'd been assured the covert team of operators had attended her house and installed the listening devices, though even she couldn't tell they'd been there Nothing had been disturbed. They told her the devices were so well hidden, no one would find them, even if they went looking.

Mia shivered. She hoped it wouldn't come to that, but she had to be prepared for all possibilities. Criminals like the Petrov brothers hadn't avoided capture by being stupid. They'd know all the tricks to look for. She just hoped she could pull this off.

She glanced around her. Though she stood in her living room, everything about the room seemed suddenly strange and unfamiliar. She guessed it had something to do with the heavy police presence that was hidden around the bushes circling the perimeter of her house. Jayde had assured her there was a response team of highly trained officers who would be watching her every move. She wouldn't see them, but they were there. If anything went awry, they'd be on the Petrov brothers before she could blink. She hoped Jayde was right.

Her palms were sweaty and her body was cold with fear. Every now and then, she shivered.

This is madness! What was I thinking when I agreed to do this? How did I think I could pull this off? What if Dimitri guesses? What am I going to do?

She'd called him yesterday and set up the meeting, promising to hand over her father's address book. He'd readily agreed to meet her at her house.

So far, so good…

He said nothing about Igor and for that she was relieved.

Maybe it would only be Dimitri? That thought gave her some relief. Where Dimitri was only slightly taller than she was and weighed maybe thirty or forty pounds more, his brother was a different story.

Igor Petrov was massive. From his huge biceps that were covered in tattoos, to his bald head and equally broad shoulders. His chest was twice the size of a normal man's. He looked like a bouncer, or a personal security guard for some high-profile celebrity. He looked like someone you didn't want to get on the wrong side of.

She'd seen him once with her father. He'd come to their home. He had an air of suppressed violence that made her think he was capable of anything. Her father had introduced them, but had then dismissed her from the room. It was right before her fifteenth birthday. She'd hidden in her bedroom with her headphones on and the music turned up loud, afraid she might otherwise overhear what they were discussing. She hadn't come out until she knew he'd gone.

Now she faced the very real possibility of coming face to face with him again. Her stomach clenched with fear. She couldn't prevent a shudder.

Logan was instantly by her side, his eyes full of concern. "Mia, you're scaring me. You're so pale. Are you all right?"

"Yes, I... I'm fine. I won't lie. I'm so nervous I could throw up, but I'll get through it." She channeled her inner determination. "I've got this. I'm just a little on edge."

"Understandably. There's a lot at risk here." His eyes filled with concern. "You don't have to go through with this, Mia. No one's going to think less of you for pulling out. We're all in awe of your courage. We will completely understand if you change your mind."

She managed a wan smile. "Thank you, but I'm not going to change my mind." She squared her shoulders and lifted her head. "I'm going to take those brothers down."

In half an hour, Dimitri was expected to arrive at her house. She'd deliberately set the meeting time for when Mikhail was safely at school. She didn't want him anywhere near the house. That was also why she hadn't arranged for

Dimitri to meet at her shop. She couldn't take the risk a customer might be inside when he arrived. No, better to keep him well away from everyone. While she was prepared to risk her own safety, she definitely wasn't going to risk anyone else's.

For the same reason, she'd arranged with Katerina to collect Mikhail from school that afternoon. Mia had no way of knowing how long the meeting would go. She hoped it would be over by then, but what if it wasn't? She couldn't risk not having a backup plan. Thankfully, Katerina had readily agreed.

"Do you want me to bring him back to the shop?"

"Yes, please. I might not even be running late, but I don't want to leave him waiting outside the school. He'll go into a meltdown if someone isn't there to meet him."

"No worries," Katerina had said.

Mia had thanked her, relieved to have that problem solved. Now for the other…

Detective Jayde Hassad came up beside her. "How are you holding up?"

"Okay." Mia's voice was shaky.

Jayde eyeballed her. "You don't have to do this."

Mia thinned her lips. She stared back at Jayde. "Yes, I do."

Jayde nodded, a glint of respect filled her eyes. "Fair enough. Do you remember what we talked about?"

Mia gave her a shaky nod. "Yes… You want me to take Dimitri into the front room and get him talking."

"That's right. Try and follow the script. And the safe word?" Jayde asked.

Jayde had insisted Mia come up with a word she could use in the event she wanted to abort the operation. If things got out of control and she felt she was under threat, or if she just wanted to call it quits, all she had to do was utter the safe word and the police would pounce. It wouldn't matter if they hadn't managed to secure enough evidence against either of the Petrovs. Mia's safety was paramount.

"Mia? The safe word?"

"Um, yes. It's dresses."

"Right. Dresses. It's a good choice. If you need to insert it into the conversation, it won't seem out of place. I'll make sure the team is aware of it." She paused and glanced at her watch. "It's nearly time. I have to disappear, but I won't be far away, along with the rest of the team. You won't be able to see any of us, but rest assured, we'll be listening to every word.

"Along with the response team, we also have sharpshooters stationed around the perimeter of your house. Stay seated at the table in the front room as much as you can. Those big bay windows are perfect. They'll give our guys a good line of sight. Someone will have a target on Dimitri from the moment he places himself there until he departs. It might feel like you're all alone in there, but believe me, you won't be. We're here for you. All of us. And we're so in awe of your bravery."

A lump of emotion lodged itself in Mia's throat. "Thank you."

Jayde gave a brief nod. Then she drew in a deep breath. "Are you ready to do this?"

Though Mia's stomach was tight with nerves and fear iced the blood in her veins, she nodded: *Yes.*

"Okay. Let's do it."

Jayde was now all business. In short order, she directed Mia to take a seat at the table in the front room. Mia turned to Logan. He immediately stepped forward and drew her close.

"I'm so proud of you for doing this, Mia. You're the bravest woman I know."

A fresh wave of fear caught in her throat. "What if he catches on that the place is bugged?"

Jayde answered. "You've given him no reason to suspect

this is anything other than a continuation of your previous conversation. As soon as we get what we want, we'll step in. You're going to be fine. I have the utmost faith in you."

Logan pulled her forward for a hard kiss. "I love you."

Her eyes widened in surprise. Though she suspected he felt as strongly as she did, this was the first time either of them had said it aloud. She never imagined they'd make declarations of love in such circumstances, but she'd take it.

With her gaze on his, she kissed him back. "I love you, too."

⌣

Katerina looked up as the door to Wishes and Dreams opened. Her stomach lurched at the sight of her brother. He always had that effect on her.

"Igor. What are you doing here?"

He looked around him like he was casing the place.

"It's all right," she said. "We're alone. Mia's already left for her 'appointment.'"

Igor's lip curled up in a half-snarl. "Good. She thinks she's meeting with Dimitri. She has no idea I'm also going to show. I'm hoping my presence will be an extra incentive to give us what we want."

Katerina eyed her beast of a brother and suppressed a shiver. His presence would definitely help Mia decide it might be best to pacify him by going along with whatever he wanted. Igor, in a rage, was a terrifying sight.

"So what are you doing here?" she repeated.

"The meeting's not until two. I wanted to come and see you and fill you in on the other part of our plan."

She tensed and waited for him to continue.

"You're going to snatch Mikhail from his school."

Katerina stared at her brother in shock. "*What?*"

Igor's expression remained determined. "Yes. I don't mean for you to tear him out of his classroom by force. You're going to collect him after school. Tell him his mother got caught up and asked you to pick him up. Whatever. I don't give a fuck what you say. Just make sure you get him."

Katerina shook her head. "Surely we don't have to involve Mikhail in this. He's just a kid…"

Anger flashed in Igor's eyes a moment before he opened his mouth. "I just want some insurance," Igor shouted, his face turning red. "In case the bitch decides not to play ball. She's called Dimitri, wanting to meet, but I've stayed out of the clutches of the cops by being smart. It's smart to have a backup plan when going to a meeting with someone who might or might not be on our side. Mikhail Ivanov is my backup plan."

"Okay. So what am I going to do with him once I get him?"

"Bring him to Amelia's place. That's where we've agreed to meet. Surprising her with Mikhail will give us extra leverage. What did she tell you about why she needed to be away from the shop?"

"Just that she had an outside appointment and would be away an hour or two."

"Did you talk about Mikhail?"

"As a matter of fact, yes. It seems you're in luck. Mia already asked me to collect him and bring him back here if she's late."

Igor smiled with satisfaction. "Good. Only he won't be coming here, will he?" His smile turned wolfish. Anticipation shone in his eyes. Katerina suppressed a shiver of fear.

"Right. I'll take him home," she said.

Igor's expression turned ugly. "And don't go blabbing to the bitch," he added in a threatening tone. "Don't forget you're a Petrov."

"Why would I go blabbing to Mia? Okay, so she's treated me fairly and it was kind of fun hanging out in a bridal wear shop, but you and Dimitri are my blood. The three of us are in this together."

The anger on Igor's face slowly eased. His tone became less threatening. He even gave her the semblance of a smile.

"That's a good girl. I knew I could count on you."

Chapter Twenty One

imitri's knock on her door came precisely at two o'clock. Mia was momentarily paralyzed with fear. Her heart beat so fast, she thought she was about to have a heart attack. She had to deliberately focus on something else and take several deep breaths before she felt up to answering the door.

Dimitri grinned at her as the door opened. "Amelia. So lovely to see you again. Can we come in?"

Mia spied Igor as he stepped forward into her line of sight. Icy terror almost nailed her to the spot. Swallowing a rush of fear, she turned her back on them without answering and walked into the front room, just as she and Jayde had rehearsed. Dimitri would be suspicious if she was too compliant. He'd been badgering her about this for months.

The line she was taking was that she'd reluctantly made the decision to come on board in order to keep her and her brother safe. She wasn't doing it with any enthusiasm and she definitely wasn't doing it to help the Petrov brothers out.

Dimitri and Igor followed. As she went to sit down, Igor grabbed her arm.

"Not so fast." He ran his hands over her body, paying particular attention to her breasts.

Mia gasped. "Get your hands off me!"

Igor grinned. "Just making sure you're not wearing a wire. A man, even a brother, can't be too sure these days."

He finished patting her down. Satisfied, he nodded toward Dimitri. "She's clean."

"Of course I'm clean, you idiot! What do you take me for?"

Igor merely shrugged. "Like I said, a man can't be too sure." He turned to his brother. "Dimitri check out the rest of the house. Make sure we're alone."

Dimitri left. Trying to control her trembling, Mia took her seat. As she'd hoped, Igor took one of the seats opposite her at the table. Mia had taken care to choose the only chair that faced the front window, which meant Dimitri and Igor had the window at their backs. Again, just as she and Jayde had rehearsed. So far, everything was going to plan, but the fear in Mia's belly didn't let up.

The presence of Igor gave the meeting an additional layer of terror. It was all Mia could do not to use her safe word right away. Instead, she silently talked herself through her fear and managed to get control of her pulse rate.

Dimitri returned and gave his brother a thumbs up. He then took the empty seat beside Igor and shot her a sly look. "We're hoping your desire for this meeting means you've come around to our way of thinking."

Mia compressed her lips. "You know how I feel about illegal drugs. I want nothing to do with them."

Igor sat forward and narrowed his gaze. Her pulse leaped with fright when she spoke. "Where's your father's address book?"

The book she'd tried so hard to forget was now in the hands of the police. Of course, she didn't tell the Petrov brothers that. She recalled the script she and Jayde had prepared.

"It's in a safe place. I'll hand it over when I'm confident we have a deal. On *my* terms, not yours."

Igor glared at her. "Dimitri tells me you're fucking a Craigdon." He hawked a glob of phlegm and spat it on her floor. "That's what I think of the Craigdons. Fucking pigs, every one of them."

With difficulty, Mia forced herself to hold his glare. "Who I choose to date is none of your business."

Igor snarled. "Fucking Nicholas Craigdon. Thinks he's king shit. He fired me from Craigdon Enterprises a couple of months ago. Fucking fired me! The prick! I'd worked for his father for years. Fucking years! And that's the thanks I get. I told him he'd rue the day he crossed me. Here's my chance to get back at him."

He leaned across the table. Mia could smell his fetid breath. Her heart thumped so hard it hurt her ribs.

"You just might be able to help me out with that, Amelia," Igor continued. "You could use your boyfriend to get close to Nicholas. I hear they're pretty tight. Once you're in his confidence, you can plant a block of cocaine on the prick. That would show him. Fucking prick."

Mia stared at him, speechless with shock. This was the last thing she'd expected. It hadn't been covered in the script. Still, she didn't need anyone to tell her how to respond to this one. She glared back at Igor.

"I told your brother when my father died I had no interest in taking up where he left off. I haven't changed my mind. You might enjoy breaking the law by selling illegal drugs, but I don't. I refuse to be part of it."

"Think of the money you could make!" Dimitri cried, oblivious to her thoughts. "You'd never have to work again!"

She turned her attention on him. "Not that it's any of your business and this might come as a surprise, but I enjoy working. I like making my own money in an honest enterprise. I love my shop."

Igor glared at her. A shiver of fear ran down her spine.

"Yes, I've heard how much you love that stupid shop. How would you feel if it happened to burn down one night? Every single fucking dress up in smoke?"

Katerina joined the slow crawl of cars that comprised the school run. She eventually found a place to park and pulled up at the curb not far from the school gate. It wasn't the first time she'd done the school run. Occasionally, Mia got caught up with a bridal party and would ask Katerina to do the school pick up. That certainly played in Katerina's favor today.

Mikhail didn't take to strangers. Ordinarily, she'd have a dreadful time trying to convince him to come with her. But it had only been a few weeks since she'd taken him to his sailing lesson. He was used to getting into her car. She hoped there wouldn't be a scene.

She caught sight of Mikhail running toward the school gate and quickly climbed out of her car. A teacher stood nearby, but her attention was focused on a small child who'd tripped and was crying. Taking advantage of the teacher's momentary distraction, Katerina strode toward Mikhail, calling out and waving to get his attention.

"Mikhail! It's Katerina. Your sister asked me to collect you."

Mikhail stumbled to a halt. For a moment he looked confused and more than a little suspicious. "Where's Mia?"

"She's running late at the shop. She asked me to come and get you."

For a long moment the suspicion remained on his face. Katerina held her breath and gave him her friendliest smile.

"I'll get you a milkshake from Joanna's on the way. Chocolate, right?"

The suspicion cleared from his eyes. Mikhail grinned. "Yay! Chocolate's the best! Let's go!"

Happily walking beside her, he tossed his backpack on the seat behind him and then climbed in the passenger seat. With her heart thumping, Katerina checked for traffic behind her then pulled out into the throng.

With an effort, Mia held Igor's narrowed gaze. "Burn down my shop? Ha! I don't think so. That's an empty threat and we both know it. Without my shop, the rest of your plan goes to hell."

Igor shrugged and sat back. "You're right. The thing is, we need you on board. We need that shop. Now that Henry Craigdon and John Hassad are out of the picture, things have been getting tough. The police are all over us. At some point, they're going to catch a lucky break.

"Laundering the money is the hardest part," Igor continued. "Your shop would provide the perfect cover." Once again, he narrowed his eyes and leaned toward her with menace. "So far, you've dealt with Dimitri. He's asked you nicely more than once. I'm not so nice. I won't take no for an answer."

Mia held onto her courage by her fingernails. She prayed the police were capturing all of this on tape and that they had enough to arrest the men who sat across from her. On a sudden burst of courage, she decided to go for bust. She recalled the words on the script. "Is that all I'd have to do? Launder drug money through my shop?"

"Yes."

"So I wouldn't have to deal with the drugs? The heroin, the cocaine, the pills?"

"No. Dimitri and I would look after that side of things. Like we always have."

Katerina listened to Mikhail's irritating chatter and wished the kid would shut the hell up. Didn't he know she had shit on her mind? She could barely concentrate through his incessant noise. He'd been talking since they'd left his school. Thankfully, they were almost at his home. Then he could become someone else's problem.

"Hey! This isn't where you buy milkshakes!" Mikhail suddenly piped up. "You promised me a milkshake!"

Katerina gritted her teeth. "We'll get one afterwards. Mia asked me to bring you straight home."

"Nooo!" Mikhail wailed. "You said I could get a milkshake! I want a milkshake!"

He was on the verge of losing control. She looked around her in a panic. There was nowhere to pull over. Thankfully they weren't too far away. She blocked her ears against Mikhail's screaming. A moment later, she spied Mia's house. With a grateful sigh, she checked over her shoulder and flicked on her indicator. She glided the car to the curb.

She looked around but couldn't see any sign of Igor's or Dimitri's vehicles. No doubt they'd parked a few blocks away and walked. They would have wanted to take the time to check their surroundings for cops. They hadn't survived all this time on the outside by being stupid.

Before she could stop him, Mikhail opened the passenger side door and bolted from the car. He tore up the path that led to the front door of his house. Katerina opened her mouth to call him back, but then closed it again. Whatever was going on inside the house wasn't her concern. Let her brothers deal with the kid. She'd done her bit. Now she was going home to take some pills and go to bed. She had a splitting migraine.

She put the car into gear, did a U-Turn and headed back the way she'd come. She'd hardly gone three blocks when all hell broke loose. Two cars spun around in front of her, blocking her path. Heavily armed men tore out of the vehicles and stormed the pavement, pointing their guns, shouting at her to step out of the car with her hands up. She stared around her in confusion and felt a trickle of fear as the officers surrounded the car with guns drawn—to intimidate her.

What's going on?

She barely got her head around what was happening before she was being arrested. Pulled out of her car. Handcuffs snapped around her wrists. Then she was forcibly removed to a police van that had come out of nowhere and roughly pushed to the back. She banged her head on the roof of the car and then half-fell against the hard plastic seat. All the while, her head spun with confusion and fear.

Somehow they knew... The cops knew I'd be here... How?

And then another thought crashed into her and it filled her with icy dread. If the police knew about the plan to use Mikhail against his sister, did they also know about her brothers? Igor...Dimitri...? With a cry, she lowered her head and prayed her brothers escaped.

Perched on a narrow seat in an unmarked police van, parked a few blocks from Mia's house, Logan listened to the conversation between Mia and the Petrov brothers. Jayde and two other officers sat at a makeshift desk, electronic equipment spread out in front of them. All of the detectives wore headphones.

Logan's gut was taut with tension. He couldn't wait for this to be over. He'd pleaded with Jayde to let him sit in and listen. She'd reluctantly agreed on the condition that he not move an inch until it was over. That was proving difficult. Unable to sit still a moment longer, he stood awkwardly and began to pace in the tight confines of the van.

Jayde shot him a look and pulled off her headphones. "I thought I told you to sit."

"I'm sorry. I can't."

Jayde's expression softened. "Hey. We've got this. Don't look so scared. She's doing very well."

Logan grimaced. "How much longer? Surely you have enough already?"

"Yes. But while they're still talking, we'll let it run. The more evidence we get the better."

Just then, a radio squawked. Jayde picked up the hand piece and spoke into it. Logan couldn't quite make out the words over the static, but he thought he caught the name 'Mikhail.' Then Jayde frowned.

Logan's gut clenched with fear. "What is it?"

Jayde hung up the hand piece and turned to him. Her voice remained calm. "We have a slight problem. Mikhail's been collected from school by Mia's assistant. She just dropped him off outside his home instead of the shop."

"Shit." Logan scrubbed a hand through his hair. "What are we going to do?"

Jayde's expression turned tense. "I'm not sure if you're aware, but Mia's assistant is a sister to the Petrovs."

Logan gasped with shock. "Katerina? She's in on this, too?"

"Yes. We don't know the extent of her involvement, but given her familial connection, we have to assume she's part of their operation."

Logan shook his head, still dazed at this turn of events. "I'm betting Mia has no idea. There's no way she'd have employed Katerina if she'd known." He looked at Jayde. "You need to do something!"

"Right. We don't know how much Katerina knows, but we have to assume she's aware her brothers are here. Maybe she brought Mikhail here at their instruction. The thing is, Mikhail's safety is paramount, but we also don't want to scare him or put him in any danger. There are plenty of officers guarding the perimeter of the property. They're well concealed, but I must admit, we didn't expect to have Mikhail turn up. It's a…complication."

Logan glared at her. "A complication? You're fucking kidding! You're putting both of them at risk! Do what you have to do to bring this to an end."

Jayde regarded him a moment longer and then nodded. "You're right."

Another squawk came from the radio. Jayde picked up the hand piece and spoke into it. The caller responded, but once again, Logan was unable to make out the words. Frustration and fear ate into him. He'd never felt so helpless. The minute Jayde hung up, he pounced.

"What is it? What's happening?"

"It seems Katerina hasn't bothered to hang around. She left right after dropping off Mikhail. A response team has been sent after her. No doubt they'll catch up with her before too long." Jayde sighed. "At least we don't have to worry about her any longer."

Logan stared at her, his gut churning with dread. "Mikhail's in that house with the Petrov brothers. And so is Mia. We need to finish this and get them out of there."

Jayde looked at him and nodded. Without another word, she turned back to the console.

⌒

Mia stared across the table at the Petrov brothers. Though she wanted nothing more than to bring this nightmare to an end, she forged on with the hope of getting more—enough that they'd both be tossed into jail for a long, long time. She didn't ever want to have to worry about them crossing paths with her—or Mikhail—again.

With a concerted effort she deliberately lightened her tone. "You've been involved in this business for so many years. How is it you've never been caught?"

Igor winked. "Up until a year ago, we had Henry Craigdon on our side. I worked for him at his company, on the side. He also had a number of law enforcement members in his pocket. Paid them well for their services, too. But Henry's dead and we don't have the same connections or protections. It's getting hotter out there on the street. We need a safer plan. That's where you come in."

She made a show of pretending to consider. "How much money would I have to launder?"

Dimitri sat forward eagerly. "No more than fifty thousand a week. Surely a high-end shop such as yours can handle that much?"

Mia took a moment to answer. "I guess so."

Igor smiled. His teeth were yellow and stained from coffee, cigarettes and God knows what. "That's my girl."

She glared at him. "Let's get this straight. I'm not your girl. I've given you what you want. Now it's my turn. If I do this, I want your word that you'll leave me and my brother alone. And you're to keep your mouth shut in front of him. He knows nothing about our late father's business connections. As far as he knows, Alexander Ivanov was a highly reputable building contractor and property developer. That's how it's going to stay. Got it?"

Igor nodded. "Fair enough."

"Good. Might I ask when you expect this little arrangement to start?"

"We'll give you a week to get your head around it."

"And how's it going to work? I mean, will one of you turn up at my shop with a bag full of cash?"

Igor gave her a level stare. "Trust us. We'll be discreet. It doesn't suit our purposes for you to get caught."

Mia twisted her lips into a grimace. "That gives me so much reassurance."

Igor shrugged. "That's all I've got."

Mia pushed away from the table. *Surely the police have enough to make an arrest…* Fear still gnawed at her stomach. Her hands were icy cold. She'd reached the end of her courage. With forced casualness, she headed toward the exit. "If you don't mind, I think it's time you left."

Before she reached the door, she heard the unmistakable sound of a gun being cocked. She froze. Her stomach clenched with dread. On the tip of her tongue was the safe word. She turned slowly and faced Igor. He now stood only a few feet away from her and held a lethal-looking pistol in his hands. The evil look in his eyes filled her with terror.

Igor's lip turned up in a snarl. "We'll leave when I say we leave. We're not going anywhere without that address book."

Mia's heart thumped. Her feet were frozen to the floor. She didn't dare move. And then another familiar sound penetrated the silence of the hallway: the sound of the front door opening, followed by Mikhail's voice.

"Mia? Where are you? Katerina won't buy me a milkshake!"

Fear like she'd never known iced her veins. She looked at Igor and then Dimitri, trying to hide her panic. She prayed they hadn't heard Mikhail. Then Igor grinned wolfishly and her hopes were dashed.

"Well, well, well. It sounds like our company has arrived."

Terror clogged her throat. "Don't you dare hurt him!" she cried. "Mikhail has nothing to do with this!"

"Mia! Mia! Where are you?"

Mikhail's cries easily reached the occupants of the room. Igor's smile widened. In desperation, Mia tried again. "Come now, Igor. Put the gun away. We're friends. Almost business partners. Right? This meeting's been very productive and I'm sure there are finer details we need to work out, but right now I must go." She paused and then added a little frantically, "I have a new shipment of dresses arriving this afternoon. So many dresses…"

Mikhail burst into the room. Mia's belly dropped. He stared at her in confusion and then turned to look at Igor. Mikhail spied the gun and his eyes widened in surprise.

"Mia! What are you doing here? Who are these men? Is that a real gun?"

"Mikhail!" Mia screamed. She went to go to her brother, but Igor pointed his gun at her and pulled her up short.

"I wouldn't do that if I were you, Amelia. We're not finished here. You still haven't brought us that address—"

Before he could finish the sentence, heavily armed police charged into the room. There were shouts and a few grunts of surprise, but to Mia's relief, the Petrov brothers were arrested without incident. As they were dragged, handcuffed, from Mia's house, the pair of them screamed threats against her, leaving her terrified and shaken. To her relief, Logan was there.

Once she ascertained Mikhail was safe, she fell into Logan's arms and burst into tears.

Chapter Twenty Two

The nightmare was over. With Logan's strong arms around her, Mia slowly stopped shaking. The sobs of relief also eased. Jayde came up to her, smiling.

"You were fantastic!" she said. "I couldn't have asked for it to go better. You said all the right things, kept your cool. There's a job on the force, if you want it."

Mia managed a shaky smile. "No. But thanks. It's kind of you to offer. Did you really get all you need?"

"You bet. There's not a defense lawyer in town capable of getting them out of this one."

"I'm so glad it's over," Mia said.

Logan tightened his arms around her and pressed a kiss against her hair. "That makes two of us."

She looked around for her brother. He was happily peppering the police officers with questions about the equipment they had on their belts. Mia's shoulders slumped on a heavy sigh of relief.

It was done.

—

It seemed to take forever, but finally most of the crowd of police officers, technicians and other people involved in the sting had left. Only Jayde remained. She came up to Mia and gave her a brief hug.

"I just wanted to tell you how proud I am of you. I've said this before, but you're a very brave woman. What you did… Most people would have run for the hills. Instead, you kept calm and held on to your courage and because of you, these two scum are off the street for a very long time."

With Jayde's words Mia was flooded with warmth and satisfaction. "Thank you. I really appreciate you saying that. I guess, at the time, I was running on adrenaline I just pushed on through. The truth is, I was absolutely terrified, especially when Igor showed up. I'd been praying it would only be Dimitri. Somehow, he's easier to handle. But Igor…"

She shuddered as the memory of his menacing glare surfaced in her mind. "Then when I heard Mikhail coming in…" She shuddered again. "I thought I was going to die. I was so scared for him."

Then she frowned as another thought occurred to her. "How did he come to be here? I arranged with Katerina to take him back to the shop."

Jayde looked at Logan who stood nearby. He nodded briefly toward Jayde and then stepped forward and took Mia in his arms. He pressed a kiss against her hair and held her close.

Jayde cleared her throat. "Popov is Katerina's married name. She's Dimitri and Igor's younger sister."

Mia gaped in shock and stepped out of Logan's arms. "Are you kidding me? She's their sister?"

Jayde nodded, her expression grim. "I'm afraid so."

Mia felt blindsided. "I had no idea."

"Don't feel too bad about it," Jayde said. "You weren't suspecting anything, least of all that the Petrovs would plant a spy in your shop."

"Is that what she was doing?" Mia asked. "Spying on me?"

Jayde nodded again. "We can't be certain, but it appears that way."

"I can't believe I let her around my brother. I trusted her implicitly and I shouldn't have. After all, she was pretty much a stranger. I should have known better."

Logan stepped forward and squeezed her arm. "Don't beat yourself up about it, Mia. None of us saw this coming."

"Why did she drop Mikhail here?" Mia asked, still feeling dazed.

Jayde shrugged. "We don't know. All we can guess is that her brothers intended to use him as leverage if you didn't go along with their scheme. Perhaps he was their insurance. It was just lucky they didn't get a chance to get hold of him."

Mia shook her head in disbelief. "I don't believe it. I just don't believe it. He could have been badly hurt."

Once again, Logan offered her reassurance. This time he gave her a tight hug. "Let's not go there, Mia. The thing is, Mikhail's all right. It's all over. You're safe. Everyone's safe."

As if realizing he was the subject of their conversation, Mikhail bounded into the living room, talking a mile a minute about the police officers and vehicles he'd seen outside. Mia threw her arms around him and squeezed him tight until he protested.

"Mia! Stop! Let me go."

Reluctantly, she dropped her arms. He turned to Logan and gave him a high five.

"Logan! Did you see all those police cars? They're everywhere! It's so cool! Almost as cool as riding Noah's motorbike!"

Mia smiled and drifted away from them and went to sit on her couch. It had been a long day. Hell, it had been a long week. Ever since she'd made the decision to assist the police in whatever way she could.

I did it! I stood up for the good guys! Sorry, Dad. It had to be done.

She picked up an imaginary champagne flute and raised it in the air.

Here's cheers to the end of your enterprise, Dad. Good riddance.

Logan insisted on taking Mia and Mikhail back to his apartment in Manly to spend the night. There was no way he was going to let her stay there in her house with the residue of all that had happened there still heavy in the air. At least at his place she might actually relax enough to sleep.

Thankfully Mia didn't take much persuasion. She threw a few things in an overnight bag for her and Mikhail and then they left.

They traveled in his car. The weekend loomed, which meant Mikhail didn't have to go to school for another two days. On the way to his place, he stopped and picked up some Chinese takeaway.

The memory of the danger Mia had put herself in still had the power to shake him. If anything had gone wrong… If he'd lost her… He shuddered to think about it.

Focus on the positive. She's fine. Everything's fine. The Petrov brothers are in jail, where they belong…

The pep talk calmed him and he reached across the gearstick to take Mia's hand. He squeezed it, not sure which one of them he was trying to reassure. She must have sensed his distress, because she frowned a little and her eyes filled with concern.

"Are you okay?" she asked quietly.

He swallowed. "Yeah. I'm… I'm fine. I'm just…still a little shaken up. I keep thinking about what might have happened if things had gone wrong and I…" He shrugged, feeling helpless.

"Hey, I'm here. I'm okay. Mikhail's okay. We're all okay. Better still, we've taken down the Petrov brothers. They're off the streets."

He blew out his breath and shook his head. "I'm so proud of you. You were so incredibly brave. I didn't think I could love you more, but I do. You're my hero."

She blushed. He could tell his words filled her with pleasure.

"I won't say I wasn't terrified to ask all those questions without making them suspicious, but I was more scared about what they might do to me, and to Mikhail if I didn't find the courage to take action. I couldn't live my life looking over my shoulder, wondering, waiting for them to attack." She pulled a face. "So, it wasn't so much bravery, as just being unwilling to live with the alternative."

Logan looked at her and shook his head. "I don't care how you justify it; you were utterly, completely courageous. I love you so much."

Her expression softened. This time she reached for his hand. "I love you, too."

After the food was eaten, the dishes done and an exhausted Mikhail settled in the spare room, Logan led Mia to his bedroom and closed the door. Slowly, tenderly, they undressed each other. Buttons slid from holes, shirts were swept from shoulders. Underwear slipped down hips, and her bra was unclasped. With infinite gentleness, Logan removed her prosthesis and the protective sock. When they finally lay skin to skin across his bed, he sighed and brushed Mia's hair off her forehead.

"I can't believe I might have lost you today," he whispered.

She gave a half-laugh. "You didn't nearly lose me."

"Okay, nothing bad happened. But it could have."

Mia sat up and then leaned down and framed his face with her hands. She kissed him on the lips. "*Shh.* I'm okay. I'm okay."

With one swift movement, Logan rolled her beneath him and kissed her like he couldn't get enough. He burned with the need to imprint every inch of her on his memory and reassure himself she was safe. She'd survived her ordeal. She was fine. They were fine. He let out a shuddering breath and then kissed her again.

Her eyelids, her forehead, her nose. He nuzzled her neck, nipped at her shoulder and then found her mouth again. Liquid heat poured through him as he plundered her mouth with his tongue. Over and over, he swept the warm recesses and then groaned when her tongue tangled with his.

And then he moved lower, his mouth tracing a path from her lips, across her chest to her breasts. He found one of her nipples and sucked the sweet bud into his mouth. She arched beneath him. Her fingers buried themselves in his hair.

"You like that?" he whispered.

"Yes. I like that a lot."

He gave the other nipple the same attention. Beneath Mia's ribcage, her heart beat fast under his ear. She made little mewling sounds of need. Her fingers kept tightening around his head.

"Please, Logan. It's too much," she gasped.

Taking pity on her, he released her nipple and then kissed his way down her stomach. His hand came up and caressed her thigh and then slid lower to stroke her kneecap. Moving lower, he replaced his fingers with his mouth and kissed his way over her stump. At the same time, his fingers found the sweet spot between her legs.

While his mouth made love to her inner thigh, his fingers plunged inside her. She cried out in passion, her breath coming fast and still he continued his sensual onslaught. With his tongue stroking her skin in time with the rhythm of his fingers, it wasn't long before she tensed beneath him and then cried out on a shout of triumph. She contracted around his fingers.

Slowly, when her breathing had almost returned to normal, he eased his fingers out. They were glistening with her juices.

"Better?" he asked.

She nodded. "So much better."

He smiled, filled with satisfaction. He swelled with pride at the knowledge he could please her. Just as she pleased him.

With that thought in mind, he reached across her to his bedside table and drew out a condom. He sheathed himself and then positioned himself between her thighs. Her legs fell open, welcoming him in.

He nudged her entrance. His cock was rock hard and throbbing. He felt like he might die if he didn't have her. He pressed forward. She was warm and wet and silky. He'd aimed to take things slowly this time, but one feel of her snug heat and he was gone.

He thrust his hips forward and plunged inside her, crying out with relief. She clung to his shoulders, digging her fingernails into his skin. Over and over again, he took all she had to give and when he reached the precipice and fell over, it was her name on his lips.

Afterwards, he gathered her close against him. His arm was around her shoulders. Her head was on his chest. He thought of the anguish and hurt he'd carried around for so long—after the accident that had stolen his future, and the fiancée who hadn't loved him the way she should have. He'd wasted so much time wallowing in self-pity, lashing out at anyone who came close. And then he'd met Mia and he'd never felt so blessed.

"Tell me about your mother," Mia said quietly into the silence.

Logan instinctively tensed and then blinked in surprise. "What do you want to know?"

"Whatever you'd like to share. My biological mother died when I was so young. I barely remember her. I bet you're grateful every day you had yours for so long."

Logan compressed his lips against the rush of guilt that

flooded through him. The truth was, he'd spent the past ten years feeling sorry for himself that his mother had been killed when he was still a teenager. He'd never stopped to consider there might be other kids who'd lost their mother even younger, or who'd never known their mother at all.

He drew in a deep breath and eased it out on a shudder of relief. All of a sudden, and with a feeling of gratitude and wonder, he felt lucky to have known his mother for as long as he had.

"She was beautiful," he began in a hushed voice. "Kind and soft spoken. She never raised her voice. Instead, when we'd done something to displease her, she'd bring us into her sitting room and talk to us, make us see without any shouting where we'd let ourselves down. More importantly, how we'd let *her* down. That was the worst. Knowing she felt disappointed in us."

He sighed and threaded his fingers through Mia's. "But everyone has their secrets. I found out recently she was having an affair with my uncle when she died."

Mia lifted her head and stared down at him, her eyes wide with surprise. "Wow. Did your father know?"

"Not at the time."

"Do you have a picture of her? I'd like to see if you take after her."

"No, I don't have any pictures here. I'm sure Dad still has some at home. I don't look like Mom, though. She had dark hair and brown eyes. I probably take more after my father, although he has brown eyes, too. My blond hair definitely comes from him. We all got the blond hair."

Mia reached up and ran her fingers through his thick, short locks. "I like it."

He kissed her. "Do you have any photos of your mother?"

Mia shook her head. Her eyes grew sad. "No. I was only five when she died. I was put into a foster home as soon as I was released from the hospital. I don't know what happened to all of our stuff. I never saw any of it again. As for other relatives, none came forward. I never knew my father. I never even knew his name. As far as I know, my mother was an only child."

His heart went out to her. "That's too bad. I wish I could undo that."

She shrugged, still a little despondent. "It wasn't your fault."

"I'll ask Dad about finding a picture of my mother for you."

"Thank you. I'd like that. Family's important."

"Yes. It is. My brothers and I have always been close. We know we can count on each other."

She bit her lip. "That must be nice."

He kissed her tenderly on the lips. "It is. And now you have me. I have your back, Mia. And Mikhail's, too."

Her eyes filled with emotion. "I'm so glad you said that. I'm sure I don't need to tell you we're a team. For life."

He brushed her cheek with the pad of his thumb. "I have no problem with that. None at all."

Chapter Twenty Three

ow that Mia had raised the topic, Logan couldn't wait to show her pictures of his mother, Janelle. Somehow it seemed even more important, given Mia didn't have any pictures of her mother. Logan thought about the fifteen years he'd had with his mother—having her there when he arrived home from school, watching him sail, refereeing disputes with his brothers…

With her mother taken from her so early and her adoptive mother a drug addict, Mia had missed out on so much. He was grateful for the time he'd shared with his mom.

"Dad? Are you there?"

Logan pushed the front door of his father's house open wider and stepped into the foyer. Mia trailed behind him.

"Dad?"

"I'm in here, son. In my office."

They found Archie seated behind his desk, a number of blueprints spread out in front of him. He looked up as they entered.

"Logan! Mia! It's good to see you."

Logan perched himself on the edge of his father's desk and looked down at the blueprints "What are you doing working on the weekend, Dad?"

"I just thought I'd give these a final look over before they're signed off." He glanced at Logan. "You know how I am. Always a perfectionist."

Logan chuckled. He reached out for Mia's hand and drew her close. Archie regarded them steadily.

"I heard about what you did, Mia. With the Petrov brothers. You were incredibly brave. I'm not sure I would have been able to do what you did."

Mia flushed and waved away his compliment. "I'm just glad they're off the streets."

"Absolutely. It's been a long time coming." He paused and then added, "Can I get you a drink? Some coffee?"

Logan shook his head. "No, thanks Dad. We're here to look for some old pictures of Mom. I assume you still have some?"

Archie's expression sobered. "Of course. But not down here. I packed up all her pictures and things and put them in the attic."

Logan regarded him steadily. "It wasn't your fault she had an affair, Dad."

Archie's eyes flared with guilt. "How do you know? According to Noah, your mother found out about me and your Aunt Elizabeth. How do you know this wasn't her way of getting back at me? Or maybe she felt the need to seek companionship elsewhere, someone who was prepared to love her the way I wished I could."

Logan shook his head. "We'll never know the answer to any of those questions, Dad. It's an exercise in futility sitting here beating yourself up. I'm not forgiving you your actions. Cheating on Mom was despicable, and while I don't want to speak ill of the dead, especially when she's no longer around to defend herself, it's obvious she must also shoulder some of the blame. You were both having affairs. I know enough about relationships to know it can't have all been your fault."

Emotion glinted in his father's eyes. "Thank you, son. That means a lot to me. I don't expect your forgiveness, but I'm very grateful for your understanding." His gaze flicked to Mia. "You've been very good for my son. I'm so glad he has you in his life."

"Thank you sir," Mia murmured.

She squeezed Logan's hand. He responded by bringing their joined hands to his lips and brushing a kiss across her knuckles. The tender gesture wasn't lost on his father.

"You can't know how much it fills my heart with joy to see you looking so happy, Logan. I was devastated for you when Virginia left, but I've always been a firm believer that everything happens for a reason. I prayed long and hard for you to find someone worthy of your heart. It looks like my prayers have been answered."

Mia looked embarrassed, but she thanked Archie just the same. "Your son is a good and decent man. I'm honored to have him by my side."

Archie stared at them a while longer and then nodded, as if satisfied. "Yes. You make a good pair."

"You don't mind if I go through Mom's things, do you?" Logan asked.

"No. Of course not. She was your mother. Nothing's ever going to change that."

Logan swallowed the lump in his throat. "Thank you. We'll be up in the attic then. Is there anything you need up there while we're at it?"

"No. There's nothing up there for me but memories."

"Fair enough."

With that, they bid him goodbye and with hands still entwined, Logan led them through the house. He came to a halt beside a staircase that led to the attic. He looked at Mia. "Ready?"

She smiled. "After you."

He shot her a teasing grin. "Don't tell me you're afraid of the dark?"

"And what if I said I was?"

He pulled her close and kissed her hard on the mouth. "I'd say I love you with everything that I am and you never have to be afraid of the dark again."

Mia followed Logan up the stairs that led to the attic. To her relief, the ceiling wasn't as low as she'd anticipated and when Logan found the light switch, the place was bathed in a soft glow. There were boxes of clothes, discarded furniture, sports equipment, toys. In the far corner, Logan found the box filled with his mother's things.

Scraps of fabric, balls of wool, books, knickknacks and framed photographs. Logan pulled one out. He looked down at it and smiled.

"This is me and Mom when I was about four."

He handed the picture to Mia. She studied the woman and the boy. Janelle was tall for a woman, slim, dark haired and dark eyed. In the picture, she was laughing at Logan who'd fallen over in the mud. His clothes were stained, along with the palms of his hands as he held them up to the camera. But there was a huge grin on his face.

Mia smiled. "How come you aren't screaming? You've obviously fallen over? Or did one of your brothers push you?"

"No. I'd been learning to ride a pushbike. Mom had been helping me. We'd been at it all morning. I kept falling off. But she kept encouraging me to have another go and finally, I got the hang of it. I went a whole round of the garden before I hit a puddle and fell off. I didn't care about the mud. All I can remember is feeling so proud. I'd done it. I'd learned to ride a bike."

In the bottom of the box was a leather-bound book that looked a lot like a diary. Logan reached for it. When his fingers closed around it, Mia noticed his hand was unsteady.

"Are you all right?" she asked gently.

"Yes."

He flipped open the first page. "It's my mother's diary. I used to see her writing in it from time to time, but this is the first time I've held it."

"Would you rather be alone?"

He looked at her and shook his head. "No. I need you right here beside me."

With a deep breath, he flipped over a few pages and silently began to read. Every now and then, he smiled. He flipped over more pages, paused to read, flipped again. And then his expression changed. His eyes widened in shock. His mouth gaped on a soundless gasp.

Mia felt a trickle of unease. "Logan? Is everything all right?"

He shook his head and lifted his gaze to hers. His eyes were so full of pain, her heart clenched.

"Logan? Please, talk to me. What is it?"

He stared at the diary. "It's true. What my brothers have long suspected. The affair my mother had with Uncle Henry had been going on for years. Even before I was born." He lifted his gaze once again and she gasped at the agony she saw there.

"He's my father. Uncle Henry. I'm his son."

Mia hid her shock. All that mattered was Logan. She could see the struggle going on inside him. Shock, anger, disbelief, pain. The emotions moved across his face in swift succession and finally anger set in and stayed.

Mia moved closer. She touched him on the arm, not sure if he was open to anything more right then. He didn't shrug her off, but neither did he turn to embrace her.

"I'm sorry, Logan. You shouldn't have found out this way."

Logan continued to look dazed. "Flynn joked about it once," he said in a faraway voice. "No one believed him. Especially not me. Then Noah discovered Mom was having an affair with Uncle Henry when she died. He touched upon the possibility that Henry was my father, but none of us wanted to go there. My brothers had their suspicions, but no one wanted to admit the truth. Now there's no denying it. Archie Craigdon isn't my father. I don't even think he knows."

Mia took him by the arms and turned him to face her. His eyes were glazed. She gave him a little shake in an effort to pierce his bewilderment.

"This changes nothing between us, Logan. I love you with all my heart. I'm sorry this has happened to you, but we'll get through this and we'll do it together. You, me and Mikhail. Okay?"

It took a long moment, but finally the tension that had gripped Logan's body eased. His shoulders slumped. He put his arms around her and drew her close.

"Okay," he breathed against her hair.

She let out the breath she'd been holding. Relief poured through her. Her heart filled with love. She lifted her head and met his halfway. Their lips met in the sweetest of kisses.

It would be all right. Like she'd told Logan. They'd get through this. Together.

It had been nearly a week since Logan had discovered he wasn't Archie's child and he was still coming to terms with that. Thanks to Mia's support, he'd managed to tell his brothers. Neither of them had been shocked. Logan realized the two of them had had more of an inkling about where the truth lay than he did. He knew they'd downplayed their suspicions for his sake, to spare his feelings, and though he was a little irritated they thought he was so fragile, he understood just the same and was grateful they cared enough to keep their suspicions to themselves. His father—no, scrap that. His *uncle*—was another matter.

Though Mia had made it clear she was more than happy to be there with him when he broke the news to Archie, Logan needed to do that on his own. He'd asked his brothers to keep the discovery to themselves until he had a chance to tell their father. They'd agreed. Now he stood outside his father's house once again. His belly was filled with nerves.

He'd called ahead to make sure his father was home. Now he made his way into Archie's office with feet that felt like they were weighted with lead.

What am I so afraid of? That he'll disown me? That he'll stop loving me? That he'll no longer think of me as his son?

Logan was sure it wouldn't make any difference to the way his father felt about him. After all, none of this was Logan's fault. He'd continue to think of Archie as his father, no matter what. As far as Logan was concerned, Archie was his father in the only sense that mattered. He'd loved him, cared for him, looked out for him. All the things a father was supposed to do.

As for Uncle Henry… Logan hadn't brought himself to read any more of his mother's diary. He didn't know if his mother had told Henry the truth about Logan, or not. He could only assume Henry had been as unaware of the truth as the rest of the family. At least in the beginning. It was unthinkable Henry had drafted his biological son into selling drugs. It was bad enough he'd done it to his nephews.

It was possible his mother had told Henry sometime later, before she'd died. After all, Henry had left Craigdon Enterprises, a billion-dollar company, to Logan. He'd overlooked his biological sons.

Logan suppressed a groan. Every time he thought about

the whole sorry situation, his head began to hurt. Both his mother and Henry were dead. There was no one around to answer his questions. Perhaps it was better that way…

Still, he had to tell Archie. He deserved that much.

Logan found him in his office. This time, he sat in one of the leather armchairs, a glass of scotch in his hand.

"Hey, there son. Would you like a drink?"

Logan nodded. "Thanks."

Archie stood and went over to the bar that stood in the corner. He dropped ice cubes into a tumbler and then poured a generous amount of scotch.

"Ease up, Dad. I'm driving."

"One drink won't hurt you."

Archie handed him the glass and Logan murmured his thanks. His father regained his seat. Logan sat in the chair opposite.

"So, how's Mia?" Archie asked.

Logan took a sip from his scotch. It burned a fiery path to his gut. "She's fine. She's at home with Mikhail."

Archie smiled. "You really hit the jackpot there, son. She's a good woman."

Logan nodded. "Yes. Yes, she is."

"Nothing like Virginia. I never could see the two of you working out."

Logan stiffened. "Really? You never said anything."

Archie shrugged. "It wasn't my place."

Logan sat forward. He did his best to hide his hurt and disbelief. "You were prepared to stand by and let me enter into a marriage you didn't think would last? What kind of father does that?"

Archie sighed wearily. "You believed you were in love. Would you have even listened?"

Logan shook his head. "We'll never know."

Archie took a sip from his glass. "I thought you must have

worked things out. That what I'd seen had just been a passing thing."

Logan felt even more confused. "What the hell are you talking about, Dad? What did you see?"

Once again, Archie sighed. He looked away and stared at the carpet. As if coming to a decision, his gaze met Logan's again.

"I saw your fiancée kissing another woman."

Shock held Logan momentarily immobilized. *"You what?"*

"Yes, it was at a family function a few months before you were due to get married. I came across them in a darkened corner out by the pool. They didn't see me. They were…too involved with each other. For a moment I thought I was imagining things. That I'd mistaken someone else for Virginia. But then I heard her speak. It removed any doubt."

Logan felt poleaxed. Though he'd known his ex-fiancée had run off with another woman, he'd had no idea it had been going on all that time.

"Why didn't you say anything?"

Archie shrugged. "As the weeks went by and the wedding wasn't called off, I thought it must have been an aberration on Virginia's part—a one-off. I had no idea she'd leave you at the altar."

Logan's shoulders slumped. "I guess I ought to be grateful she did. Breaking off an engagement was a whole lot less messy than divorce, even if she did break my heart."

Archie looked at him, askance. "Did she? Break your heart?"

Logan took his time in answering. "If you'd asked me that a month ago, I would have given you an immediate affirmative response. But that was before Mia… Now I know what true love feels like. What I felt for Virginia didn't even come close. I didn't realize that at the time, of course. But looking back, she did me a favor by breaking things off."

"She did both of you a favor. She would have been just as miserable as you. I hope she's found true happiness. It's a tough road, being married to someone you don't love wholeheartedly, or who doesn't think you're the love of their life."

Archie sounded so sad, Logan was moved to ask. "Is that how it was for you and Mom?"

Archie compressed his lips and slowly nodded. "Yes."

Logan gathered his courage. He drew in a deep breath and asked the next question. "Was that because of the way she felt about Uncle Henry?"

Archie tensed. Logan kept his tone low and full of compassion. "It's okay, Dad. It's okay to admit they were having an affair. Noah found irrefutable proof during his investigation. And I did, too. Up in the attic."

Archie frowned in confusion. "What are you talking about?"

"Remember when I came here last week with Mia and we went through some of Mom's things?"

"Yes."

"I found her diary. There's no doubt she and your brother were having an affair." He paused and drew in another breath. "She also writes about how I was the product of their affair."

Archie sat bolt upright. His mouth agape. His face pale. "What... What are you saying?" he croaked.

"I'm Uncle Henry's son, Dad."

Archie began to turn his head from side to side. Pain in his voice was palpable. "No! No! No! It can't be true."

Logan twisted his hands in his lap, feeling helpless. "I'm sorry, Dad. I'm so sorry."

His father turned anguished eyes upon him. "I had no idea it had been going on so long. Noah tried to tell me about it, but I refused to believe him. You and Nicholas were born only weeks apart. She must have known Henry was still sleeping with Elizabeth and yet she obviously didn't care."

"I don't know how it went Dad," Logan answered honestly. "But does that really matter? You both cheated on your spouses. You both had children outside your marriage. I don't think either of you hold the higher moral ground." He threw his hands up in an act of surrender. "It happened so long ago, Dad. Does it really matter who was the first to cheat?"

Archie slowly shook his head. "No, I guess not. I'm sorry, Logan. I'm so sorry. I didn't know. Your mother never said…"

"It's all right, Dad. This doesn't change anything. I just thought you had a right to know."

"Thank you. I appreciate your kindness. If you don't mind, I'd like to be alone for a while."

Logan set down his glass and stood. "Of course. Will you be okay?"

Archie stood with him. He reached out and the two men embraced. Logan was flooded with relief.

"Yes. And don't doubt I love you, son."

"I love you too, Dad."

Long after Logan left, Archie sat staring at the wall of his office. He sipped from his fourth glass of scotch. A low buzz had started in his head, but nothing could wipe out the knowledge his wife of two decades had given birth to someone else's son. No, not someone else's—his brother's.

Good old Henry.

Henry had always been a winner with the girls. First, Elizabeth. Then Janelle. He just couldn't help himself. Henry always wanted what Archie had. And he made sure he got it, by fair means or foul.

At last, everything made sense. No wonder Henry had left his company to Logan. All that time, they must have been laughing at him, knowing he was oblivious to what they'd done. And all that time they'd known he was Sophia's father, and they hadn't said a word. Archie couldn't help but wonder why.

Was it because they didn't want to expose their own dirty little secret? Have their world blow up in their face. Messy divorces, bad publicity, children tugged from pillar to post?

Archie ought to be grateful. They were the same reasons he and Elizabeth had hidden their love. Were still hiding their love…

A wave of irritation went through him. He was tired of all the subterfuge. Tired of hiding the way he felt. He loved Elizabeth. He always had. But she'd belonged to Henry. It shamed him to admit he'd married Janelle only because Elizabeth was out of reach. Now he and Elizabeth were both free to love whomever they pleased, yet Elizabeth was still resisting his pleas.

It wasn't the right time… The children were still grieving… There have been so many shocks…

She had a ready list of excuses, but he was well and truly over them. She either loved him enough to come clean to their children about what they meant to each other, or she didn't. He wondered if he had the courage to give her an ultimatum.

And now this. He'd just learned Logan was Henry's son.

I'm not going to tell Elizabeth…

The thought popped into his mind and startled him. He frowned. Of course he'd tell Elizabeth. They didn't keep secrets from one another. At least, not anymore.

But she had kept Sophia a secret. For twenty-one long years, in fact. She'd known all along who Sophia's father was and she hadn't breathed a word. The knowledge still hurt.

With a sigh, he tilted the glass to his lips and emptied the contents down his throat. He'd tell Elizabeth about Logan eventually, but first they were going to talk about *them*. They were going to tell the world about the way they felt about each other, about the way they'd felt right from the very beginning. This time, he wouldn't take no for an answer.

Chapter Twenty Four

Mia filled the vase of fresh flowers with water and set them in the middle of her dining table. Leaning over, she inhaled their sweet scent. The flowers were a thoughtful gift from Logan. When she'd asked him about the occasion, he'd merely smiled and told her there didn't need to be one.

She'd never felt so happy. She'd managed to find another assistant to help out in the shop and her relationship with Logan was going from strength to strength. Most nights, he spent the night at her house. It was better for Mikhail that way. Her brother liked consistency and was not so good with change. Besides, his school was only a short distance away and it was important not to disrupt his studies.

For Logan's part, he didn't seem to mind. Though they hadn't spoken of a more permanent arrangement, for now things were just fine. Logan had taken her to a Craigdon family dinner and she'd been properly introduced to all of the gang. Jayde had regaled them with stories of Mia's bravery the day Mia had invited two members of a notorious drug gang into her home.

Then Nick had announced he and Harper were expecting a baby and the talk had turned to the pending arrival.

Elizabeth had suggested they move the wedding date forward. Nick and Harper agreed.

Archie had remained mostly silent at the head of the table. Elizabeth sat opposite at the far end. Logan had told Mia he'd spoken to his father, but no one knew what had gone on from there. Logan insisted it wasn't his business to tell Aunt Elizabeth. He left that up to his father. Still, from the tension that emanated from the oldest people in the room, Mia could only guess the news hadn't gone down well.

The beep of a horn outside her front window interrupted Mia's thoughts. She parted the curtains and saw Logan sitting in his car out front. Mikhail ran to the door and opened it and bolted down the stairs.

"Come on, Mia! Let's go! Let's go sailing!" he shouted on the way out.

Mia smiled and gathered her things—a hat for her and Mikhail, her sunglasses, towels, her handbag. Then she pulled the door closed behind her. Brimming over with happiness, she went to join her men.

Note to Readers

I do hope you have enjoyed reading Logan and Mia's story. If you've enjoyed this book, I would really appreciate it if you could leave a review at Goodreads and your favorite digital retailer. Every review increases visibility and helps other readers to find books they enjoy.

Receive a free book when you sign up for my newsletter if you like to receive news on upcoming stories, release dates, book launches and other snippets. I love to receive feedback from my readers. Please feel free to contact me at chris@christaylorauthor.com.au.

Elizabeth is the next book in the Craigdon Family Dynasty series.

Keep reading below for a sneak peek at *Elizabeth*:

Chapter One

Ever since her husband's untimely death a year earlier, Elizabeth Craigdon had avoided Henry's study. It was a well-appointed room, with luxurious leather couches, high backed chairs, floor-to-ceiling bookshelves and an impressive hand-carved cedar desk, but it was a place that had always been her husband's domain. She was sure, even a year after his death, the scent of his expensive cologne still hung faintly in the air, mocking her.

Theirs hadn't been a happy marriage. They'd both had affairs. Henry's were too numerous to mention. Elizabeth had only strayed once, but the love she felt for Henry's brother had continued to deepen as the years went on. So much that she was still in love with him. Not even their children knew the affair that had started so long ago was still ongoing. It was a bone of contention between her and Archie. He couldn't understand why she wouldn't come clean with the children, now that their respective spouses were dead.

Elizabeth couldn't explain her reluctance either. She loved Archie with all her heart. Apart from his work commitments at Craigdon Super Yachts and Elizabeth's devotion to various charities, they spent most of their time together. Even the nights. A few times they'd been caught together by one or other of their children. It had been past the time when she could have explained their presence together in one home or the other as nothing more than a casual visit. Thankfully, so far none of their children had pushed for answers. She wasn't sure what she'd say.

Why can't I just come out and tell them? They already know about the affair. They know Archie's Sophia's father and she's nearly twenty-two…

The thing was, everyone assumed the affair that produced Sophia had ended long ago. After all, both she and Archie had remained in their marriages. They'd given no one reason to suspect it was still going on. But Archie was growing impatient for them to be open about their love; to live together; to do what other couples did. She understood his impatience and she hated to see him upset. Perhaps when this meeting Henry had decreed was over, she'd finally be able to move on.

"Are you ready, Mrs Craigdon?"

"Yes thanks, John. I think we're all here."

She forced a tight smile for her late husband's lawyer, who'd come in behind her into the study. John Edgerton Junior had been the Craigdon family lawyer for years. Slight of stature and soft of voice, he was the antithesis of Henry Craigdon. Elizabeth wasn't the only family member who'd wondered at Henry's choice for legal counsel. Still, Edgerton was more than competent and Henry had prized that above all else.

Callum came up and touched her elbow. The strain around his eyes was noticeable. "What about Christopher?"

"He said he couldn't make it," she replied. "Actually, I think his exact words were more along the lines that he would rather kill himself than be subjected to more self-serving bull—nonsense—from the mouth of Henry Craigdon."

Callum grimaced, but nodded in acceptance. "Fair enough." He moved away to take a seat.

Elizabeth looked around the room and sighed. A year

earlier to the day, Edgerton had gathered the family together for the reading of Henry's will. It had been the same day as Henry's funeral. A difficult time for everyone. But twelve months down the track, time had started to heal raw wounds. Now there was every chance those wounds were about to be re-opened.

A week ago, Edgerton had called her to advise that part of Henry's final instructions included a letter he wished his lawyer to read aloud to Henry's family a year on from the day of his funeral. Elizabeth had been taken aback, but wasn't surprised. Henry had always demanded the last word. She'd phoned around the family and they'd all gathered together in Henry's study.

She gazed at their faces as they slowly took seats. Their expressions were filled with a mixture of boredom, curiosity and concern. They sat on the leather couches, the high backed chairs and other seats that had been brought in from the dining room to accommodate the large group.

There was her eldest, Jett, and his wife, Danielle. This time, their children had been left in school. Elizabeth agreed with their decision to keep the children away. No one had a clue why Henry had insisted on this meeting, but knowing how malicious he could be, it was probably something the children best not hear.

Next to them sat Callum and his wife, Grace. They'd also elected to keep their children in school. Though Seth and Alyssa weren't Callum's biological children, he'd taken to his role as step-father with eagerness, generosity of spirit and love. Callum had recently confided in her he was keen to adopt them and had already begun the process. Thankfully, Grace's ex-parents-in-law had given their blessing. It warmed Elizabeth's heart every time she heard them call him "Dad".

Her gaze drifted further along the row of chairs. Her son, Joel, and his fiancée, Sheridan, were seated next to Grace.

The loved-up couple sat with their shoulders touching and their fingers entwined. Next to them was her youngest son, Nicholas and his fiancée, Harper. They'd recently celebrated their engagement, along with her daughter, Isabella and Raine. It had been a splendid family affair and one that filled Elizabeth with fond memories.

Now Nicholas and Harper were expecting a baby. Everyone was delighted with the news. After the year of sadness and turmoil they'd all endured, it was nice to set all the tumult aside for a few hours and concentrate on what really mattered: family and togetherness. There was no better way to do that than to celebrate new love and new life.

As Elizabeth took her seat in the front row beside Jett, she acknowledged the others in the room. Her youngest daughter Sophia, sat with her husband, Jarrod. In the row behind was Elizabeth's nephews—Flynn, Noah and Logan. They were also flanked by the women who'd stolen their hearts. Elizabeth was full of gratitude and gladness knowing the younger generation had found true love. Though she and Henry hadn't enjoyed a happy marriage, she still yearned for that kind of safety, security and contentment for the people she loved.

Then her gaze snagged on Archie. Henry's brother. The love of Elizabeth's life. He sat slightly apart from the rest of the group. His expression was closed and dark. Elizabeth's heart ached. Archie had been even more distant than usual over the past few weeks. She guessed he was still upset over the fact she'd never told him he was Sophia's father.

He'd only found out when it was a matter of life and death and though they'd talked about it and as far as Elizabeth was concerned, the matter had been dealt with, it was obvious Archie was still battling over her deception. Either that, or there was something else weighing on his mind. Something else that had kept him from her bed this past week.

Lately, between his work at Craigdon Super Yachts and her endless charity pursuits, they'd barely shared half a dozen conversations and Archie always seemed to have an excuse as to why he couldn't stay the night. She wondered if this was his way of punishing her for refusing to come clean to their children; if he was trying to force her hand. A silent protest. A withdrawal of affection until he got what he wanted.

No. She refused to believe Archie would be so immature. They had a deep and abiding love for each other that spanned more than two decades. In addition, there was respect, admiration and a genuine friendship. No. Archie wouldn't stoop so low as to use those kind of tactics against her. There must be something else playing on his mind.

Perhaps it was simply the fact that it had been a whole year since his brother's death; that as the anniversary of Henry's passing drew nearer, Archie had been reminded of the fact his brother was gone and never coming back. Or perhaps it was something else entirely. After all, Henry and Archie had never been close. More like rivals. They'd even competed for her love.

Then there was Archie's late wife, Janelle. The family had recently discovered Henry and Janelle had been having an affair at the time Janelle was killed. It was a shocking discovery and though Elizabeth had had her suspicions, Archie had been taken completely by surprise.

"Are we ready to begin?" the lawyer asked, seated behind Henry's desk.

Elizabeth shook her head slightly to clear it of her thoughts and nodded. "Yes. Thank you, John. Let's get this over with."

The lawyer's gaze moved over the people gathered before him. He cleared his throat. The low murmur of voices fell silent.

"Firstly, I'd like to thank you all for coming. As you're aware, Henry Craigdon was my client. I prepared and witnessed his will—the same will I read to you a year ago. What some of you might not know is that at the time of executing his will, Henry left me a letter he'd written, along with instructions this letter be read to all of you a year after his death."

The lawyer paused and once again, his gaze moved around the room. "So here we are. Like you, I have no idea about the contents of this letter. It has remained in a sealed envelope since the day Henry handed it to me." Once again, he paused and his expression turned grim. "Let's hope there aren't too many surprises," he muttered.

"Okay, here we go."

"So, it's been a year since I died. I hope at least some of you are still grieving, but I can understand if you're not. A few of you didn't think too highly of me. That's your loss. I didn't get the chance to say these things to you before my death, so I'm saying them now. Like it or not. I don't care.

"Jett—my firstborn. I'm so proud of you and the man you've become. You always had your heart set on being a detective. I'm so glad you got to realize your dream. And Danielle and the kids… I hope they're enjoying your inheritance. Hey, you deserved it. You always were a good and dutiful son."

Edgerton glanced in Jett's direction. Elizabeth saw the grim resignation on Jett's face. He reached for Danielle's hand and she shot him a reassuring look. Some of Elizabeth's tension eased.

So far, so good…

"Callum. My second born. The night you came into this world, I didn't think you were going to survive. You were so tiny, so fragile. Every breath was an effort. I spent the night on my knees in the hospital chapel, praying for God to save you, to give you the strength to live. I made a foolish promise that night, one I had no right to make. I'm sorry I forced you into the priesthood. Though I was prepared to barter anything in return for your life, it wasn't fair to chain you to a promise I made. I could tell

it wasn't your calling; that you'd only entered the seminary because of me. I was filled with guilt at the knowledge you were there under sufferance, but I couldn't bring myself to release you from that bond.

"So I did what I thought was the next best thing. I left you ten million dollars. I had no way of knowing how long I had on this earth, but I hoped whatever time you had left, you made good use of it. My generous gift was my way of releasing you from the burden of my promise. I hope you've abandoned the idea of becoming a priest and made a good life for yourself with the money I left you. I hope you're finally happy."

Once again, Edgerton paused. Elizabeth looked in Callum's direction. He and Grace sat close together, their hands clasped, their shoulders touching. The strain Elizabeth had noticed around his eyes had disappeared. She breathed a surreptitious sigh of relief and focused once again on what the lawyer was saying.

"Joel. Headstrong, passionate, stubborn and determined. You remind me a lot of me. That's why I let you ignore my wishes that you go into the law. You would have made a fine lawyer. That's something I even considered at one time. But life took me in another direction and I was okay with that.

"I thought about sabotaging your efforts to enter the police force. I had friends at the Academy. A word in the right ear and your policing career would have been over before it began. But I decided against it. Call it a moment of weakness. God knows, I didn't have many of those. I hope you appreciate that.

"But it was obvious you had no desire to be a lawyer; that your heart was set on a different kind of law enforcement. Though I was disappointed, I finally accepted that. I wish you all the best with your career in the police force. Even though you went against my wishes, I'm proud of all you've done.

"The police force need good people like you on their side. I should know. I've dealt with plenty who are far less scrupulous. It's a disgrace. It shouldn't be that easy to corrupt a member of our finest. I left you ten million dollars, the same as Callum and Jett. I hope you've made good

use of it. Bought yourself something nice. Be happy, Joel."

Elizabeth slowly released the breath she'd been holding. So far, it hadn't been as bad as she'd feared. Perhaps Henry had been feeling more generous, more compassionate while he penned what would be his final words? She'd never know.

Edgerton cleared his throat and kept reading.

"Isabella—my little girl. The keeper of my secrets. The light of my life. You'll never know how much I loved you. So much it frightened me. I wanted to give you everything. I wanted you to have the best. You were my shadow, my conscience, my co-conspirator. God, we had so much fun… At least, I hope it was as much fun for you keeping secrets as it was for me…

"I left you twenty million dollars. I hope that was enough. I gave you more than your brothers received. I did that deliberately, of course. I hope you understand you were my favorite. Live well and be happy, my darling girl. I miss you."

Elizabeth bit down on a surge of anger.

How dare he? How dare he come right out and say it! Okay, so it had been obvious he'd favored Isabella over the others, but to be so blatant about it… Especially now, in his final words to his family, when he was no longer around to rail against, to take out the anger and hurt on. It was so wrong, so selfish, so hurtful… So utterly Henry…

She glanced over her shoulder to where Isabella sat straight and tall in her chair. She stared blindly at a spot on the carpet, but her lips quivered, her eyes glinted with anger and tears ran silently down her cheeks. Raine leaned close and whispered something in her ear. She offered him a shaky smile. Elizabeth briefly closed her eyes. She didn't dare look at her other children. She couldn't bear to witness their pain all over again. It wasn't Isabella's fault. She'd never asked for special treatment. No, this was all on Henry.

You bastard…

Elizabeth was immediately filled with remorse. It was uncharitable to think so unkindly of the dead. But still…

Henry didn't make it easy. She didn't know what she expected. He'd been just as selfish in life. She was grateful when Edgerton continued.

"So, my dear wife. I turn to you. I'm sure it comes as no surprise I left you nothing but our family home. I only left you that because I knew you'd get it anyway through the courts. If it had been up to me, I wouldn't have left you anything. That's more than you deserved.

"You thought you'd been so clever keeping your feelings for Archie from me. You were a fool. As if I couldn't tell how he mooned after you, right from the very start. It was sickening to watch, but it was also fun. Archie was in love with you even before we said our vows. He stood beside me as my best man and watched the woman he loved commit herself for life to someone else. I got a kick out of it, don't you worry. Best day of my life.

"While Archie pined from a distance, you and I had a good life. In the beginning, at least. You were everything I wanted. A trophy wife. Beautiful, poised and passable in bed. But it didn't last. It couldn't last. I wasn't built to be faithful to just one woman, least of all my wife.

"Fancy being married to the wrong man. How long did it take you to realize that? Not long, I'll bet. Not with Archie always sniffing around."

Elizabeth's face flamed. She kept her gaze fixed on her hands that were now twisted in her lap. Though her family knew of her affair with Henry's brother, none of them knew the full story. She wanted to rail against Henry's accusations; tell them it wasn't like that. She'd remained faithful to her wedding vows until it became impossible not to.

But the truth was, she *had* been unfaithful and her family would judge her for that. She only hoped that now they'd all found true love, they'd understand how complicated matters of the heart could be. She silently prayed for their forgiveness while the lawyer continued to read.

"What about you, Nick? Have you done something with your sorry life? I hope you're still not moping over the fact I gave my company to Logan. See, the thing is, a scant eight years into our marriage, I was convinced my dearly beloved wife was having an affair. Though your

mother always denied it, I didn't believe her. It didn't take me long to work out who was her partner in crime.

"My brother was always sniffing around her, looking like a lovesick puppy. By now he had a wife of his own, but that didn't seem to matter. I knew how hard it was to remain faithful—hell, I was the king of affairs—so I had no problem believing Archie had also broken his vows.

"I didn't care that he'd cheated on Janelle, but I did care he'd done it with Elizabeth. She was my wife. She belonged to me. It didn't matter that I was unfaithful to our marriage vows almost from the beginning. That was me. My wife was another matter.

"Awhile ago, I decided to get a DNA test. I'm not sure why. But I did and what do you know? You're mine, after all. So there you go. I was wrong. Not that it makes any difference. I've spent most of your life believing differently. What's done is done. I left you one million dollars and not another cent. I won't be changing my will. Your beloved Craigdon Enterprises has gone to someone else."

Elizabeth was filled with so much anger toward her husband, she could barely contain her rage. Her body shook with the force of it. Fury burned her cheeks. All this time, Henry had known. He'd known Nicholas was his son and yet he'd still carried out his despicable, hurtful act. He'd left Nicholas almost nothing. A scant million dollars. And the company Nick loved so much had been left to his cousin.

She risked a glance in Nick's direction and her heart clenched. His face was pale, his eyes wide with shock. Though he'd had a year to come to terms with his father's callousness, it seemed no amount of time would lessen the hurt. Elizabeth burned with a rage that frightened her. Digging her fingernails into her palms, she prayed for the strength to forgive the man who'd caused them all so much pain.

Chapter Two

Edgerton stopped reading. He looked up, a resigned expression on his face. Elizabeth could tell the contents of the letter brought him no joy. He seemed as reluctant as the rest of them to continue.

"Would anyone like a drink?" he asked. "A glass of water? Something stronger?" he half-joked.

Elizabeth offered him a tight smile. She looked at the family gathered around her. They all wore equal expressions of anger, sadness and resignation.

"I think we should just get it over with," she said and heard the surreptitious sighs of relief from those around her.

Edgerton nodded. "Very well." Like he had at the outset, he cleared his throat.

"And so we come to Sophia. Of course, there was no doubt at all you weren't my daughter. This time, your mother didn't deny it. I put it right on her: she was having an affair with Archie and the baby was his. You arrived six months later and you were the spitting image of him. You still are. I can't believe my stupid brother is still oblivious. Even funnier, that my darling wife didn't see fit to tell her lover he was the father. Poor Archie. Always the loser.

"So I'm sure you won't blame me for being less than generous with your inheritance. Like Nicholas, you were lucky I left you anything at all. Only the advice of my trusty legal counsel who told me if you challenged

the will in court you'd end up with a whole lot more than I was willing to give you changed my mind. So I left you enough to pay off your student loans. I hope you're grateful. It was more than I wanted you to inherit.

"And then I decided to have some fun. I added the clause about *inheriting the five million if you married and stayed married for at least a year. I'm sure you accepted the challenge, though I bet you struggled with it for a while. You tried so hard to win my favor, but no matter what you did, you could never change my mind. You were my brother's child. A constant reminder that my wife had strayed.*

"But five million dollars is a lot of money. I almost feel sorry for the *sap who's been roped into marrying you. Have you had the guts to tell him you're only doing it for money? Or are you just as deceptive as your mother? Oh, that's right. She was honest about Nicholas, after all and she didn't deny you belonged to Archie. Maybe you get your deceitful streak from me? Ha, ha.*

"I can't help but wonder if you'll make it to the end. Twelve months *married can seem like forever. I bet you've come to realize just how hard it is to stay faithful. Your mother and I sucked at it. I hope you have better luck."*

A soft gasp filled the sudden silence. Elizabeth glanced over her shoulder to where Sophia sat softly crying. Her husband, Jarrod, looked fit to kill, but when his gaze fell on his wife, his expression softened, filled with tenderness and love. He kissed her gently on the mouth and pulled her close. She gave him a wobbly, grateful smile.

Once again, Elizabeth's anger spilled over. With hands clenched into fists, it was all she could do not to give voice to her fury.

How dare you treat our children like this! Sophia loved you! By tacit agreement, we raised her as our daughter. And now this! A betrayal of the worst kind. I hope to God you've gotten what you deserve…

The nasty thought pulled her up short, but right then, with white-hot anger still coursing through her veins, she refused to apologize for it. There would be time later to beg forgiveness from her maker. She was sure God would understand.

Edgerton glanced down at the contents of Henry's letter. From the disgust that pulled down the lawyer's lips, it was obvious he took no pleasure from what he was forced to read. He shot the gathering an apologetic look before continuing.

"And so we come to the question you must have all asked yourself, time and time again since my death. Why did I leave Craigdon Enterprises to Logan? Have you worked it out yet? Yes, that's right. Logan is my son."

Elizabeth froze in shock. There were audible gasps from around the room. Her gaze immediately went to Archie. Though she'd suspected as much, Archie wouldn't have a bar of it. He'd refused to believe his wife had cheated on him, let alone produced a child. And yet, strangely Archie's expression remained closed, his eyes shuttered. He gave no outward sign that he'd even heard the announcement.

Strange… Is he in that much shock that he's beyond any reaction?

And then another, more insidious thought occurred to her: *Did he already know?*

No, she refused to believe that. The night Noah had come over and told them about Janelle and Henry's affair, Archie had stormed off, refusing to listen. Despite the evidence, he wouldn't accept his wife of two decades had cheated on him— and with his brother, no less. Elizabeth and Archie hadn't spoken of it since.

But now there was no denying it. Or the fact that the union had produced a child. It was written in black and white. Still taut with shock, Elizabeth forced herself to listen as Edgerton continued.

"Did that shock you? Probably. Not many people knew. Yes, I had an affair with my brother's wife. Janelle. It started out as a petty act of revenge, back before Nicholas was born. I was so sure Elizabeth had cheated on me. I wanted to get even with her. How dare she make a fool of me with another man! And not just any man, but my brother! So naturally I did what any self-respecting male would do—I sought revenge. Who better to do it with than my brother's wife?

"So I set out to seduce Janelle. I charmed her with my wittiness. Won her over with my good looks, my charm. Our families spent a lot of time together, which made things easier. Even still, it took longer than I anticipated, but eventually she capitulated. I still remember our first time together…"

Edgerton broke off. He squirmed on the seat, looking uncomfortable. Elizabeth squared her shoulders and spoke.

"Please continue, John. Let's get this whole sordid ordeal over with."

A flush of embarrassment tinged the lawyer's cheeks, but he gave a jerky nod and continued.

"Anyway, I digress. Within months of our affair, she told me she was pregnant. She wasn't sure which one of us was the father. I was a little taken aback she was still sleeping with Archie. Then again, I was still being intimate with my wife. I guess we were even.

"I wanted to believe the baby was mine. You see, by that time I'd fallen in love with Janelle. Yes, the joke was on me. She still cared deeply for Archie and didn't want to hurt him. She refused to tell him about our affair and swore me to secrecy. What could I do? I loved her. Also, she refused to leave her marriage. I guess that was fair. I wasn't prepared to leave mine, either, though my reasons were a lot less noble than hers.

"We increased the times we spent together, making love whenever we could. Thank God for Harriet Young. She made it so much easier. She covered for us more times than I can count. Thank you, Harriet. You were a true friend to Janelle. And to me.

"For years we met in secret. By this time, my darling wife had confessed she'd been unfaithful and Sophia was the result. I felt justified in my affair with Janelle, though I continued to keep our secret. The subterfuge made it all the more exciting, although there were times when I wished we could love each other openly. She was the love of my life. And then I killed her. With my stupidity, my lack of self-control, I killed her. It was an accident, but I blamed myself for her death right up until the end. If I hadn't been drinking, we might never have crashed and she'd still be alive. God! How could I have been so stupid?"

The room was so quiet, Elizabeth could hear the chirping of a bird outside the window. Everyone appeared to be holding their breath. She didn't blame them. It was the first time any of them had ever heard Henry express anything that even resembled regret. And it was all because of Janelle. Apparently the love of his life. Edgerton kept reading aloud.

"That's why I left Flynn and Noah some money. Guilt money. I stole their mother away from them. It wasn't fair. She could have still been alive and living a happy life, going to weddings, baptisms, birthdays. Watching her sons make a life for themselves. They were her world. She loved them with everything she had. I took all of that from her when I crashed that car. All because I was drunk.

"It was also my fault she wasn't wearing a seatbelt. I asked her to go down on me. She was happy to comply. That's the kind of person she was. Always happy to put herself out for someone else. For me."

Edgerton's face flamed with embarrassment. Elizabeth was beyond caring. She just wanted the whole thing to be over with so that they need never speak of it again. A little impatiently, she urged him to continue.

"I'm sorry about getting you into drugs, Logan. I didn't know at that time you were my son. I had my suspicions and so did your mom, but we never knew for sure. She kept up her deception with Archie right until the end. She didn't want to hurt him by throwing our affair in his face.

"Of course, when Sophia came along, I couldn't wait to tell Janelle the truth. She was devastated to discover Archie had cheated on her with Elizabeth, but she knew she'd also been deceitful. It troubled her. Deep down, she was such a good person. But she came to accept she and Archie were even. Neither owed the other anything. She refused to say anything to him. She refused to allow me to tell him the truth, Right to the end, she protected her husband. She stayed with her spouse out of respect for him and for the sake of her kids. As did I.

"Logan, you were fourteen when I finally learned the truth about your parentage. By then, it had become an obsession of mine. I had to know if you were mine. Janelle insisted it didn't matter, but to me it did. Your

mother stole some hair from your hairbrush. It was a simple matter after that to submit it for D.NA. I'm so proud to call you my son. I wish I'd been able to do it to your face, but your mother forbade me. I honored her wishes until the very end.

"So there you have it. Like me, love me, hate me. I'm done."

As Edgerton folded the letter and set it quietly down on the desk, the occupants of the room sat frozen, no one sure of what to say. So many questions had been answered, but in some respects, Elizabeth was certain they would have rather remained oblivious.

Good old Henry. He had to be the star of the show. Right to the very end.

Elizabeth risked a glance around her. Varying degrees of anger, devastation, resentment and pain were reflected on the faces of her family. Nicholas was breathing hard, his face flushed. Harper held his arm and spoke quietly to him. Isabella's tears had dried, but her expression remained full of sadness. Sophia looked the most upset. As Elizabeth watched, her daughter shrugged off Jarrod's arm from around her shoulders and stood and made her way over to where Elizabeth sat.

"How could he, Mom? How could he be so cruel?" she cried, her eyes flooding with tears.

Elizabeth shook her head. "I'm so sorry, honey. I don't know."

"He knew how much I loved him, how much I yearned for his acceptance, his approval. He treated me with disdain at every turn. Even his final words to me were mean and cold. It wasn't my fault he wasn't my father. I treated him like he was. I loved him like he was. And he threw it back in my face. It was like he blamed me for being Archie's daughter. What kind of sick son of a bitch does that?"

Elizabeth reached out in an attempt to soothe away Sophia's pain, but she was having none of it.

"I'm sorry, Mom. I just can't do this right now. I know we've talked about this, sorted through our feelings, but right now things are too raw for me to deal with. I hate knowing he despised me, right to the very end."

"Oh, Sophia!" Elizabeth cried, her heart breaking at the pain on her daughter's face. "He didn't despise you. It was *me* he despised. And Archie."

"Then why did he take it out on *me?*" Sophia shouted.

Elizabeth shook her head, overwhelmed with sadness. "I don't know. He was like that. Cold and unforgiving. Please, God. Don't let yourself become the same."

Sophia remained mutinously silent. With a last devastated look in Elizabeth's direction, she stormed out of the room. Jarrod hurried after her.

Elizabeth's head ached. A pulse beat behind her eyes. The stress of the occasion was getting to her.

Damn you, Henry! You always had to have the last word! You've ripped open wounds that were barely healed over. Your family are once again reeling with pain. I hope you're proud of yourself…

She looked across at Archie. He was surrounded by his sons: Flynn, Noah and Logan. No, not Logan. Logan belonged to Henry. The longer she looked at her lover's family, the more she realized there was a somber air of acceptance encircling them. It wasn't the shock she expected upon discovering Logan was Henry's son. It was almost as if the four of them already knew…

And maybe they did…

Convinced she was right, Elizabeth stood and made her way over to them. Archie looked up at her approach. She tried to read his mood, but his eyes were still shuttered. It was like staring at an obelisk.

"You knew, didn't you?" she stated flatly.

He didn't bother to ask her to clarify. Instead, he offered her a brief nod, his mouth tight. "Yes."

Though she'd been expecting that answer, it still shocked her. She tensed and then shook her head in disbelief. "And you didn't tell me?"

He held her gaze almost defiantly. "No."

She stared at him in bewilderment. "Archie! I... I don't understand."

Instead of answering her, offering her reassurance, he simply stood and regarded her steadily.

"I don't suppose you do, but that's not my problem. Now, if you don't mind, I'd like to leave." He turned to his sons. "Come on, boys. Let's get out of here."

Logan shot her an apologetic look. Flynn and Noah both mumbled goodbyes, their eyes downcast. Elizabeth stared after them, beyond words.

"I'm really sorry you had to go through that."

Elizabeth blinked. Edgerton stood beside her, holding Henry's folded letter in his hands. She gathered her wits about her and responded.

"That was Henry, wasn't it? Selfish and spiteful to the end."

Edgerton lowered his gaze and nodded. "I'm sorry," he said again.

Elizabeth's anger suddenly deserted her. Whatever the fallout from Henry's letter, it wasn't the lawyer's fault. She compressed her lips.

"Thank you, John. I appreciate this hasn't been easy for you, either."

The lawyer accepted her words with a brief nod of acknowledgement. He held the letter out to her. "Would you like to keep this?"

Elizabeth stared down at the innocent-looking sheaf of paper and shuddered. "No. You keep it. Or burn it. I don't care what you do with it. I never want to see it again."

Edgerton nodded once again. "I understand."

Belatedly remembering her manners, Elizabeth offered him refreshments. He politely declined. Relieved, she saw him out and then returned to the study where the rest of her family remained quietly talking among themselves.

Well, you did what you set out to achieve, Henry. You had the final word. Now I'm left to pick up the pieces. Again.

And this time, she wasn't even sure she had the love and support of Archie…

A wave of helplessness poured through her, momentarily snatching her breath. But then she remembered who she was and where she'd come from. Elizabeth Grace Louise Doherty was made from sterner stuff. This wasn't the first time she'd faced adversity and come out the other side. No, whatever Henry had hoped to achieve with his letter, there was no way she'd let it break her. Nor would she let it destroy the family she loved above everything else.

He can go and shove his malice and spite up his ass. I refuse to let it affect me… Or the ones I love. Take that, Henry Craigdon!

Chapter Three

While Sophia and Jarrod's places at the family table remained conspicuously empty, and Archie hadn't yet returned with his sons, the rest of Elizabeth's children and their partners gathered together for a meal. It was a little past one and Elizabeth was sure some of them were hungry. It would also give them a chance to come together, reconnect and talk through what had happened.

She'd asked Amy to prepare lunch ahead of time. As they filed into the generously proportioned formal dining room, the housekeeper came in bearing platters of cold meats—ham, thinly sliced chicken, and roast beef. They were quickly followed by fresh buns, a bowl of lettuce leaves, sliced tomatoes, boiled eggs and a plate of sliced cheese. Butter, mayonnaise and other condiments accompanied the rest of the food. Everything was set down on the long wooden dresser that doubled as a serving board.

"Thank you, Amy. You've gone to a lot of trouble. This looks great," Callum said quietly.

The old housekeeper's face creased with wrinkles as she smiled. "Thank you, Callum. Nothing's too much trouble for my babies. Now, eat up."

Callum and Grace formed a line that snaked along the

serving area. Fine china plates, cutlery and linen napkins were stacked in a neat pile at one end. As each one filled their plates and found a spot at the table, Elizabeth allowed herself a tiny portion of food and eased out a weary sigh.

The worst part was over. Now for the inevitable dissection, mulling over and no doubt some more heated discussion. Not that she blamed them. Her children were entitled to vent. There was much to be upset about. While they'd already discovered much of what Henry had revealed, there was still an almost palpable sense of shock and anger that permeated the air.

Joel pulled out a seat beside her and set his plate down in front of him. Sheridan took the chair opposite. He reached across and patted Elizabeth's hand.

"How are you doing, Mom? It's been a rough day."

Hearing the kindness and genuine concern in his tone, a rush of emotion burned behind her eyes. She managed a tight smile. "You can say that again."

"What happened to Uncle Archie?"

"He… He left with your cousins." She realized what she'd said and hurried to correct herself. "I mean, your half-brother and cousins." She stared at the table. Her face burned.

"It's all right, Mom." Joel's tone remained gentle. "I understand." He paused and then added, "It must have come as a shock to all of them."

"Yes. No. I mean, I'm not sure about the boys, but your uncle already knew."

Joel's eyes widened in surprise. "He knew about Logan?"

Her lips thinned. "Yes."

Joel frowned. "How? When?"

Elizabeth shook her head. "I don't know. We didn't get that far."

"I take it he hadn't told you?"

Once again, Elizabeth's lips thinned. "No," she said grimly.

"I guess that's just one more thing I'm going to have to deal with."

Joel looked sympathetic. "Don't worry, Mom. I'm sure he'll come round. He's probably still feeling a bit put out about the fact you didn't tell him about Sophia."

Elizabeth sighed. "I didn't think he could be that childish, but it seems I was wrong."

"Don't be too quick to judge him," Joel said quickly. "You don't know what went on. Give him a chance to explain before you convict him of any wrongdoing."

She managed a weary smile. "Thanks, Joel. I appreciate your support. For both of us."

Joel merely shrugged. "You're my family. That's what we do. Support each other."

She blew her breath out on a sigh. "Yes. I wish your father had felt a bit more like that while he was still alive."

Joel's expression darkened. "Dad had his problems, that's for sure. I won't pretend I understand where he was coming from with all that stuff. It defies reason."

"Yes. But we're not going to let his pettiness destroy us. We Craigdons are stronger than that."

Joel smiled. "Of course we are."

"I'm annoyed that he didn't enlighten us any further about Stella Taunton," Isabella grumbled. "I mean, he left the orphanage fifteen million dollars. A not insignificant sum. It would be nice to know his connection to the place and his reasons."

"You're right," Nicholas agreed with a grimace. "He was oh so generous with me. I'm intrigued what motivated him to leave the institution so much money. None of us have ever heard of it."

"I did a little digging," Joel admitted. "All I came up with was a private company established about two years ago. Only the bare minimum of information was publicly available.

Without knowing who's behind it, I came up against a brick wall."

The sound of stilettos on the travertine tiles that traversed the foyer reached all of them. A moment later, Sophia and Jarrod appeared. Elizabeth's heart jumped for joy. When Sophia immediately went up to her and gave her an awkward hug, tears came to Elizabeth's eyes.

"I'm sorry, Mom. Jarrod and I have been talking. He made me see things from your point of view. I'm sorry," Sophia said again. "I behaved badly."

Elizabeth shook her head. "There's no need to apologize, honey. I understand. It was like finding out all over again. I'm sorry you had to go through that."

Sophia grimaced. "I'm sorry, too. I wish none of us had to be subjected to that. I don't care how Daddy tried to justify his behavior. The truth is, he was an asshole. Right up to the end."

"Sophia," Jarrod admonished quietly.

Elizabeth touched Sophia's husband on the hand. "It's all right, Jarrod. Sophia's right. He was an asshole."

It was the first time she'd said the words aloud. They felt good on her tongue. She said it again, this time louder.

"Asshole. Asshole. Asshole."

Sophia cheered. "Way to go, Mom!"

The rest of those gathered around the table turned to look at her. Embarrassment heated her cheeks, but she refused to apologize for her behavior. She held their combined gazes defiantly. One by one, they began to smile. Then Callum got to his feet. He wasn't the firstborn Craigdon, but he'd always been the unofficial spokesperson for the group.

He lifted his wine glass. "I'd like to propose a toast. To Mom."

"To Mom," came a chorus of agreement. Elizabeth smiled with pleasure and pride. These were her children and their chosen life partners. Jett, Callum and Sophia had already said their vows. Joel, Nicholas and Isabella were engaged. No doubt there would be wedding bells in the near future. Especially for Nicholas who'd announced only a week earlier that he and Harper were expecting.

With her throat clogging up with emotion, Elizabeth gazed around at her family. She took a sip from her champagne flute and smiled.

"Thank you. Thank you, all of you. We've endured a tumultuous year, but we've managed to hold it all together. I appreciate your love and support and I hope you know you have mine. Now and for always."

They turned their attention to eating and the murmur of conversation mingled with the sound of cutlery as it struck the china plates. Elizabeth thought about Christopher, her late husband's illegitimate son. Once again, Henry had completely ignored his firstborn's existence. Once again, he'd been unbelievably malicious and cruel.

"What is it, Mom?" Callum asked softly from where he was seated next to Joel.

She blinked in surprise and looked at him. He'd always been her most sensitive child, the one most in tune with her moods.

"I was just thinking about Christopher," she said honestly.

Callum's mouth twisted in a grimace. "It was a good thing he wasn't here. Once again, Dad was completely insensitive."

Elizabeth nodded. "Yes. I'm glad Christopher made the decision to stay away. He didn't need another reminder of how little his father cared for him, to the point where he completely ignored his existence. First in the will and now in the letter. It would have caused Christopher unimaginable hurt."

Joel's lip curled up in disgust. "I don't know why you're so hell bent on worrying about Christopher's feelings, Mom. He doesn't seem to care about anyone else's."

"I understand what you're saying, Joel. And you know that better than most. You and Sheridan bore the brunt of one of Christopher's stunts. But let me say this. I think he's trying to put that bad behavior behind him. Look at what he did to help that police officer. If he hadn't done what he did, the police commissioner would have gotten away with murder. Then there's the tip he gave to Noah about Logan's girlfriend being in imminent danger. Who knows what might have happened if Christopher hadn't spoken up."

She paused and then added in a quiet tone. "I think it's time to cut him some slack. After all, none of us is perfect. We all have rough edges. Some more than others. Christopher's trying hard to be the kind of man he can be proud of. We should applaud him and give him our support."

There were various grumbles, mostly of agreement. Elizabeth had to be content with that. She didn't expect her family to embrace Christopher overnight. After all, he'd gone out of his way to put most of them offside. But lately, she'd seen a change in him and she believed very strongly that everyone deserved a second chance.

The dirty plates had been cleared away and the leftovers packed up to be taken back to Callum and Grace's soup kitchen. At Elizabeth's suggestion, they all withdrew to her music room for coffee. Amy brought in a steaming pot, along with a tray containing coffee cups, teaspoons, milk and sugar. There was also a plate of petit fours.

"Thank you, Amy. These look delicious."

"When I knew my babies were going to all be here, I did all their favorites. I hope you approve."

Elizabeth smiled. "Absolutely. And I'm sure they do, too."

Amy departed. Elizabeth picked up the pot and began pouring. As she handed out cups of coffee, she took another moment to appreciate what she had. Most of her thirty-three years of marriage had been difficult. She'd been married to a selfish, egotistical man. But he'd also given her six beautiful children. Well, five not counting Sophia. Her children were her life and now she had their significant others to welcome, to nurture, to love. She looked forward to the time when they provided her with grandchildren. She might have faced some difficult challenges, but she wouldn't swap her situation for the world.

A knock at the front door caught her attention. She stirred, on the verge of getting up, but then heard Amy's footsteps as she traversed the travertine tiles. A moment later, the door opened and conversation could be heard. The words were too muffled for Elizabeth to hear clearly, but it sounded like the visitor was a woman. A moment later, Amy appeared in the doorway of the music room.

"I'm sorry to interrupt, Elizabeth. But you have a visitor. I told her you were otherwise engaged, but she insisted she see you right away."

Elizabeth frowned. "Oh, did she give her name?"

"Yes. Stella. Stella Taunton."

Elizabeth froze in surprise. "Did you say, Stella Taunton?"

"Yes. Do you know her?"

"No. That is, her name's familiar, but we've never met." She looked back toward her family who were all looking equally shocked. "It seems we're going to have the pleasure of meeting Ms Taunton after all. Let's hope she can answer our questions." She turned back to Amy. "Please send her in."

Isabella sat beside Joel on the couch. She nudged him with her elbow. "This should be interesting."

"You bet," Joel replied.

"Make sure you mind your manners," Callum admonished quietly. "We don't know anything about this woman."

"Except that she impressed Dad enough that he left her orphanage fifteen million dollars," Isabella retorted.

"She might not even know Dad," Callum insisted. "Perhaps her having the same name is merely a coincidence."

Isabella rolled her eyes. "Then why is she here, Callum? Outside Dad's house?"

Callum was spared from replying when Amy appeared once again in the doorway of the music room. Behind her stood a young woman who looked about Nicholas' age. Elizabeth started in surprise. Stella Taunton looked nothing like she expected. Call her naïve, but Elizabeth somehow had the impression the woman whose name fronted a home for widows and orphans would be mature, matronly, over fifty at least.

The young woman who stood before her had long, brassy blond, messy hair. She wore a sapphire blue, figure-hugging, low cut dress that only emphasized her assets. She was big-breasted, slim of hip and with enough height that she'd tower over the average woman. And that was without her four-inch stiletto heels.

Hiding her shock, Elizabeth got to her feet. A whiff of cheap perfume almost made her sneeze. She resisted the urge with an effort and held out her hand toward the woman.

"I'm Elizabeth Craigdon. Welcome to Craigdon Manor."

"Stella Taunton. Nice to meet ya," the woman replied around a wad of gum. She gave Elizabeth's hand a perfunctory shake. "You're not what I expected."

Elizabeth frowned in confusion. The woman spoke like she knew her. But how could that be? Elizabeth was certain she'd never met the woman.

"What did you expect?" she heard herself ask.

Stella shrugged nonchalantly. "Oh, you know. Old, fat and frumpy."

Elizabeth was momentarily silenced by shock. Before she could respond, Stella began to move around the room, looking this way and that. She gave a low-pitched whistle.

"This is one cool house. I had no idea Henry was so loaded. I mean, I guess I should have, given everything that happened, but at the time, I didn't have a clue." She walked over to where a collection of priceless figurines stood on a shelf beside the bookcase. She picked one up and looked at it, turning it this way and that before setting it back down in place and picking up another one.

Once again, Elizabeth hid her surprise. She wondered how her husband had known this woman. She couldn't imagine Henry giving Stella the time of day, let alone fifteen million dollars, albeit to her company, or at least, to the company that bore her name.

Belatedly remembering her manners, Elizabeth invited the woman to sit down. With another insouciant shrug, Stella crossed the room and perched on the edge of one of the sofas. Callum and Grace shuffled over to make room.

"Would you like some coffee?" Elizabeth asked.

"Sure. Why not. White with three sugars," came the flippant reply as she continued to chew on her gum.

Elizabeth concentrated on pouring the coffee and adding the teaspoons of sugar. She didn't dare catch the eye of any of her children. She was sure they were as bemused as she was as to what this woman was doing there and what was her connection to Henry. Handing the cup to Stella, Elizabeth regained her seat. She folded her hands in her lap and looked at the woman expectantly.

Stella slurped loudly from her cup and then set it down on the coffee table that stood between her and the opposite couch. Isabella frowned with annoyance. Sophia hid a giggle behind her hand. The rest of Elizabeth's family regarded the woman with varying degrees of anticipation and incredulity as they awaited her next move. Suddenly impatient, Elizabeth took control.

"So, Stella. I'm sure you understand our surprise at your

visit. I must admit, you have us at a disadvantage. You seem to know about us, but we know nothing about you."

The woman smiled brightly. "Of course you do. You were there for the reading of the will, weren't you?"

"Y-yes," Elizabeth replied uncertainly.

"Then you know Henry left me fifteen million dollars."

"Um, no," Joel said. "He left the Stella Taunton House for Widows and Orphans fifteen million dollars. I looked into it. It's a charitable trust."

Stella smirked. "Trust, huh? Good old Henry. He was always smart as a tux."

Elizabeth's eyebrows rose in surprise. She regarded the woman steadily, doing her best to hide her concern. "What do you know about the Stella Taunton House for Widows and Orphans?" she asked.

"Just that it doesn't exist."

"Of course it does," Joel insisted. "I did a company search."

Stella rolled her eyes and grinned. "You're obviously a lot smarter than I am, so I'm gonna take your word for it. I don't know anything about what Henry did behind the scenes to make it all legit. All I know is he told me he'd taken care of me, if anything were to happen to him. Which it did. But ya ready know that, right?"

ELIZABETH is available for preorder at all of the digital retailers.
It will be released on 18 July, 2021.

About the Author

Chris Taylor grew up on a farm in north-west New South Wales, Australia. She always had a thirst for stories and recalls writing her first book at the ripe old age of eight. Always a lover of romance and happily-ever-afters, a career in criminal law sparked her interest in intrigue and suspense. For Chris to be able to combine romance with suspense in her books is a dream come true.

Chris is married to Linden and is the mother of five children. If not behind her computer, you can find her doing the school run, taxiing children to swimming lessons, football, ballet and cricket. In her spare time, Chris loves to read her favorite authors who include Richard North Patterson, Sandra Brown, Kathleen E Woodiwiss and Jude Devereaux.

You can find out more about Chris and sign up for her newsletter at her website:

http://www.christaylorauthor.com.au

9 781925 119886